£2·99

Simon Raven was born in 1~~...~~
Charterhouse and King's Co~~...~~
Classics. Afterwards he serve~~...~~
Infantry. In 1957 he resigned his commission and turned ~~...~~
book reviewing. His first novel, *The Feathers of Death*, brought
instant recognition and his popular *First-Born of Egypt* series
encompasses seven volumes. His TV and radio plays, of which
Royal Foundation is the best known, are classics. He also wrote
the scripts for the *Pallisers* series and *Edward and Mrs Simpson*.

SIMON RAVEN

Doctors Wear Scarlet

HOUSE OF
STRATUS

This edition published in 2001 by House of Stratus, an imprint of
Stratus Holdings plc, 24c Old Burlington Street, London, W1X 1RL, UK.

www.houseofstratus.com

Typeset, printed and bound by House of Stratus.

A catalogue record for this book is available from the British Library.

ISBN 1-84232-180-3

The Provost

and Fellows of Lancaster College, Cambridge

Request the Pleasure of the Company of

MAJOR ANTHONY SEYMOUR, MA

At the Annual Michaelmas Feast

To be Celebrated on October 31st, 1959

at Half Past Seven O'Clock

Evening Dress with Decorations

Doctors Wear Scarlet

R.S.V.P.

Author's Note

At certain stages in this story the holders of actual offices – Princes, Bishops or Headmasters – appear briefly on the scene. It is not to be inferred that I intend portraits of those who are the present holders of such offices. The Headmaster of Eton, for example, who appears at the Michaelmas Feast, is a generalised figure who stands for all headmasters whatever; he is *not* my old and respected acquaintance, Mr Robert Birley.

S R

PART ONE

Chimes and Meadows

I

One evening in the May of last year, one of those evenings which are so blue and beautiful that you start thinking everything will be all right forever, I came home to my flat in Chester Square at about ten o'clock and found Tyrrel sitting by the window. He was reading a translation of Cavafis and looking very young and tired.

"I'm sorry, Mr Seymour," he said. Then he produced an identity card which said he was Inspector John Tyrrel of the Metropolitan Police.

"How did you get in?"

"I'm sorry, sir," he said again. "The caretaker... I showed him my card."

"My telephone number's in the book," I said. "As far as I'm concerned the police can ring up for appointments just like anybody else."

"I'm sorry," he said; "but you see this isn't really an official visit. I've just come – "

"If this isn't an official visit," I said, "then so much the more could it have waited until some reasonable and pre-arranged hour of the day."

"I'm rather busy just now, sir."

And then his face seemed to crumple a bit, like that of a worn out child on the verge of crying at the end of a long day. I've come to know Tyrrel much better since then, so that now I realise that this can only have been a trick; but on that evening in May we were still strangers and I fell for his trick straight away, thinking how pompous and futile I was being – and that in any case the best way of getting rid of him was to find out what he wanted and settle the matter. So I asked him to have a drink, since he was only unofficially present, and gave him the brandy which, to my surprise, he preferred to whisky or beer. Then, still treating him like the harassed and pathetic child he was still pretending to be, I settled him in a comfortable chair. Finally, after he had been sipping his brandy for five minutes and showing no signs of saying anything at all, I found the strength of will to bring him to the point.

"What," I said, "do you want?"

"I should very much like some more of this excellent brandy, Mr Seymour."

This was cool behaviour by any standard. But Tyrrel was still looking so much like an orphan standing over his mother's grave that Herod himself could not have refused his request. I got up and fetched him some brandy. By now it was quite plain that he had beaten me hands down; there was nothing for it but to wait until he himself saw fit to state his (unofficial) business. Perhaps, however, he was satisfied with the degree of moral ascendency he had achieved; in any event, after only another minute's sipping, he condescended to converse.

"You are the friend, sir, of Mr Richard Fountain."

"Certainly. But I haven't seen him for nearly a year. He's away in Greece."

"Ah, yes," said Tyrrel sadly; "that's the trouble."

"Trouble?"

"As far as we can make out."

"You're not being very plain."

"I know... Tell me, sir, how well do you know Mr Fountain?"

I rallied a little.

"It might be more to the point if you were to explain exactly why you're so interested."

4

"I dare say it would be," Tyrrel said – so humbly and wistfully that I felt like the ogre in a pantomime. "I dare say it would be," he said; "and I'll try – oh yes, I'll certainly try. But first of all, sir, if you could tell me how well you know him?"

"Well," I said, "I'm four years older than Richard Fountain and I've known him since he was thirteen. He came to Charterhouse at the beginning of my last year there, and I had him for my study fag." ("Study fag," said Tyrrel gravely to himself.) "So naturally I knew him quite well then. But in 1944 I had to go away from school to the war, and I didn't see him again until October four years later, when we both came up to Lancaster College, Cambridge, as freshmen."

"This would be in 1948?" said Tyrrel.

"It would."

"So Mr Fountain must have been allowed to come straight to college from school? Without doing his National Service?"

"In those days," I said rather sharply, "you could choose whether to do National Service before or after your time at the University. Richard wasn't getting out of anything."

"I know that, sir," said Tyrrel.

"Then why ask?"

"Just to make sure I've got everything dead right. And that *you've* got everything dead right, Mr Seymour."

I decided to let this pass. If I don't get on, I thought, Tyrrel will be here till the birds start singing in the square.

"Well then," I said. "We were both Scholars," ("Scholars," mumbled Tyrrel appreciatively), "so we both had rooms in College for our entire time as undergraduates. And we both read the Classics," ("*Ah*"), "so we saw a lot of each other for three years. We got to know each other very well. We went abroad together once or twice. We were…close. And then in 1951, when we graduated, I came to London – "

"Were you lovers?" said Tyrrel, very quickly and without a trace of insolence or malice. Something in his manner demanded and deserved a sensible answer and would have rendered expostulation merely absurd.

"No. We neither of us...went in...for that kind of love."

"I thought not," he said. "So. In 1951...?"

"...I came to London late in the summer and started to live here. But Richard had got a further two years' deferment from call-up so that he could write a dissertation" – ("Dissertation," said Tyrrel with silky admiration) – "in competition for a Fellowship. He stayed in Cambridge to do this, and of course we still saw quite a lot of one another. But it wasn't what it had been because it wasn't so continuous. I mean, when we were both up together, we'd plan the whole day – day after day. Once I'd left..."

"I know what you mean, Mr Seymour," said Tyrrel. I was certain, too, that he did.

"In any case," I went on, "after two years Richard duly finished his research, and then he had to go off and do his National Service. Some six months later he heard that his dissertation had been successful – which meant that he was awarded a Fellowship and would be able to return and take it up as soon as he was out of the Army. Meanwhile, he was just about to be commissioned – into the same Regiment, incidentally, as I'd been in – and once that happened, he went to the Middle East and was seen no more in England for a year and a half. He wrote occasionally, and I heard something of him from friends of mine in the Regiment who came back home from time to time; but I didn't meet him again till he returned to Cambridge as a Fellow of Lancaster in September '55 – "

"...with a brand-new MC glittering on his chest," put in Tyrrel.

"That's right. Well, after that he stayed in Cambridge for a year, and we saw quite a lot of one another again. But then, at the end of last summer, he left to do some research in Greece; and, as you seem to know well enough for yourself, he's still there."

"You've heard from him?"

"Not a lot. He's not a great letter writer unless there are some actual arrangements to be made. Once or twice, soon after he got there, he wrote that he'd settled in and his research was ticking over... But I've heard nothing since Christmas... So there you are. Have I been telling you what you wanted to know?"

"Up to a point, sir, only up to a point."

I found this rather deflating. Once again, I attempted to rally myself.

"Nevertheless," I said, "it's your turn to tell me something. You did say you would, you know."

"Yes, yes indeed," he said. "The trouble is that there's almost nothing to get your tongue round. It's just the Greek people have been getting...impressions."

"The Greek *people*?"

"The police, I mean. The authorities. '*They*', you might understand."

"I understand nothing."

"Neither do I really," said Tyrrel. "But I was hoping that what you would have to say would give me some sort of clue. Then I might have been able to explain to you as well. But as it is...you've really told me nothing, have you? Just a string of dates and places. Now, you're a...a humanist, Mr Seymour. You've read the Classics. You must know that dates and places, necessary no doubt, never tell one what one wants to know. Particularly in cases like this. Now, sir, I'm asking you: put a little flesh on all these bones."

"Why should I? You've as good as told me that there is nothing in all this except for some vague feeling...some impression...harboured by '*them*' in Greece...that there's something odd about Mr Fountain. So vague is it all, indeed, that you seem to want me to tell you his life history in the hope that this will give you something concrete to latch on to at last. It strikes me that you might seize at anything. Now why should

7

I help you to give body to some entirely nebulous suspicions? Just answer me that, Inspector Tyrrel."

I had rather expected Tyrrel to start looking winsome or pathetic again. Instead, he suddenly looked very grave indeed.

"Oh no, sir," he said slowly. "You've got it wrong. Assuredly you have. I may not *understand* this but I know there's something in it. Something not a bit nice, either. The Greek people made that quite clear."

"So now they've stopped having vague impressions and become models of precision?"

"No, sir," he said steadily. "Their impressions are still vague; but they are the sort of impressions which neither they nor anyone else could possibly have unless something...very odd indeed...was going on. Put it like this. You or I might have a vague impression, about some politician, say, that he was a genius or a crook or a sexual misfit; and we might be right or we might be wrong, but in any case these are the sort of vague impressions people have every day and, as such, do not command respect. But suppose we suddenly got a *vague impression*, about this politician of ours, that he might be the Son of God, or even just that a lot of other people thought he might be. Now, sir, whether he was the Son of God or not, there'd have to be something very odd going on before we could *begin to think in these terms.* You see what I mean? However vague, it would be an altogether different impression from those people normally have. Not at all an everyday affair."

"So Mr Fountain thinks he's the Messiah?" I asked with heavy sarcasm.

"I didn't say that, sir. I'm just saying that this impression the Greeks have got, however...nebulous (and thank you, sir, for *that* word), is nevertheless so much out of the run of things that it couldn't have begun to arise unless there was something – whatever that something might be – something very peculiar in the air."

8

"In the air over Greek territory, Inspector. Which makes it no business of yours."

"They're going to get rid of him, Mr Seymour. Send him home. It'll likely be my business soon enough."

"After all of which, perhaps you can at last tell me what *is* in the air?"

"I'll try, sir. But it would be better – far better – if you'd fill in a bit more about Mr Fountain first. Put the flesh on the bones, as I said. Tell me about him when he was your study fag, when he was at Cambridge with you. What you know of his service in your old regiment. All that."

"I still think that first I've a right to know – "

"This is *important*, sir, and it is *serious*, and I must ask you to accept my judgement. Please do as I request," said Tyrrel leaning forward with urgency and looking straight into my eyes with what I can only call authority. "*Please*, Mr Seymour. *If you want to help your friend.*"

So then I capitulated finally and utterly. I fetched two fresh drinks and told Inspector Tyrrel all I knew about Richard Fountain, just as I have set it down below.

II

Richard Fountain arrived at Charterhouse in the Autumn of 1943, at the beginning of my last year there. He was at that time a well built, clean spoken and slightly arrogant small boy – with more than a suggestion of self-satisfaction and priggishness in his demeanour. He had come to us as a Scholar (he had achieved, I think, the third place in his year's list), but also with a reputation as a fine games player and as a boy of "sound" character. Now, it is not a good thing when boys of thirteen are praised for their characters; it usually means that they are either pushing or hypocritical or, more probably, both; and when such moral excellence is accompanied by athletic tastes and the whole is crowned by intellectual ability, then one is well advised to approach the child with wariness or not at all.

Certainly, the brains, games, character formula seemed at first to make Richard unapproachable, thick skinned and self-sufficient. In his case, too, as in the case of all young boys who are good examinees, there was a very pertinent question to be asked: how far is this boy just an efficient parrot, learning his grammar with diligence and potting 100% in the syntax paper? Or how far does he in fact possess originality, curiosity, intellectual courage? If the answer was in his favour, his stiff bearing and proud formality did nothing to help us discover this; and for some time, for this reason and others, he was regarded with reserve and without sympathy. After all, we had seen the type so often, the stern-faced little delator who slipped along to the Housemaster's study to report that all was not well with the "tone" of the House (somebody having used a four-letter word in his hearing), the blue-eyed but frowning teacher's darling who got full marks for Latin composition and then led the under-sixteen eleven to victory that very afternoon. Intolerant, interfering, self-righteous boys, who won early positions of authority for themselves, brought nothing but trouble on their more easy-going contemporaries, and ended up as Heads of Houses, lashing themselves into frenzies and nagging their subjects silly over petty discoveries of "slackness" or of "smut". Tiresome and prurient busy-bodies, who eventually won minor scholarships to obscure colleges (there are always a few closed scholarships reserved for boys of "character") and were then mercifully never heard of again in the world − would have been as though they had never existed, indeed, had they not left squads of pestiferous imitators behind them, who took the baleful torch from their mentors as these left the race and continued to illumine the corridors and cubicles with the same sulphurous rays of disapproval, recrimination and guilt. Oh, yes; we knew all about boys of this type − the type to which Richard Fountain so clearly seemed to belong.

Small wonder then that the more equable and good-humoured among us did not look on Richard with much favour for a time. But after he had been at Charterhouse for about two months, it began to become apparent that he had, after all, several qualities of an unexpected and pleasing nature. True, he was impeccably correct and punctual, severe in manner and quietly contemptuous in aspect; but then again his contempt seemed to be turned, not so much on lax morals or human fallibility, as on the sheer waste, stupidity and muddle so common in gregarious life of this kind. He may have been rather pleased with himself, but he was not, it turned out, a delator or a "sneak". The only time, in fact, that he had been known to approach Authority at all was to tell it to its face that some minor arrangement which concerned himself and the other new boys was ill conceived, unnecessary and burdensome; and Authority had been so taken aback that it had conceded Richard's point out of sheer shock and withdrawn the offending edict. This and other incidents unmistakably argued his integrity and, indeed, his courage: a favourable impression which was only increased when his form mates reported that he did not "grub" for the extra marks which he might have been expected, as a Scholar, to obtain, but simply set himself with modest efficiency to fulfil allotted tasks, to do adequate work which was completed without frills and presented without comment. He was always, it was said, ready to help others in a crisis over exercises or preparation. Not that he could be said to unbend: it was just that he was prepared, if his advice was sought, to give cool and swift assistance. And to cap all this, there was his performance as a footballer: this had come fully up to the expectations aroused by the reports from his private school, and it seemed that he was one of the most promising players the school had had for several years; but here again, he matched achievement with good sense; and so far from being prideful in the matter, he quietly gave it to be understood that he held team games as being of little importance in the scheme of things and considerably overrated even as a pastime.

In fact, his modesty and good sense began to be so generally applauded that I now became almost as suspicious on this account as I had formerly been for entirely opposite reasons. All this "efficiency," "coolness," "diffidence" – they could only be, I thought, the careful products of some really inordinate form of pride reinforced by some truly monstrous degree of self-control. It was too good to be true: it just wasn't natural: no boy of thirteen had a right, if he was natural, to be so unexceptionably moderate and unassuming. And then, whatever anyone might say, there was no real abatement, if one took a general view, in the self-satisfaction and priggishness so evident at his arrival: "modest" about his football he might be, but there was still something behind his eyes which let one know that he thought Richard Fountain a pretty adequate creation. So all in all, I was for reserving judgement (I had not, at this stage, yet chosen him to be my study fag); until one day something happened which, if it did not precisely settle things in his favour, ensured that he must henceforth be the object of the closest possible attention.

I myself was not present when the incident in question took place. But I heard a number of eyewitness accounts at the time – which were confirmed, years later, by Richard himself. So you can take what follows as being tolerably exact.

Know, then, that there was in our House at this time a loutish and pustular boy called Westerby. Opinionated but near-cretinous, loud-mouthed and pea-brained, overgrown, over-bearing and over-sexed, Westerby was now starting his fourth year at the school. Still in some remote and unbelievably inferior form, he was the soundest candidate for superannuation that ever I heard of. But this, you must remember, was during the war; and the war-time policy, discreetly urged on Head Masters by the Heads of Services, was that boys, however stupid, who were "potential officer material" should by hook or by crook be kept at school till the age of seventeen and a half, in the hope that they might learn *something* and because, if they were superannuated at an earlier stage, there were technical difficulties in getting them commissioned with all the speed thought necessary. Now, I should have thought Westerby would have been better placed as a convict than as an officer; but in those days "public schoolboy" automatically meant "potential officer," no matter how degraded the creature might be, and so Westerby was allowed to stay, and his sixteen year old presence was suffered by the harassed little master of the lower fourth (who was supposed to be teaching rather backward boys of fourteen), and there he was, the brute, eating enough for two and taking up the room of three. But just because of his size and his seniority in years, some minor place in the official hierarchy of our House had to be found for him: so that Westerby was declared "Head of Longroom", which, as its name implies, was simply a long room inhabited by all boys too junior to have studies, in which category, though he was a Scholar, Richard was inevitably to be found during his first year.

Now, among all the other miserable little boys who sat in Longroom and were governed by the ineffable Westerby was a Jew called Stein – a sweet-natured and sensitive boy who, however, by some unfortunate biological irony, had an exterior every bit as loutish as Westerby's and, despite his mental delicacy, an ungovernable passion for eating. And indeed, poor child, he needed to eat with a frame that size – a frame, I should add, the bulk of which was in no way balanced by its strength: for Stein was only fourteen, so that, unlike Westerby, he had not had time for his muscles to match his growth. Physically, he was a shambling, inflated, utterly frail and uncoordinated creature, with, as I say, this monstrous but necessary lust for food – yet in other respects as kind, intelligent and finely tuned an individual as one could wish to meet. It will not surprise you, then, to hear that Westerby hated Stein. He hated him because of his intellectual ability, his courteous but clumsy manners; because his physique was a parody of Westerby's own; and because he was a Jew. Nor could it be said that Stein was popular in other quarters. I have neither time nor inclination to discuss the attitude shown towards Jews, during the war, by well to do little boys; in some schools it may have been better, in others it was no doubt worse: but at Charterhouse it was, at any rate among the younger boys, uncharitable. A Jew was a Jew. Was in this case the unfortunate Stein. So that when Westerby baited or bullied Stein, the performance was received, if not with approbation, at any rate without protest. Westerby was a lout and much disliked; but then Stein was a Jew. No one was going to risk trouble with Westerby by sticking out his neck on behalf of Stein.

Well, one day towards the end of Richard's first quarter (which was what we called a term) Stein got hold of some sausages from God knows where, and started grilling them over the Longroom fire and wolfing them up like a besieged man. In the middle of this (not very pleasing) exhibition, in came Westerby.

"Ah," he said, "snorkers. Do as you would be done by, Stein."

(Lest you should think that this quotation shows a trace of wit, I should say that it was the common formula for begging food or sweets off another boy.)

At this Stein, being something of a realist, gave Westerby two well grilled sausages and started to cook another one. This he was just about to eat when Westerby, who had guzzled up his two like the hog he was, snatched it away from him.

"That won't do, Stein," Westerby said. "Anyway, these are pork sausages. Jews can't eat pork."

Stein made some ineffectual scrabbling movement to get his sausage back; but Westerby drew back out of reach and, as he went, scooped up the pile of still uncooked sausages which were warming up ready in the grate.

"I'm confiscating these," Westerby said. "My conscience will not allow me to watch a Jew eat pork."

He walked jauntily away towards the grandiose desk, markedly separate from the rest, which custom allowed the Head of Longroom. As for poor Stein, his eyes blinked behind his thick, uncomely spectacles, his cheeks went very red, and two large and deplorable tears came dribbling down on either side of his nose.

"Give me back my thauthages, Wethterby." Stein, of course, had to have a lisp.

"I've told you, Jew. You can't eat pork."

"Give me back my thauth — "

"YES," said another voice from behind Westerby. "Give Stein back his sausages."

So Westerby turned round, and there was Richard Fountain, fists clenched and face quivering with anger; a well built boy for his age but seemingly half the size of Westerby; Athenian versus Barbarian, lithe wrestler against hired tough.

"And who do you think you're talking to?" said Westerby: "new bug."

"That has nothing to do with it. Just give Stein back his property."

"You just mind your own business."

"All right."

And then Richard jabbed Westerby very hard in the pit of the stomach with his left fist and, as Westerby started to double up, caught his head from behind with his right hand. Jerking it down as hard as he could, he raised his left knee with a vicious crack into Westerby's face. After which, as Westerby slowly began to lift his head again, Richard, stepping one pace back and making a wedge of his right palm, swung it backhanded straight into the elder boy's throat just below the jaw. Westerby flopped on to the ground: Richard picked up the remnants of the sausages, gave them to the gaping Stein amid the complete silence of the other onlookers, walked straight out of the room, and never, as far as I know, referred to the incident again until I asked him about it years later at Cambridge.

But of course everyone in our House heard about it within the hour. Nothing official was ever done – what could be done? For the future, Westerby was a little more mannerly, Stein a little less oppressed, and Richard, as I say, remained totally unaltered. As for myself, hot with admiration and curiosity, I chose him there and then to be the study fag to which I was newly entitled. I say "curiosity", because that in the end was the chief emotion the incident aroused in me when I heard of it. To my mind, the really interesting thing was not that Richard had shown moral and physical courage of a high order, but that he should somehow have known, or at any rate have devised for the occasion, such peculiarly devastating and unpleasant methods of hand to hand fighting. It was not that he was unjustified in using such methods: Westerby was twice as strong as he and had deserved, in this instance, absolutely everything he got. On the other hand, however, such questionable forms of attack as the knee to the face or the backhanded wedge blow sorted very ill with what was known of Richard's character. Had he simply squared up to Westerby in Queensberry fashion, like Tom Brown against Flashman, or even shown some slight knowledge of Judo, I should not have been surprised: but as it was, he had demonstrated some back-alley tricks of the nastiest possible kind. Here, plainly, was an indication of some entirely alien yet possibly vital element in his personality: here was one more tantalising inconsistency in a character, at first sight dull and conventional, but which was rapidly coming to present a riddle of the highest quality. Just what was it that made Richard Fountain tick? One might well ask.

For certainly I got no nearer an answer during the remainder of that year. There were no more dramatic incidents, no more overt hints of mysterious attributes. But even so, I found him increasingly fascinating. Why, I wonder? He performed the small menial tasks I set him unselfconsciously and with dignity – nothing peculiar here. He continued to put out a rather self-righteous, a consciously *noli me tangere* air about him, while at the same time maintaining his unspectacular efficiency in the classroom and accepting with modesty the praise he won for his performances on the football field – and later, during the summer, as a cricketer. But I already knew about this aspect of his life, so there was nothing of novelty here. In his relationships with others he was quiet, reliable and unaffectionate. Towards myself he was courteous, respectful and more or less friendly; but friendly only in the most superficial way, showing no desire to give or take, to enquire about my life or to reveal his own. It is possible, of course, that he just found me rather boring at that time. Or was very shy. Or was simply too busy for confidences. But whatever the case might have been, only two things are certain – and those contradictory. Firstly, my own growing and almost obsessive suspicion that here was a being, not only outstandingly talented, but, in some fashion, marred by a gigantic yet undetectable flaw, deformed by some hideous twist of the spirit. And secondly, the fact that this suspicion was based on no concrete reason whatever. Outwardly Richard remained just an able and rather pompous little boy, straight-eyed and clean-minded, conventional in utterance and unexceptionable in manner – if a good deal too stiff-necked to be immediately pleasing. To go beyond this was to proceed entirely in the dark: to search for mysteries was to hunt alone and without a scent. It was all a matter of feeling, of intuition on my part. Evidence, save possibly for the brief and savage bout with Westerby, there was absolutely none.

And since, to be candid, intuition has never been my strong point, and since Richard's career now seemed to proceed in an entirely normal fashion, I began to think, towards the end of my last quarter, that perhaps I had been wrong after all, that probably there was nothing there other than what purported to be there – a healthy, intelligent, reserved child of the kind which always did well at schools. During my last month this feeling became steadily stronger; and when I finally tipped Richard and said goodbye to him, I found myself reflecting that here was just another monitor parting from just another study fag – nothing more and nothing less – neither of whom would have either desire or reason ever to meet again... And so I went to the war. During my four years odd in the Army, I heard of Richard from time to time: but everything I heard only confirmed the thoughts I had had during my last weeks at school – that he was, when all was said, just a conventionally able boy. For he had prospered as a games player, it seemed, and he had done his work thoroughly, and the "soundness" of his character had been unwavering. So he had become Head of the Classical Sixth and Head of the School and Captain of Cricket; and he had got a good Classical Scholarship to Lancaster

18

College, Cambridge. The latter was the most hopeful item: but even this proved nothing, other than that he was dexterous in the formal manipulation of the ancient tongues: for the study of Latin and Greek, which can be the most thrilling study of them all, yet lends itself sooner than any to be exploited, for examination purposes, by clever and superficial boys who are adept at wielding words while having no understanding whatever of the meaning which lies behind them. This might be the case with Richard, and it might not. Since I was to go to Lancaster myself in the autumn of '48, and so, it appeared, was he, I might shortly find out about this and much else − if I still had the interest and the energy to do so. Meanwhile four years in the Army had sapped my energies; and as for my interest, I found little in anticipation of meeting Richard again. For it seemed to me from what I had heard that he had simply passed the years in strict and dull accordance with the brains, games, character tradition, and that all I was likely to find at Lancaster was an empty husk inside the most suitable sort of blazer.

"But you didn't find that at all," said Tyrrel, rising and stretching and looking out on to the midnight square.

"No."

"What did you find, Mr Seymour? Not a lover − which in any case you did not want. But a friend, a real friend this time. So the reserve must have gone − some of it anyhow. And you must have learnt some of Mr Fountain's...secrets."

I remained silent.

"Because there were secrets, weren't there?" he went on. "You had been right at the very beginning − when you thought there was something mysterious, something disastrously twisted even, about Richard Fountain. You were right then and wrong later − when you gave him up as an ordinary and priggish little boy. And you were wrong to expect...a husk in a suitable blazer...when you went to Lancaster College. So what did you find, Mr Seymour? *I want to know,*" he said, striding fiercely back across the room and sitting down sharply and without relaxation in the armchair opposite me.

"You may be disappointed," I said.

"Not if you tell the truth, Mr Seymour. The truth is never disappointing – in the end."

So once more I fetched us both drinks. And once more I tried to conjure up the past for Tyrrel: a nearer past this time and, despite Tyrrel's hints of black secrets, a brighter one: the meadows and the chimes of Cambridge, the slow river moving through the summer afternoons.

It is not easy, now, to tell you exactly what seems to be required of me. It is true that when I arrived at Lancaster and met Richard again for the first time in over four years, I did not find him boring or unpleasing, as I had expected, but indeed became his very close friend. It is also true that my original interest in him, the kind of almost obsessive interest I had felt after the Stein incident, was revived and did not, this time, give way to indifference. But these secrets... I knew of no secrets as such; and yet I did come to feel, with more and more conviction as time went on, that there was...something, something impalpable in essence but definitely wrong, some dissatisfaction or perversity or flaw, that had a great deal more to do with Richard's life than was evident from its apparently smooth and successful progress. Perhaps this was really all I did learn – that I had been right to have doubts about Richard at Charterhouse, wrong to abandon them and write him off as just a gifted but conventional schoolboy. But, you will say, if I got as far as deciding this, I must have had some clear reason – something concrete must have happened. Perhaps it did, but I never knew of it: my surmise was based, I can only tell you, on a feeling in the air. I have already admitted, of course, that intuition is not my strong point; but in this case it seemed altogether too insistent to be ignored. Yet how to convey the quality of this feeling to you? I can best do so, I think, by trying to describe Richard's relationship, not with myself (though you will hear something of that), but with Walter Goodrich. For the more I think of it, the more Walter seems to have dominated those years at Cambridge, to have joined in the conversation at the crucial point, to have poured the wine when one was thirsty, to have made the casual but memorable comment, to have been always and inevitably *there*.

Doctor Walter Goodrich was the Senior Tutor of Lancaster College. This meant that he was broadly responsible for discipline among undergraduates and their correct pursuit of academic studies. Of course, he only actually taught in his own subject, the Classics; and then again, disciplinary questions only came to him if they were too serious for one of the Deans to handle. But this was just what Walter liked: not for him the petty irritations of minor administration and everyday misdemeanour; his was the big picture, the vaguely outlined but all-embracing sphere of influence, the final decision when all the painstaking reports had been drawn up by other people. Next to the Provost, he was the most powerful man in the college; and indeed the Provost's overlordship was scarcely more than theoretical, for it would have been unthinkable that this kindly, withdrawn and scholarly old man should either desire or dare to upset a decision of Walter's.

Nor was Walter without influence outside the college gate. He was one of the senior lecturers in the Classical Faculty. A professorship had never been likely and was by now out of the question, but he was well enough regarded by his fellow scholars and had indeed been allowed a Doctorate of Letters on the strength of some five or six general and wholly readable books – *Day to Day Life in Periclean Athens*, that kind of a thing. Furthermore, Walter was by way of being one of those dons with a network of well sorted strings outside the University, one of those smiling and dining *eminences grises*, whose "nights up in London" were always resulting in some nice little appointment, in the Foreign Office, the City, or even the lower reaches of Government, for one of his many protegés. Walter's protegés, I should add, by no means ceased to be so when they left Lancaster. He battened them to his soul with hoops of steel, and many middle-aged Civil Servants have had good reason to be thankful to Walter. And Walter, of course, to them: for men whom he had advanced (or merely pre served) in their careers were inclined to be helpful when fresh cheeked candidates in their last year at Lancaster were presented for accommodation … You will always hear his name if you happen to be in the haunts of the great world, in the clubs or the chambers or the country houses.

"Oh, so you're at Lancaster?" an Admiral, a Press Lord, an Impresario will say: "well, give my love to Walter."

In this and other ways, Walter Goodrich was not very typical of Lancaster. For it is not a worldly college. It is a puritanical institution – in the intellectual sense at least: its Fellows follow with dedication the most remote paths of scholarship, those least rewarding in money or sensuous enjoyment; and its graduates, who tend to come from poor homes, go out to be of service to the world (despite Walter's efforts on their behalf) rather than to make their mark there. I myself must be almost alone among my contemporaries in having had a substantial private income as an undergraduate and in being able to live, when I came down, a comfortable life with an undemanding job – a job I only do for the mildly cultural value it seems to possess. But if I too was untypical of Lancaster, at least I had an inkling of the austere tradition of learning and service which the college represented. I don't think Walter understood this at all; certainly he could not have raised much sympathy for it (beyond discreetly smiling lip-service) any more than he could find sympathy for the rather joyless left wing politics which most of his colleagues professed or the highly moral brand of rational agnosticism for which the college was famous.

This brings us to a further and very significant point. Just as Walter showed undeniable equivocation in professing a scholar's humility but relishing worldly success, so his attitude to religion, which should have been founded, in his circumstances, on an honest intellectual appraisal, was in fact dictated by the requirements of convenience and mere good form, these in turn being slightly discounted by his anxiety to appear neither gullible nor unsmart. Such various and shifting factors placed him in what might have been an intolerable situation. As the humanist, on the one hand, which he claimed through his books to be, he had to acknowledge – and probably genuinely admired – the non-Christian tastes and virtues of the pagan world: on the other hand, however, he could neither adopt these tastes wholeheartedly nor even link them with the traditional agnosticism of Lancaster, for the world he wished to influence – the established, Athenaeum world – required at least a nominal deference to the Christian faith. As far as that went, Walter was quite happy to go to church occasionally, to refrain from attacking Christianity in his published works, and even partially to accept its tenets as a form of life insurance policy; but one would have thought that the consequent and enforced modification of his enthusiasm for Greek and Roman values might have made even books so general in tone as Dr Goodrich's rather difficult to write with conviction. But if one thought thus, one thought wrong. For Walter, with impeccable insight, had adopted a thoroughly respectable and well tried formula for the reconciliation of these conflicting interests: it was the old schoolmaster's trick of enthusing over the Ancients with one breath and then lamenting, in the next, that Christ had not been born a thousand years earlier so that they too could have had the benefit of his teaching. "Socrates was a truly great philosopher – but he might have been a Christian saint." "Virgil was obviously reaching out, though he did not know it, towards the Christian faith." "Catallus...humph...well, Catallus would have diverted some of his undoubted passion away from the lusts which clearly made him so unhappy: Catallus would have been a natural convert." And so on. An excellent fashion of having it both ways, if, that is, you are not deeply concerned with either. No doubt Walter quite liked the Classics and what they stood for: but in the last resort he was not deeply concerned about the Classics or anything else save for his satisfying and slowly seeping influence in the College, in the University and in the World. A realist if ever there was one, he saw that one must offer the right brand of every commodity – from cigarettes to religious faith.

For the rest, you should know that he was a widower and had one daughter called Penelope, with whom he lived in a pretty house at Grantchester. But this did not prevent him from spending nearly all his time in the college – often he spent the nights there – and from making it the centre and base for his social activities. There he gave many entertainments – far too many by the plain standards of his colleagues; but then none of them was given just for the joy of it, they all had some official or covert purpose. At such of these as were sexually mixed, Penelope acted as hostess; and it was at a "mixed" party of Walter's, given the day after my arrival at Lancaster and designed to introduce the freshmen to the Fellows and their wives, that I met Richard Fountain again for the first time since I left Charterhouse.

Having gone, quite literally, to the wall in order to recover from the barrage of introductions which Walter had levelled at me, I was surprised, for I thought I knew no one there, to hear a very firm voice saying almost into my ear: "And how are you, Anthony?"

Turning towards the voice and failing to recognise the owner, I reflected that if manners at Lancaster entailed addressing strangers by their Christian names, then I had chosen the wrong college. And then the contours of the face I was looking at fell into place, as it were, and I was examining the grown Richard Fountain, a tall, well cut, mature young man, who smiled faintly and said: "I knew you were going to be here. You don't mind if I use your Christian name? Now we're no longer at school?"

"No... Richard."

"People call me Dick."

"I dislike abbreviations," I said, "though I can see what people mean."

For "Dick" was clean and manly and sensible and short, and would have had great appeal in the world of school which Richard had, after all, so recently left. "Dick" meant centuries against Winchester and defending the North West Frontier; and of such was the kingdom of Fountain.

"What have you been doing all this time?" he said.

"Just soldiering. The war was nearly done by the time they commissioned me. I saw a little fighting in Germany. And you?"

"Just being educated. Do you think they did a good job?"

"I wouldn't know," I said; "I'll tell you in a month or so."

"You would like us to see something of each other then?"

"Why not?"

"I just thought... There was something very final about the way you said goodbye at Charterhouse."

So you spotted that, I thought, you sharp little cookie, you. And remembered it. Another talent for Richard Fountain: long memory for potentially important subtleties of behaviour.

"I thought that I was going to a war and would probably be killed. In such circumstances it is prudent to say firm 'adieux'."

"Very plausible, Anthony," he said, "but untrue. You were bored with me and hoped you'd seen the last of me."

Before I could reply to this remark, or even think about its significance, Walter Goodrich was standing in front of us with his hand on the shoulder of a tall and lumpish girl — badly dressed, thick in the calf and ankle, but with a sweet face; a face in no way beautiful or even pretty, yet thoughtful, charitable, and possibly handsome in consequence.

"So you've met each other," Walter said succulently. "But of course you were at Charterhouse together… Richard was your study fag," he said to me with the suspicion of a leer. "Was he…industrious?"

"Passably so."

"Well, now you must both meet my daughter… Penelope, this is Richard Fountain and – er – Major Anthony Seymour."

I had already told Walter that I had no intention of using this ridiculous title, which represented the most tenuous of temporary appointments. The fact that he used it now, with the slight hesitation, could only mean that he wished to imply that I was wilfully clinging to an artificial sense of my past importance which he himself deprecated but was prepared, out of courtesy, to humour. For whose benefit was this deceitful little charade? Penelope's? Richard's? And why?

But Penelope had scarcely noticed what her father said. Her eyes, her ears, her being were for Richard. In a well bred way, of course. She stood there, superficially placid and cow-like, but gazing at him, taking him in, with a fierce intensity that was almost the more indecent for its surface calm.

"I've got someone I want you to meet," said Goodrich to me. Clearly he wanted his daughter and Richard left alone. What a lot of different games he seemed to be playing. But of course it was all really the same game. Discredit the old, and supposedly influential, school chum in front of Richard: make him seem pompous and ridiculous in front of Penelope: then leave Penelope and Richard together. You crafty brute, I thought.

As Walter was leading me away, however, Richard turned from Penelope and said very clearly: "Come to my room tomorrow morning, Anthony. T 5. Come early, and then we can look at Cambridge together. New places are more exciting in the company of old friends."

I think the remark was sincere. But its secondary purpose – to annoy Walter and shake his possessive smugness – was very plain. Good for you, Richard, I thought. As for Walter, he turned a defensive smile in Richard's direction, and then led me up to a tall and angular man who was apparently sitting with some difficulty on the fence which divides youth from middle-age.

"This is Mr Honeydew," said Walter, "College Tutor in mathematics."

"But you may call me Marc, Anthony Seymour," said Honeydew in a precise and high-pitched voice, "Marc, my dear child, with a '*c*'."

Marc Honeydew, who had been imported, I found out later, from King's, was even less typical of Lancaster than Walter or myself. I suppose that was why Walter had introduced us. But if Walter's social sense was not at fault, his sense of tactics very definitely was. For Honeydew missed very little, had observed the scene between the four of us against the wall, and now started immediately on analysis and speculation.

"So of course you know Dickie Fountain," he said. "Now that one, my dear, has really caught our Walter's eye. You should have heard Walter when Dickie came up to take his scholarship exam. 'A real *winner*,' Walter said, as though poor Dickie were in for the Stewards' Cup. 'Will go a *long way*,' Walter boomed. But of course we should have elected him anyway, if only because he wrote such a charming essay. Do you know what he wrote about?"

"No."

" 'The Dying Gods', my dear. Not original, you think? Ah. But you see, it wasn't one of those dreamy, melancholy little pieces, pretending to think Pan is still alive but only just, you know the kind of thing, and sometimes to be seen crying in the woods if you look very carefully. It was a great big angry essay, saying that the Gods were dying indeed but *not fast enough*, that they were still a menace and ought to have been done with long since. He got very cross about it and seemed really to believe what he was saying."

"I don't quite see why this ensured his election," I said.

"Well, it didn't really, because all his translations and things were so good anyhow. But it made an *impression*. Such style, you see. Such vigour. Such *attack*."

"I'm glad to hear it," I said. And then for some reason I felt impelled to tell Honeydew about my own view of Richard. How I still wasn't sure whether he was just an efficient examinee, or something very much more. How his school career supported the former view; whereas I did not yet know enough about him, as he now was, to say whether there was anything to uphold the latter.

"As to that, my dear," said Marc Honeydew, "it's early days to say yet. Though you might think about that essay... But I'll tell you something that *is* for sure. Conventional public schoolboy or little monstrosity, Walter's taken to your Richard and he's going to give him the works. He's going to push him and groom him and drill him; and by the time he's finished, Dickie's going to be one streamlined little go-getter − in whatever line Walter chooses for him − just for a start. The University's a good taking-off point − if you know when to take off..."

He looked at me quaintly and sadly, and smiled with considerable charm.

"I didn't know, you see, so I'm still here, and will be till they throw me out. But Walter will see nothing of the kind happens to Richard... And I'll tell you one more thing, Anthony Seymour. Walter thinks Richard might suit that daughter of his − poor Penelope − and she, my dear, thinks the same. Look."

And so I looked towards where Penelope, still grave and upright, was nevertheless clearly doting with the force of her whole body on the conversation and presence of Richard.

"He's not nineteen," I said.

"Don't you worry about that, dear. Walter won't have any nonsense till everyone's at least twenty-three − he's too old a hand for that. It's just that he'll contrive to see that there's some sort of understanding... A nice, vague, but in fact cruelly committing understanding... And then he'll leave everything nicely on ice until he's ready to get it out and serve it up."

"But... Walter...scarcely knows Richard," I said. "How can you be so sure of all this?"

"Walter," said Marc Honeydew, "picks them on sight, as quick and clever as a cat. And as for me, Anthony Seymour, I've got two sharp eyes in an idle head, and I'm a bugger for watching Walter at his larks."

I paused for a moment to offer Tyrrel a cigarette and light one for myself.

"Please go on," he said gravely; "all this is more interesting − more relevant − than you might think."

"It's also rather exhausting."

"You mustn't stop now, Mr Seymour. Just when some sort of...pattern...is beginning to emerge."

He got up and placed an ashtray on the arm of my chair.

"And so...?" he said.

It may be that I have taken rather a long time describing one uneventful and very ordinary party. But if it is desirable to look for patterns, then this party reproduces, in a sense, the pattern of all our lives during my three years at Lancaster College. Walter watching over Richard Fountain, planning for him, throwing him together, as much as possible, with Penelope. Penelope quietly doting. Richard accepting this situation, but from time to time making it pointedly plain that he also had ideas and arrangements of his own; seeking my company constantly − often, I thought less for its own sake than for contrast to the uncritical adulation of Penelope, for relief from the paternal and mellifluous coaching of Walter. And then there was always Marc Honeydew some where in the background, thrilling to the latest rumour, vibrating with new hypotheses, a sort of evil fairy who was acting, however, only in the capacity of chorus, taking no real part in events but hoping for the worst. Not but what I was fond of Marc. For all his malice, he was more sympathetic than Walter, who was supposedly working only for Richard's good. Marc only wanted to be amused: Walter wanted to enslave.

The day after the party, I went to Richard's room as he had suggested and we explored Cambridge together. It was one of those fine but melancholy autumn mornings which invite reflection about the past rather than anticipation of the future. We didn't in fact discuss the past; but Richard was quiet and confidential, falling into the mood of the day, and I was pleased that he responded in the same manner as myself. We lunched together, went to some film in the evening, had dinner, a few drinks... A very ordinary day, you might think, but a very happy one – one of those days one looks back on with pleasure years later when other events, which seemed at the time so full of colour and significance, are more than half forgotten.

There were to be many such days. But, as I say, I came to feel more and more that they were of value to Richard as release from Walter rather than because of his affection for myself. So as time went on, there was a shadow. As for Walter, he had at first slightly resented my apparent influence over Richard; but it did not take him long to realise that this influence, while genuine, was neither deep nor harmful. So like the diplomat he was, he took to professing a liking for me, and often asked me even to the more exclusive dinners or whatnot that he was giving on Richard's behalf. That he proposed, in this way, to make an ally of me I had little doubt, for frequently he would take me on one side in great confidence and say, for example, "Don't you think that such-and-such is an excellent plan for our young friend?" And since an assumption of comradeship, even on the part of someone you dislike, is difficult to confute, I found myself drawn gradually into an unwanted and dishonest understanding with Walter – which, crudely expressed, would have amounted to, "You help me with this boy, and I'll see you get your share." Richard realised this, for Walter took care that he should; so that Richard sometimes thought of himself as in a sense deserted, and the shadow between us grew.

But it never entirely separated us. We spent holidays abroad together, during which Walter was left so far behind that the shadow would disappear altogether. Even in Cambridge itself there were, right up to the end of my last year, many meals and parties, conversations and expeditions, afternoons on the river and evenings in somebody's rooms. But more and more, when I accepted an invitation of Richard's, I would find unexpectedly that Walter or Penelope were to be of the party. It was as though Richard were saying, "I know you're really with Walter in all this, for all the jokes you make about him when we're alone: so don't you think we'd better have him here just to make everything quite plain?" And then I would be as hurt as if he had said this aloud to my face, I would remain silent throughout the evening and leave as early as I decently could, wondering where Richard really stood in relation to us all, and what final use he intended to make of my friendship, of Walter's interest and assistance. What is Richard's angle, I used to think, as I walked back through the little courts to my room by the river? What does he want of all this? What manner of man can he be?

But whatever the questions I asked myself in the midnight courts near the river, there was no doubt Richard was achieving great outward success. A very solid first in Part I of the Classical Tripos. Two of the more demanding University awards. An occasional place in the University Cricket XI – though he didn't, in the end, get a blue. And then there was the matter of his poems…

For one day, when I went to Walter to have one of my proses corrected, he handed me a thin sheet of paper.

"Look what our young friend has done," he said. And there it was –

> *Who incense for my pyre,*
> *Who wine and spice shall bring,*

31

Who heaps high the fire,
Makes vain offering.
While yet I live, be kind;
No wine on ashes pour:
For thus only mud is made of him
That's dead and drinks no more.

"There are a lot more," said Walter. "I'm arranging with Michael" – and here he mentioned the name of a very well known publisher indeed – "to have them done next spring."

And appear next spring they did, charming, tinkling, derivative – meaningless in the last resort – and because they reminded some of Fitzgerald and others of the Greek Anthology, they sold very well in a small way and brought Richard a definite reputation: "...young man with a talent, undeniably slight, but gently evocative, wistful, delicate and sad," said The Times Literary Supplement.

"Nicely wrapped chocolates," said Marc Honeydew, "with a nymph and a shepherd in a bower on the box."

"Oh?" I said.

"Yes, my dear. Soap bubbles. Candy floss. You must understand. Walter's intellectual influence is proving fatal for poor Dickie. Never mind Walter's plans for his *career* at the moment – must consider what he's actually teaching him to *think*. Academically, I mean."

"Well, what?"

"Perhaps it's not so much *what*, but the *way* he's teaching him to think. All this business about 'the pagans were good but only the Christians really knew'. Aristotle and Aquinas. Christ and Socrates. Virgil writing poems about the virgin birth. Having it both ways, Anthony Seymour."

"What makes you think Richard accepts that point of view?"

"*Look* at these bloody awful poems, dear. They're not *meant*, you see. They're an exercise. Like some old dear writing elegant

Latin elegiacs in praise of cricket or his favourite cat. Listen to this."

He took Richard's book from his table and read out loud –

> *"Love in his mother's lap,*
> *A child at his morning play,*
> *Threw his dice at a hazard*
> *And gambled my life away.*

"Very pretty, Anthony Seymour. But it means nothing because Richard's plainly not running the slightest risk of anyone gambling his life away for love or anything else. It's a 'let's pretend' poem. Let's pretend we're a young Greek poet who's unhappy in love. Or let's pretend we've spent the whole night crowned with garlands and swilling down wine and ended up having sex in a mountain grove as the sun rises... When all the time we're just a cute little English boy with blue eyes, good at cricket, spending a lot of time with a bulging virgin called Penelope Goodrich, and getting ready to cover ourselves with glory in Part II of the Classical Tripos. It is all, my dear, a fake."

Now, what Marc said was undeniably true. You could hardly have had a better indication than those poems of how far Richard seemed to have succumbed to Walter's juicy spiritual compromises, his sly intellectual equivocations. (Leaving alone, as Marc said, the whole question of how far he accepted Walter's proposals and machinations for his future career.) But I promised you I would try to show how I became aware, at Cambridge, that there might be something odd, something violently twisted even, about Richard; and it is at this stage I can best do it. As I say, I have nothing really concrete; but these poems...it is something Richard told me about them which may show you what I am trying to get at.

You see, I thought them facile and artificial. Walter praised them – and effected their publication – because he regarded them as charming verses which in no way committed anyone to anything. Marc damned them for the same reason. But Richard... Richard regarded them as the real thing. They had come from the heart. In Richard's view these poems, so far from being influenced by Walter's dishonest habits of thought, had been meant to express that side of his life which was in revolt from Walter – from whom, indeed, he had tried to conceal them, but who had been too sharp eyed to miss the fact that something was going on.

"And when he called while I was out and found one of the poems on my desk," Richard told me, "I thought he was going to be very angry. It was that one about Bacchus coming to Ariadne after Theseus had left her. It was meant to convey...wildness...lust."

In fact, it had conveyed nothing but a familiarity with a poem by Propertius and a painting by Rubens... But it was *meant* to convey lust...

"So naturally I was very surprised," Richard went on, "when he said how charming he thought it was and could he see more? Because what I put in that poem – well, it's hardly Walter's thing."

That's all you know, I thought. Then, struck by a sudden idea, I said aloud, "How does this wish of yours to express pagan wildness square with that essay you wrote in your scholarship exam?"

"Essay?"

" 'The Dying Gods.' I'm told you condemned pagan survivals."

"In a way I do. We've all got lives to live and careers to make. We've all got to marry sometime, settle down. And this seemed to me a point of view which might do one good in an exam of this kind."

"Really, Richard. You calculating – "

"Please, Anthony. I wanted that scholarship: I *needed* it. I'm not rich, you know. And in any case, I believed what I wrote

34

about pagan survivals...being in some way a threat. But then again, sometimes I think that the very things which are most threatening about them are the most deserving of...of respect. The idea of wine or sex being in some way divine, because they lead beyond mere pleasure to ecstasy and so to release. So that revels or routs are not just obscene – they represent the desire to escape oneself and – become part of...the god. This was the kind of thing I was trying to express in some of my poems and what I thought would make Walter angry... But somehow it didn't."

"Did it worry you – the fact that he might be angry?"

"Yes. But then in a way I wanted to make him angry. Sometimes I hate Walter" – this in an ugly tone I had never heard before – "and that daughter of his, great heavy bosom and cow eyes." Then he calmed down. "But of course he wasn't angry and the poems have been published, and I suppose it's all for the best."

He couldn't realise, you see, that he'd failed to put his message of pagan liberation across. Despite the Times Literary Supplement and its references to "delicacy" and so forth, he just did not see that his supposedly fiery poems had gone down as softly as orangeade at a tennis party. But there's nothing twisted, here, you will say: just an adolescent outbreak of petty rebellion, so innocuous that it resulted only in a few feeble and tinkling verses. Yes; but what you don't see, if you think that – what Walter didn't see and Marc had unaccountably missed – is that he was looking for a weapon to get at Walter and to get at the respectable side of himself. He hadn't found the weapon. All he had done was to produce some saccharine stanzas about nymphs and satyrs and theoretical priapism. The whole thing just spluttered out. But that didn't mean he wouldn't go on looking for a weapon – or that he might not find a dangerous one. Because for all his long sessions with Walter, his polite social attendances upon Penelope, his academic and athletic successes and his thought for the future, there was something of

35

a very different kind waiting to get out; and the fact that it hadn't yet found a channel, or was most of the time damned up by self-control or hypocrisy, only made the whole business a great deal more perverse.

But now I will tell you of something which happened during our last summer – and may make what I mean rather plainer. It was still nothing really definite; for the incident, though nasty, was a small thing and perhaps not uncommon in kind. But you may feel, knowing what you now do, that what was or might have been behind it gives valuable matter for thought.

At the end of our last summer term, we made up a party, at Walter's suggestion, to go to the college May Ball. It was agreed that Richard should partner Penelope, that Walter should preside in bachelor splendour, and that I should find someone external to give a little novelty to the gathering. So I invited a distant cousin who was then up at Girton, and duly presented the pair of us in Walter's rooms, where we were to dine before going on to the Ball.

I anticipated a routine and mildly tiresome evening. But Walter was exerting himself as host, while Penelope was visibly pleased both with her dress and her situation – as partner to the most distinguished undergraduate in the college on the social occasion of the year. Richard was relaxed and happy because he was finished with his exams; and my cousin from Girton was personable and knew how to conduct herself. Under these auspices the evening started and continued well – so well, that towards the end of dinner Walter could no longer resist the temptation to exploit the prevailing good humour in the interest of his latest scheme.

"So," he was saying, "here you both are – and about to graduate inside a week. It seems only yesterday you arrived…" And then to me, "What are your plans, Anthony?"

As a matter of fact he knew very well, for he had asked this question and been answered several times in the last month. But I let him have his cue.

"I'm going to London," I said. "I've invested some money in a new magazine they're starting, and I shall act as one of the editors."

"What magazine?" said my cousin.

"*Metroland Topics*. It will be literary in tone and expensively produced."

"And will make no money at all," said Walter, "but will carry high prestige. I was talking to Stephen and John about it last week. You will be well employed, Anthony. And easily available," he added, "to come up and see us all here."

"I shall come often," I said.

"Because you see," Walter burbled on, "I'm arranging for young Richard to stay on and do some research. A good idea, you think?"

Since everyone in the room, except my cousin, had known for at least two years that this was Walter's intention, and since we had also known for a month or more that he had taken very definite steps to implement it, there was a certain superfluity about this speech. I immediately thought — rightly — that it could only be the preparatory process for something more dramatic.

"And now we're all here," said Walter, "the family as you might say, I'm sure Miss — er," — a swift bow to my cousin — , "will forgive me if I mention a little proposition I have in mind. You see, my dear boy," he said to Richard, "I have come to be very fond of you, and so has Penelope, and so I thought…" — clearly Walter had bitten off something rather craggy even for him — "…well, let me put it this way. What are you doing about digs?"

"Digs?"

"Yes. Research students can't keep rooms in college, you know. You'll have to move out of your comfortable T 5 and find somewhere in the town. Had you thought of this?"

"No," said Richard crossly.

It was very plain what was coming now. You bastard, I thought. Bringing this up in front of myself and, what was more, a complete stranger, so that Richard would have to behave politely and might thereby find himself more than half committed before he properly knew what was happening.

"Well," said Walter soothingly. Penelope was gazing at Richard with evident anxiety, hope and fear written all over her honest face. "Well," said Walter, "there is plenty of room at Grantchester. You could have a bedroom and a sitting-room of your own. You could have your meals with us, or, when I'm in Cambridge, with Penelope. And what is more, dear boy," said Walter with the air of a conjurer who produces a bird of paradise instead of a chicken, "It wouldn't cost you a penny."

"Oh, Richard," said Penelope, touching his arm.

Now, at first sight, this was a kind offer which would be very helpful to Richard. He had only a tiny allowance from his father, the stipend paid to him as a research student would be minimal. But it was equally obvious that Walter, who never did anything for nothing, would be receiving excellent value for his money – in the form of Richard right under his eyes and under his thumb, in almost permanent contiguity with Penelope. It was really an outrageous suggestion, and the more so for the circumstances in which it was made. It had something in it variously of the slave-dealer, the procurer and the vampire. Walter, one felt, wanted to suck Richard dry and infuse God knows what noxious mixture back into him in place of his own blood.

"Don't you think it is a good scheme?" said Walter to me.

"That is for Richard to decide."

"Well then... Richard?"

Richard was white but collected. He simply said, "You're very kind, Walter. I shall think it over and talk to you later, if I may."

But he said it in such a manner as to close this discussion firmly and for good; and from that moment he devoted the evening to revenge.

His method was very simple. He behaved, except in matters of formal courtesy, as though Walter and Penelope were not there. He passed them the cigarettes and offered them his lighter, he answered them, though as shortly as possible, if they addressed him; but in general he contrived to give them the impression – and this in Walter's own rooms – that he was spending the evening *à trois* with my cousin and myself and that Walter and Penelope were merely strangers who happened to be at a nearby table. Walter, who realised that he had gone too far (it was odd, if one considered his experience, how many tactical errors the man made), was apparently prepared to see the matter through without complaint. Certainly he contrived to play the host quite adequately and without abashment. Penelope, on the other hand, began to be very distressed indeed. Nor was her unhappiness in any way lessened when we moved on to the Ball itself; for here Richard, having danced dutifully for a while with my cousin and never looked in Penelope's direction, left us without a word and was then variously to be seen dancing with the partners of friends or drinking with other parties. He knew how to make his presence felt, how to be brilliant on brilliant occasions; he went hither and thither winning admiration and undisguisedly warm glances in every part of the room except for where his business lay – with us. It was cruel for Penelope. An evening which was to have been a rich source of personal happiness and social triumph had been effortlessly turned by Richard into one of outrage and humiliation.

In other circumstances she might have had the spirit to fight back, for she was a plucky girl and not without resource. But where Richard was concerned she was a blushing and hesitant fool. So she simply sat quiet and miserable, if not without dignity, blankly staring when he was not to be seen, following him avidly with her eyes (but not her head) when he was. We all did our best to treat her with sympathy and yet at the same time as if nothing untoward were happening. But by the time I rose to dance with her for the fourth time she was clearly near breaking point.

"Why does he have to be so hard?" she said to me. "Why does he go on? He's made his point."

"He doesn't like people organising his life."

"Oh, he doesn't." She snorted – that, I'm afraid, is the only word. "He's happy enough to let Daddy organise his life when it suits him. When it means getting books published or being allowed to stay on here as a Research Student. But when Daddy asks him to do something which will give pleasure...not to mention saving him money...out of pure kindness..."

"He has his pride. And perhaps he doesn't want your father...to have too great a share of his existence. After all, to go to live in someone else's house is an important step. It is very committing."

"I suppose you're on Richard's side," she said bitterly; "boys together."

At this moment we were dancing towards a table at which sat a large and rather raucous party whom Richard had lately joined. He was talking with some animation; and there was a kind of glitter about him which made me wonder what and how much he had been drinking.

"I'm going to settle this," Penelope said.

Before I could stop her, she had detached herself from me and was moving squarely toward Richard. For a moment I thought she had found the spirit to confront him in anger; but if so her sudden animus had flagged before she reached him, and when she finally came to a halt in front of him she was standing as a supplicant.

"Richard," she said, "won't you dance with me? I'm sorry if... We didn't... Please dance with me."

For about ten seconds Richard looked into her face with a charming smile as though he were about to agree to her request. Then he rose, took a step towards Penelope, turned to one side and, without speaking, helped an attractive and sly-looking dark girl to her feet and swept her away across the floor. Penelope, who had already started to hold her arms out, let them fall in a gesture of utter defeat, turned about and walked with head drooping into the night. No spectacle I have ever seen has ever filled me with such horror and shame.

A few days later Richard and I went to the Senate House to receive our degrees; and then I left Cambridge, to return, henceforward, only as visitor or guest. Richard's quarrel with Walter and Penelope was soon healed. He excused himself on the ground of the strain of his examinations followed too soon by too much drink and excitement; and they were only too ready, with their various motives, to forgive him. But of course it had been nothing to do with strain; Richard had started the evening in a relaxed and pleasant mood, and would have stayed that way had not Walter's mistimed gesture of possession called up the evil in him. Evil? Certainly some quality of which his friends had little previous notion: with the exception of myself, who remembered the Westerby incident at Charterhouse and the vicious manner (albeit in the cause of justice) in which Richard had then acted; who remembered lots of lesser and impalpable but curiously suggestive things over the three years we had been at Lancaster together; who was by now certain that there was something deeply and perhaps incurably... wicked?...perverse?...at any rate something *wrong* in Richard Fountain.

But, as I say, I was now leaving Cambridge and going to live in London. I saw quite a lot of them all during the next two years, but there was no longer the same revealing everyday contact. As far as I could make out, Richard settled very steadily and contentedly to his research; in any case I heard nothing, even from the inventive and trouble-relishing Honeydew, which gave any hint of the diseased soul which I thought I had seen revealed at the May Ball. Richard never went to live with Walter in Grantchester: the offer was never again referred to. But now as ever he was Walter's boy, and Penelope's too, I suppose; for towards the end of his period of research, it was made plain to everyone that there was now an "understanding" between them – just as Marc Honeydew had presaged at Walter's party for freshmen so long before. Still, there was to be nothing official about this as yet – one obvious and quoted reason being that Richard would now have to go away and do his National Service. For while Walter had easily got this deferred for another two years so that Richard might do his research, even Walter could not get it deferred forever. So in August 1953 Richard completed his dissertation – "Some Observations on the Survival of Minoan Rites into Classical Times" – , and handed it in to meet success or failure when adjudged the following Spring. And then, leaving Penelope happy in her "understanding" and Walter busied with manifold ambitions on his behalf, Richard Fountain went for a soldier; being at this time in his four and twentieth summer, as handsome and likely a lad to look on as ever swore loyalty to the Queen.

III

For some moments Tyrrel remained seated, still in the poised and tense position he had maintained throughout my narrative. Then he rose and went to my bookcase. After a time he said, "There are two books by Richard Fountain here."

"The second is also poetry. Written in the Army this time."

"As artificial as the first?"

"Yes and no. Some of the poems are only a hangover from the state of mind which induced the earlier ones. Look at page 73."

Tyrrel turned the pages, and then began to read in a sensitive voice which was somehow made the more impressive by a slight Midland flatness:

> "*O aves nunc in silva canunt,*
> *The wind of the South is on the wing.*
>
> *Duri magistri mox abibunt,*
> *The lawyers cease from their chattering;*
> *Deserta stant in urbe turres*
> *And men make ready for journeying.*
>
> *Tristis est hiems et longa dies,*
> *Time for the old men's lecturing –*
> *Time for the priest crudele locuto*
> *Pestes et oras, of death and sin.*

Sed animus omnis nunc solutus,
The girls are ripe for the gathering;
Laete per campos mittitur amnis,
The bells in their towers this rhyme do ring:

O aves nunc in silva canunt,
The wind of the South is on the wing."

"You see?" I said. "Youth going on the rampage despite the muttering of lawyers and old men – for whom read Walter Goodrich."

He nodded.

"But what about the poems which aren't just a hangover?"

"War poems – of a kind. Genuine, I suppose, but a trifle reminiscent of Rupert Brooke. And a little inflated, when you consider that the sort of action Richard saw was really only police work."

"Yet he seems to realise that was all it was," said Tyrrel. "Here.

"Shall death find me?" he read,
"Find me where the river ends?
And shall I come to darkness
For old men's dividends?

"Keeping the Empire ripe for the shareholder," Tyrrel said. "For shareholder read Dr Goodrich again?"

"I dare say."

"Did this book do as well as the first?"

"Better. A soldier's poems are almost the only kind that sell. And then you should remember that Richard became a hero in a small way."

"Yes…I can see he might have done well in the Army. Competent, intelligent, good physical specimen. Fully prepared to tell others what to do – and to take his own share in it. Brave.

44

And with a very suitable outlet for this violence you speak of. Not popular with his men though?" said Tyrrel shrewdly.

"No. Too good to be true. To be popular with his men an officer must be fallible."

"You remarked earlier," said Tyrrel slowly, "that from time to time friends of yours in Fountain's regiment – your old regiment – returned to England and told you of him. So what did they tell you?"

"Mainly gossip. How the men trusted him but didn't like him, as I say. How the officers found him superior and rather unsympathetic. Of course, he heard just before leaving for the Middle East that he had been awarded a Fellowship. This was hardly calculated to make him more amenable to military society."

"Ah," said Tyrrel; "but from what you've just said it looks as if he was disliked, not because he was an intellectual or a scholar, but because he was more military than the military. Too good to be true, you said, Mr Seymour. Too efficient? Too keen? Too…ruthless perhaps?"

"Perhaps. The Army in peace time can be very easy going."

But I knew Tyrrel was right. It was only fair that I should confirm his hypothesis more definitely.

"No, not perhaps," I went on rather angrily. "You're dead bloody right, Inspector. Dead bloody right. They didn't like Richard, partly because they knew he had another and in some ways superior world to go back to – a world they none of them could aspire to or even understand – but mainly because he was just a damned sight too good at his job. Not but what he was as unassuming about this as he used to be about his games at Charterhouse. But he got everything much too right. And if anybody got in his way, when he was told to get something done, he'd slap him down as smartly – "

" – as he slapped down Westerby in Longroom," said Tyrrel, using the expression as easily as if he had been an old Carthusian himself.

"Yes. No little compromises over gin and tonics. No convenient delays. No little hints to people of the trouble that might be coming their way. Just do whatever it was, wham, wham, wham, and let the dead bury their dead. He was a very awkward colleague."

"And no doubt an awkward enemy, Mr Seymour. We should be fair. But it rather looks as if Mr Fountain's brother officers spotted what a lot of his clever friends — except yourself of course — had missed. That there was this *twist* — a very ugly twist — in his make-up."

"In a crude way they may have spotted it. But they couldn't see into the...subtleties...of it all."

"Nor could you, Mr Seymour."

"At least I knew they were there... But you mustn't think, Inspector, that he was *hated* by the other officers. One or two were even very fond of him. Or at least interested enough to relish his acquaintance. The colonel found him rewarding. Several others. There was Major Longbow — who put him up for his MC."

"What about this MC? You say he was made quite a hero out of it all?"

"It was more for displaying persistence and resource than actual courage... Though God knows there was that as well... That poem you were reading, Inspector: 'Shall death find me?' Read out the rest of it."

With evident pleasure, Tyrrel complied:

> "*Shall death find me?*
> *Find me where the river ends?*
> *And shall I come to darkness*
> *For old men's dividends?*
>
> *And shall old Charon have me,*
> *To ferry me clean away*

To the end of the river,
To the end of my day?

And shall my love follow me
Over the river?
Give me heart's blood, that brings
Life from the giver?

O the bank I left is fairer
And there my love will stay;
Listening for the safe sweet chimes
In the meadows of May."

"Apart," I said, "from the unfair implication that 'his love' –
Penelope one supposes – would soon forget him, what do you
notice?"

"A lot about a river."

"Yes. It isn't only an image. This poem refers to an expedition
led by Richard – a very unpleasant expedition down a
particularly sinister river."

"Go on, sir."

"I've never talked to Richard about this, but I know the
Sergeant Major who went with him as Second in Command
quite well. He was once a corporal under me. I met him at the
Depot a year or so back, and from his account what happened
was this…"

We were up there in the jungle on detachment, Sergeant Major
Meredith had said. That is, the Company was, with Major
Longbow commanding, and only Mr Richard and one other
subaltern to help. The rest had all been taken with jungle belly,
see, and a good third of the men besides and more getting it
every day, so that things weren't what they should have been,
sir, very awkward, with everybody doing everybody else's job
and most of the men spending most of the day just cleaning up

their mates who had this jungle belly. Which is a kind of dysentery, sir, fierce and runny like a geyser. And in the middle of all this there comes the District Commissioner from Nianga, and says his District Officer's in trouble up the river.

Now, sir, this District Officer had his headquarters with a clerk and a handful of nigger police thirty miles up the river at a place called Akoru, if you could call it a place; because all there was was a few raggy huts and a piss-run, and the only way of getting there was going up the river in boats, being as how there was thick jungle, like a hot-house crammed full with coiled barbed wire, for ten miles on either side of the river. And what they wanted to have a District Officer or any other of God's creatures at Akoru for is more than I can say; though I did hear talk that he was responsible for the River Tribes, which lived further up the river and scratched some sort of living up, like the birds picking meat from the holes in a crocodile's teeth. Nasty work, I wouldn't wonder, and no miracle they sometimes got a bit tired of things and should need for to take it out on somebody.

Any road, this District Officer had come up on his wireless set and told his chief he didn't like the smell of things up his perishing river, and would he send some more police at the double? After which his wireless goes out with a noise like a room full of drummer boys all farting at once, which makes the District Commissioner think he's likely telling the truth. Only there wasn't any more police to send, see, because they were all sorting out trouble in Nianga. All there was to go was us. And us two officers short, and half the men shooting their guts into buckets twice a minute; not to mention poor Colour Baines as yellow as pepper and floating round his bleeding stores like a prick-shaped balloon at a kid's party — you only wanted a cigarette end or a pin and he'd have been a handful of damp rubber.

But Major Longbow says, "We're here to help the Civil Power, Sergeant Major, and help the –ers we will. There's Mr

Fountain," he says, "and you can go as his 2 i/c, and you can take two corporals and twenty men and four of those large canoes. Six of you with your rations and bedding to each canoe."

So off we went, Major Seymour, sir, and very simple I dare say it sounds. Follow your nose and you can't miss Akoru. No more you could – provided you could heave the boats through the weed, because the river's just a marsh, a lot of it; and provided you didn't get eaten whole or just nicely poisoned by some hell-creature in the mud when you were in the water pushing; and provided the mosquitoes and the dear Lord knows what left a drop of your own blood in your body. And, on top of it all, provided that six men in twenty didn't get jungle belly eight hours after starting. You see, sir, normally you get natives who know the river and its ways to take you down. But with the trouble in Nianga and all over... Not a nigger could we get. Not a one. And after twelve hours we'd covered just ten miles, all of us dead beat and, as I say, six men with their innards turned to hot Steinhager ripping its way out of them like a saw.

"Leave 'em here with Corporal Symonds and one canoe, sir," I said; "and we can make our way on in the morning."

So Mr Richard got on his wireless to the Major and asks him to make what shift he can to collect Symonds and the other six. The Major didn't like this, but he quite saw that six sacks of gut fluid wouldn't be no help in getting us twenty miles further, and so he agrees. Then we spend a few hours trying to sleep, and off we go again, leaving Symonds doing nursey and looking back down the river, where his help would come from, as though he thought to see Jesus Christ come walking over the water at any minute.

Well, sir, by the time the sun went down that second day, we'd got a further twelve or fourteen miles and we could reckon to reach Akoru late the next afternoon. Which was lovely as far as it went. Only another five men, including the second corporal, had come down with jungle belly. Which left us with just nine fit men and me and Mr Richard.

"We can't leave them here this time, Meredith," he says. "It'd take two days for the Major to send them help — if he's got any help to send. And we can't spare good men to stay here and look after them. They'll have to come on with us in the morning."

Which was fair enough, sir. They'd not be too comfortable in the canoes, but we'd be able to do something for them when we got them to Akoru. Or so we hoped. So then he gets on the wireless to let the Major know how things are, and the Major says to take the sick men on the next morning like he's decided, and once again we try to get some kip.

But in the morning, sir, there's four men more as sick as you please, and one that was sick the night before — Private Buxton — lying there dead. Which means only seven of us is properly on the move. Not to mention that if you carry a dead man you carry more than his weight.

"All right," says Mr Richard. "It's no good thinking us seven can get three canoes and all these sick men through this shit to Akoru. The only hope is for a few of us to get to Akoru quickly, try to organise help there and send it back."

Which is all very nice, I thinks to myself, only you don't know, bonny boy that you are, what sort of games they're having in Akoru just now.

But he has the sense not to give me or any other —er much time for thinking.

"Which of the five fit men is the most reliable, Sergeant Major?" he says.

"Private Thorpe," I says.

"Come here, Thorpe," he says.

And Thorpe comes.

"Private Thorpe," says Mr Richard, "it is my duty and privilege to promote you, here in the field, to the rank of full corporal. You have my word that this appointment will be confirmed and honoured by my superior officers after we get back. You will now select one of the remaining fit men to stay here with you and assist your sick comrades until such time as I send help back from Akoru. Understood?"

Well, sir, Thorpe looks a bit green, and he's just going to open his mouth to say something, when Mr Richard says, "I'm particularly glad to have you to call upon, Thorpe. I was reading the other day in the History of the Regiment how your grandfather won a VC at Ypres."

It was a long shot, because there's a lot of Thorpes in the regiment, being as it's a Ludlow name, but Mr Richard had come up with the right number. Private Thorpe stands up like double his height, and he salutes Mr Richard as though he were saluting the Prince of Wales, and off he goes like the Lord Harry himself to choose a mucker to help him.

"You and I and the other three will go on," says Mr Richard, " – with Private Buxton."

"Bury him here, sir," I says.

"No, Meredith. Private Buxton may well be the most useful member of the party."

Then he gets them to making a sort of bier for poor Buxton. Tent poles, a couple of blankets and some cording. A pillow for his head. Gets some green and a few of these jungle flowers and decks it all up a treat.

"Now. Buxton in one canoe with two men to paddle and keep the flies off. You and I and the other man in a second canoe. The third stays here."

And off we go once more. There's a rough patch soon after we start, where it's every live bugger in the water pushing, but it's not too thick at that, sir, and later on the going's good enough. So that by about three in the afternoon Mr Richard says he reckons we're nearly there.

Then he stops us to make some preparations. First of all, he has the canoe with Buxton lying in it attached to ours with a rope, so that we can tow it behind us. Then he routs about in his bedding roll, and damn my heart if he doesn't come up with his Sam Browne belt and sword case. He fits his Sam Browne and gets me to buckle on his sword.

"You two," he says to the boys in the second canoe, "one at Buxton's head, one at his feet. Arms reversed."

And on we go, Mr Richard standing at the bow end of the leading canoe with his sword drawn, and me and the other chap paddling him and towing the one behind, where Buxton's having his last ride, all decked out with jungle green and two good men to guard and mourn, as is fitting for a soldier of Her Majesty's forces. Round a bend in the river we come, and there it is — a few miserable huts on the bank and a couple of native boys going screaming in among them to give the word. A flag post but no flag. A sentry point but no sentry. And then half a hundred ugly bloody wogs, some of them with rifles and some with those cutlasses they carry, coming out of the jungle and out of the huts, crowding down to the water's edge with a sort of mutter hovering in the air above them, and all of them waiting for us.

"Akoru," says Mr Richard. "Just keep a steady pace into the bank, Jim Meredith," he says, "or you'll never make RSM."

So very slowly we move in towards the bank. And as we get nearer, the wogs start fiddling with their rifles and fingering their cutlasses, and I start wondering what it feels like to have two feet of rusty iron up your crutch, and Mr Richard stands there as stiff as though he's outside Buckingham Palace and whispers out of the corner of his mouth: "Easy does it. That's my good boys. Easy… Easy…"

And then, when we're only about thirty yards from the reception committee, and the mutter they're making is like a cloud of angry bees in summer time, Mr Richard lifts his sword hilt to his lips and brings the point down in a salute as lovely as ever you saw. Then he raises the point again and sweeps it round, very very slowly, till he's pointing straight at poor Buxton lying there in the second canoe, with the two lads making shift to lean on their arms-at-the-reverse and their heads bowed like a pair of weeping angels. And at that moment the crowd stops its muttering and takes a good look, and then starts jabbering again twice as loud but in a softer tone, if you see what I mean, sir; and then damn my soul to hell if they don't start sort of shrinking away from each other, till lo and behold there's a clear passage made through the middle of 'em, wide enough for three good men to march abreast.

Well, we don't need to be told what to do now. When we reach the bank, Mr Richard walks about ten feet up from the water and then stands still. Me and the other lads unloads Buxton and lays him down. Then I and another picks him up again, the remaining two form up behind us, and at the word from Mr Richard we slow-march up through the crowd and forty yards or so into the village, till he halts us just by this flag pole which hasn't got a flag. We put Buxton down at the foot of the flag pole, and Mr Richard steps forward and calls out, "Who speaks English here?"

Then a funny little chap, all wizened and shrinking and bowing, comes scratching out of the crowd.

"Where is your leader?" Mr Richard says.

The little chap calls out, and a big man with a rifle, and a cartridge belt slung across his chest, comes slowly out of the ruck of them, looking at Mr Richard as if he wants to chop him apart for fire wood – and no doubt would have done if poor Buxton hadn't been lying there with the flies starting to settle on him now and a faint stink coming up, which gets me to wondering how long we shall have to keep him above ground for our protection.

Any road Mr Richard points to Buxton and then to the flagpole, and says to the interpreter, "Tell your leader that my dead friend would wish the flag of his fathers to fly above him."

So the interpreter tells the big bloke, who mutters and curses and shakes his head, but the crowd have heard too and come edging forward, chattering and mumbling; and somehow it's plain that they agree with Mr Richard, for some of your natives can have a powerful respect for the dead, so that the big bloke, after he's looked at them once or twice as cruel as a barrack square on a February morning, lumbers off to one of the huts and comes back with the flag and hands it to Mr Richard. And Mr Richard and me, we start fiddling with the hoist ropes, and all I can think of is "Now which way up is the –ing thing meant to go?" But up it goes in any case, Major Seymour, sir, right to the top of the pole. The lads present arms without having to be told, bless their hearts, and then we lower away again till the flag's at half mast above Private Buxton, who deserves the compliment if ever any bugger did, for stink as he might he'd saved the lives of his five comrades.

And many more too, I wouldn't wonder. For once that flag went up, and the natives saw it where they were used to seeing it, there was an end to trouble in Akoru – and all the length of the river, as we afterwards heard. The crowd melted away like the beer in a quartermaster's pot, until there was only the big bloke and the interpreter left for Mr Richard to question. Well, the District Officer was dead and so were most of his police, bar those that had joined the rebels. But with the flag up and the crowd gone, and the big bloke seeing that the best he could do to save his skin was to help us all he knew, we soon settled to get everything to rights. Disarmed everyone in the village. Got on the wireless to Major Longbow, who said he'd tell the District Commissioner and send fresh men as soon as possible. Fixed up a team of natives who really knew the river to go back with me and collect Corporal Thorpe and the rest. And there it was, Major Seymour, sir, everything sweet and cosy again, and all done with a silly toy of a sword and a dead man who was already fit meat for the flies...

"And so he came home a hero," said Tyrrel. "And his proud Penelope was waiting to go to the Palace with him and see him get his medal."

"She went to the Palace all right," I said; "but after that things didn't go quite as she might have hoped."

"Oh?"

"You see, Inspector, when Richard got back to Cambridge in the autumn of 1955 he was a bit restless at first and rather difficult. But Walter and everyone put this down to two years away in the Army; and so when, after a time, he seemed to settle more or less, they thought everything was all right. He was getting on quite well with a new line of research Walter had suggested, and taking the part expected of a young don in college life, and you might have thought all was well."

"And wasn't it?"

"From Walter Goodrich's point of view, there was still one thing very much amiss. The 'understanding' which Richard was supposed to have with Penelope…nothing whatever seemed to come of it. Oh, he was polite and nice enough when he saw her. But he didn't go one step out of his way in order to do so."

"Perhaps he'd met someone else…while he was in the Army?"

"If so, there was no sign of her. So both Walter and Penelope began to get a bit restive about this. And matters were not improved when he began to avoid them – not merely to make no effort to see them, but actively to keep out of their way. Nor was this all: at about the same time he began to see a very great deal of a young first year undergraduate called Piers Clarence."

"I thought you said – "

" – I did say. There was nothing about Richard's friendship for Clarence," I said firmly, "which could even remotely suggest a homosexual entanglement. I saw them together several times and I'm sure of this. It was just awkward that he should suddenly make of Clarence an almost constant companion at the same time as he started to see as little as possible of Penelope – not to mention Walter."

"And what did you deduce from that?" said Tyrrel.

"Much the same as Marc Honeydew did," I said. I went to my desk and routed for a few moments until I found what I was after.

"This letter," I said, giving it to Tyrrel, "sums up the whole matter very shrewdly. Marc wrote it to me just when Richard first started to see a lot of Piers Clarence – before I myself had met the boy. You will notice that Honeydew on the whole supports me in saying that this was not a homosexual affair – though one or two of his innuendos indicate that he might like to have believed it was. Ignore those, and you have a very tolerable account."

Dear Anthony Seymour, (Honeydew had begun,)
  It was lovely seeing you in London last month, though I don't think much of that stuffy old club of yours. Any way, it's high time you came to pay us a visit again, my dear; and I have a little news which may tempt you from the gay metropolis quicker than our other poor attractions.
  The fact is that Dickie Fountain has started a kind of affair with a new undergraduate called Piers Clarence. Of course you know what a hysterical old thing I am, so when I say "affair" I'm exaggerating a bit, because I don't think there's anything wicked going on, my dear, like holding hands under the table in the Arts' Restaurant or taking luxurious double bedrooms in five star hotels. The plain truth remains that Dickie and this boy are together a very great deal – lunches, walks, theatres, the *lot*.
  So what's he like, this Piers Clarence, I hear you asking in that serious way of yours, and is he a good thing for Richard? Well, Anthony Seymour, Master Clarence is a very gay nineteen, with manly cherub looks (the contradiction is purposeful) and reputed to be highly intelligent. He is also known to be very lazy, prone to spend money he has not got, and given to much wine and

merriment; the ushers at his school reported him as being "unsatisfactory"; so all in all you can see he is an attractive character, and it's a bit of a puzzle to my addled old brains how he ever came to get into Lancaster. Because you know, my dear, what long and austere faces we all have here.

Anyway, here he is, the friend of Dickie Fountain's bosom, and I don't think it's what Dr Goodrich ordered at all. It isn't that Dickie is being distracted from his work – that goes quite well from what I hear, and of course those Army poems of his have been doing him a deal of good in a generally cultural way. Nor is it that there is any particular likelihood of overt scandal, because after all Master Clarence is reading the Classics and so can be assumed to have that most respectable asset in common with Richard as well as his (less respectable) youth; when all is said, dons aren't positively forbidden to go about with their pupils. No. Walter's trouble is that a lot of people are already beginning to enquire what has happened about the famous "understanding" Richard was supposed to have with Penelope, and this means that the Clarence business has come at the most unhelpful time possible – just when it is absolutely *vital* for Walter to have the strongest grip on Richard he can contrive. Which is exactly what he hasn't got. Because you see, my dear, the real point is this: Dickie is using Piers Clarence in much the same way as he once used you – as an embodied contrast to, and a means of escape from, the burdensome influence of possessive Walter. So frustrating for Walter.

Not, I hasten to add, that Richard isn't fond of both Piers and yourself for your own delicious sakes; but you've both come in handy, at one time or another, as *Walter-antidotes*, and this does make you even more desirable than Dickie might otherwise have found you… But there is, Anthony Seymour, one important difference, which I now beg you to note, between Richard's friendship for yourself and his affection for this Clarence child. In your case, he'd known you before, and even though you were conceived by him as an "anti-Walter" you were a pretty sober and serious companion. So much so that even Walter had to recognise and respect you as such. This Piers Clarence, on the other hand, might have been deliberately chosen as a Walter bait. He is a positive banner of rebellion. Pagan and dissolute in habit, mocking in demeanour, racy in speech and casual in conduct – anti-church, anti-establishment, even anti-education – I tell you, my dear, he's a joy to have around. And it very much looks to me as if Richard, after years of plaudits from the schoolmasters and Walters of this world (if we forget his *occasional* naughtinesses), is at last beginning to think he's been in the *wrong* gallery all along and is bent on letting everybody know it by the simple expedient of flaunting Piers Clarence in front of them. Not that he actually joins in Piers' frolics; but he never rebukes him, and even, I think encourages him, if only indirectly, by lending him little bits of money – and on one occasion by letting him use his rooms for a party while he himself was away for the weekend. *Rather* naughty, I thought – and so did all the Porters.

Of course, one can't help feeling sorry for poor Penelope with all this going on. I'm so afraid we shall wake up one morning to find she's become a *nun*. But then you know her, bags of guts and officer-like quality, so I expect she'll face it out somehow... Anyway, my dear, I do beg you to come up and have a look at this ménage, and possibly to counsel Dickie against becoming too outrageous. (He hasn't yet, but he's in an odd mood, and he won't take any notice of silly old me.) And don't delay too long. For a little bird tells me that Richard is keen to get away, at the end of the academic year, and prosecute his researches in Greece. Which is the last thing Walter would have allowed normally, since he's only just got back from the wars; but what with this Clarence affair bubbling away so gaily, I wouldn't wonder if Walter doesn't lend hearty support to the idea, in the hope that a year away from Piers may bring Dickie back to his senses – and to Penelope – again. But then just think of what he might get up to in Greece! Poor Walter. Poor Penelope. Poor Marc Honeydew, for that matter, who has nothing better to do than send you these pages of provincial gossip and tons and tons of love.

"Quite a correspondent, this Mr Honeydew," said Tyrrel wryly.

"He does run on rather a lot. But he was none the less right," I said, "for all that."

"About Clarence being…a banner of rebellion?"

"Yes. I went down there a few weeks later and met him for the first time. He was all Marc had said – witty, attractive, dissolute. There was only one thing Marc had left out: except in money matters, Piers Clarence was very, very honest. He saw things very straight and clear. And one of the things he saw was that Dr Walter Goodrich was a monumental sham. His books, his parties, his influence in high places – his whole set-up, for all its front of culture and graciousness, was just a frowsty doss-house for the shelter of half-baked ideas and the incubation of intellectual vermin."

"And he said as much to Mr Fountain?"

"Frequently."

"And Mr Fountain agreed?"

"Not directly. He smiled a lot – sometimes rather uneasily. It almost seemed, for all his competence, as if he couldn't quite cope with Piers Clarence… Meanwhile there was no doubt that things were getting very awkward. Because although Richard's affection for Clarence *was* sexually innocent, their association was being talked about, Penelope was bitterly distressed that Richard would hardly ever see her, and Walter, so to speak, had plainly lost both his compass and his map. It must have hurt him a lot – one of the most promising protégés he had ever had, and one that once seemed so co-operative and malleable, coming back to a position more or less created for him by Walter himself and then behaving so disloyally. But Walter never entirely lost his grip. Whatever else, it was quite clear that if Richard stayed in Cambridge the situation would just become more and more humiliating. So he made a virtue of necessity, and saw to it that Richard got all the permissions and grants he needed to go off and research in Greece…which Richard did – but not without one parting act of defiance."

"Oh?" said Tyrrel.

"Walter had put Richard on to researching into the Roman conquest of Greece – how far the Romans became Hellenised culturally and institutionally and *vice versa*. But Richard now said that he was going back to his original subject – the one he'd written his fellowship dissertation about."

"The survival of Minoan rites?" said Tyrrel with speed and interest.

"Yes," I said, faintly surprised that he should have remembered.

"He told Walter he still had a lot to clear up. Walter said that all the arrangements had been made on the assumption that he was to investigate the Roman conquest of Greece. Richard said he didn't care what arrangements had been made; when he got to Greece he was going to spend a lot of his time in Crete, and it was Minoan rites he was going to look into, and they could like it or lump it. So finally Walter, who was still crazy to get him out of the way, pretended to like it and got the various College and Faculty boards concerned to allow the change of plan. It cost Walter a lot of *hard* work. But he managed."

"And Mr Fountain left in the August of last year?"

"Yes."

"And you've heard nothing since Christmas?"

"Little enough before then."

"And Miss Goodrich was sorry when he left?"

"Very, I believe. She was hoping…well, that things would straighten themselves out."

"What about Piers Clarence?" said Tyrrel with a grin.

"Piers is a realist. No doubt he was sorry to lose an ally. But he knows that people come and go and it's no good getting into a state about it."

"Yes," said Tyrrel, still grinning. "I imagined he thought that…I hope I shall meet this Mr Clarence… So when had you expected Mr Fountain back?"

"This September, probably. But there was also some sort of idea that he might be enabled to prolong his stay for another year…if he seemed to be on to anything good. I fancy this was Walter's scheme; because Clarence still had two years to do at Lancaster when Richard left, and no doubt Walter felt he might as well keep Richard out of the way till Clarence had finally gone."

"I can tell you one thing," Tyrrel said grimly. "Mr Fountain will be back *this* September and even a good while sooner."

"Ah," I said, "I hoped you'd volunteer something sooner or later. It's very much your turn. How do you come to be so certain, Inspector Tyrrel? Expand."

"Because the Greek authorities, sir, will not allow him to stay."

Not for the first time that evening, he wandered over to my bookcase and looked carefully along the shelves.

"Go on, man."

"One of the pleasing things about this case," mused Tyrrel, disregarding my remark, "is that it has so many…intellectual implications."

He took from the shelves a book by Carl Kerényi called *The Gods of the Greeks.*

"When did you last read this, sir?"

"As an undergraduate. Before one of my exams."

"Read it again, Mr Seymour. Particularly the early chapters. Or perhaps you remember them?"

"Not in any detail," I said.

"Very well... Now, let me remind you of one or two things that have emerged very clearly from our discussion. One: Mr Fountain wrote an essay as a boy of eighteen – an essay which created some impression – called 'The Dying Gods'; and in it he complained that the old gods were not dying fast enough and constituted a menace to society. Correct?"

"Yes," I said, "but – "

" – Two," said Tyrrel firmly: "his fellowship thesis was concerned with the survival of Minoan rites into classical times."

"Granted."

"And three: after he came back from the Army Dr Goodrich put him on to another line of research; but before leaving for Greece, Mr Fountain insisted on changing back to his Minoan interests. And what do you conclude from all this, Mr Seymour?"

"That he is interested in ancient religions, particularly the earlier varieties."

"Good enough. And necessarily of course he would have to know, not only about Minoan or Cretan carryings-on, but also about the early imported Northern practices, which were brought down into Greece from Central Europe or Asia or wherever?"

"Presumably."

"So. Now, Mr Seymour," said Tyrrel, as if he had occupied a lecturer's dais all his life, "if you will be so good as to reread Mr Kerényi – or any other of the great number of books on this subject – you will not be slow to recollect that the ideas and rituals associated with Minoan religion were a trifle unsavoury. Mind you, the Cretans were an attractive people, and there is no doubt that their whole conception was being gradually softened, that a strongly pleasurable element was creeping into their observances. Still, even the Cretans are not exactly a model guide for contemporary procedure. Agreed?"

"Most heartily."

"And if this can be said of the Cretans, what are we to think of the primitive Northern and Asiatic deities, who also occupied an important place in the original Greek theogony? They were not *at all* pleasant, Mr Seymour. There are little tales of rapes, castrations, wholesale devourings of offspring: their qualities, as befitted the harsh and uncharitable regions whence they came, were in every way destructive, vengeance primed and lustful. There is no need to go into detail. You take my point?"

"Very clearly," I said with some admiration.

"Well, sir. Some say that the Female Principle – Mother Earth or the Mother Goddess – is on the whole a Cretan or Southern speciality; and that the Male Principle – Uranus the fertilising sky-god, perhaps – came from the North. What concerns us here is that *both* principles were celebrated, in early times, with sacrifice, violence and assorted indelicacy. And that is all I am going to say about that."

He tossed Kerényi on to the table in front of me.

"Well?" I said.

"I do not permit myself, sir, to make connections without strong factual evidence. But you may care to bear in mind what I have just been saying; and then to hear, in return for the facts you have told me, the very limited set of facts which I can tell you.

"*My* facts are just these. Firstly, the Greek authorities are concerned because there have lately been two or three very nasty discoveries – discoveries associated with the unexpected disappearance of certain people and which suggest peculiar, not to say abnormal, conduct on the part of some other – unknown – people. Secondly, the Greek authorities have made it plain that Mr Fountain must be out of the country at the end of one year's residence – which is to say by this September. Thirdly, they have given him no reason for this. Fourthly, they have informed Scotland Yard both that they are requiring Mr Fountain to leave, and also of their concern about...the incidents I have just mentioned. And those are all my facts."

"I can see no connection anywhere," I said petulantly.

"Of course," said Tyrrel, "the Greeks know nothing of what you have been telling me. But with regard to what they *do* know, they did just hint that considerations of time and place were...indicative. There is a link or two, though admittedly no chain."

"For Christ's sake be more precise."

"And the Greeks did observe that some of Mr Fountain's scholarly investigations, on sites and in libraries, had been of a curious nature."

"Of course they had," I nearly shouted at him: "his *subject* is of a curious nature. Tell me what you *mean*, man. What anybody means."

"I'm afraid we must leave it at that," said Tyrrel abruptly. "You've been most helpful, sir. And believe me, I've told you all I can."

He walked smartly towards my bookcase, carrying the Cavafis he had been reading when I first found him. Then he hesitated and turned round.

"Might I borrow this?" he said.

"If you wish," I said, with as much annoyance as I could get into my voice. "Only remember to send it back – at some reasonable hour of the day. It is a rare book."

"That," said Tyrrel, "is why I asked to borrow it. And don't worry about its being returned. You will be seeing something of me."

"Oh?"

"We shall be needing your help, you see."

"What more do you want of me?"

Tyrrel had picked up his hat (a brown trilby of the cut favoured by the more offensive type of young officer), but he now came back into the middle of the room.

"To keep your ears open. To let us know what you hear of Richard Fountain's activities in Greece from his friends or from himself. Indeed, sir," he said more humbly, "we should be grateful if you would make a point of going to Cambridge in a week or two to see if any of your friends – Mr Clarence, perhaps – have picked up anything of interest. They might have had news…or dreams," he added oddly. "Though I must ask you not to tell them what I've told you."

"You've told me very little, Inspector… But I'll go to Cambridge – if you'll trust me with one more thing to keep quiet about when I get there."

"And what would that be, Mr Seymour?"

"These incidents…these discoveries the Greeks claim to have made. You must know more about them than you've said?"

By now Tyrrel was working his way slowly toward the door.

"Oh, *those*," he said almost gaily. "Well, sir, you're a man of education – and imagination. You don't really need me to tell you what a place looks like after a butcher's been in it. No," he said, slipping lightly through the door, "I shan't presume to instruct you further. Good night… Anthony Seymour."

"Goodnight, John Tyrrel," I said, acknowledging, half in pique and half with pleasure, the bond formed by the night's discussion.

When I went over to my window, I could see Tyrrel disappearing out of the square and into Chester Row. He had both hands in his pockets; he was walking slowly with a kind of scuffle; his gaiety and jauntiness had gone. It was now impossible (just as it had been impossible earlier in the evening, when he looked at me like a tired child) to feel anything but sympathy for him. But you might have told me more, John Tyrrel, I thought – after all I told you. Particularly as you want more help. You might have stayed my questions. But then again, what questions? What useful question remained, at this juncture, to be asked? The facts, as far as they went, were really plain enough. There was a disagreeable mystery abroad in Greece, and the authorities, thinking but being unable to prove that Richard had part in it, were keen to get him out of the country. For the rest — it simply remained to be seen. So, "Keep your ears open"…"Let us know what you hear"…"Go to Cambridge if you will"… Well, I thought, I can do all that and gladly, John Tyrrel; but whether I keep mouth shut, as you request — that is another matter. Because the people involved are my friends, John Tyrrel: even Dr Walter Goodrich, if only because of the length of time I have known him, must count in some sort as a friend.

But now the birds were chattering in the square, and the light blue dawn was at hand, and it was time to sleep.

IV

In the end, I went to Cambridge early in June. Not the best time to go there, because the place is filled with outsiders who flock in for the alien gaieties of May Week, sweating mothers and proud but watchful fathers, hopeful and happy girls who cackle like geese along the river and far into the night. But in a way this was just the kind of thing I wanted. For there are a lot of people and a lot of drink about in May Week; and the sort of information Tyrrel had asked me to look for was far more likely to come leaping off a pleasure-loosened tongue over champagne after luncheon than to be soberly delivered during the long walks more typical of normal Cambridge afternoons.

I had arranged for a guest room in Lancaster, and also to give dinner to Walter and Penelope on my first evening there. I had warned Marc Honeydew I was coming, and in any case the bachelor flexibility of existence which both he and Piers Clarence enjoyed would make them easy of discovery and access at any hour of the day or night. There was only one thing which really bothered me. In order to find out what I wanted, I should have to proceed in a rather questionable fashion. It would be no good just saying "Heard from Richard lately?": for I was after anything, however trivial, which might point to anything (however slightly) odd; and in order to come at that degree of detail I should have to nag and probe and cross-question in a manner which would at once strike my informants as being eccentric. They would realise there was "something up", enquire what it was, and in part at least I should have to tell them. Well, I thought at first, and why not? These are my friends and Richard's and they have a palpable right to know if something is amiss with him. And yet... You see, there had been something about the hours I had spent with Tyrrel which had not only made me like the man but had also enjoined on me, or so I felt, a definite loyalty towards him. Tyrrel had asked me not to reveal what he had told me, and, friends or no friends, I was ill disposed to breach the trust.

Still, as Tyrrel himself would have been the first to admit, it was very difficult. And so, as I lay resting on the outrageously uncomfortable bed with which Lancaster College saw fit to provide its guests, listening, as the evening deepened, to the gentle admonition of the clock across the Court, I pondered the matter without pleasure or certainty: loyalty to my friends, loyalty to Tyrrel, loyalty to Richard; not to mention my wish to achieve efficiently any available information; what did these conflicting interests require of me? (And for that matter, were they really conflicting? Did not *all* of us, at bottom, want Richard's good?) In the end, glimpsing Tyrrel's face pressing close to mine in my half-sleep, − "Now, you're a man of education and resource, Mr Seymour" − , I came to the only possible decision. I should just have to use my wits and play the ball as it bounced. But whatever happened, I thought, I must try to keep as much as possible from Walter and Marc (the former an intriguer, the latter a common gossip); whereas it would be possible to let Penelope, with her courage and resignation, and Piers Clarence, with his fierce, improbable integrity, have any information they might chance to ask of me.

Having decided which, I walked two hundred yards round the Court to the nearest bathroom; and then I set out to meet Walter and Penelope where I had bidden them − a Restaurant which was my favourite, not so much for its food as its position: for it was opposite that college which, in its serenity, grandeur and magic, is and will remain above all colleges whatever – the Royal College of the Blessed King Henry VI: King's.

Walter looked pleased to see me in his usual rather squelchy way; while Penelope was also pleased, but at the same time wearing a general aspect of strain and dissatisfaction. For a long time (as the shadows over King's lawn lengthened and the pigeons swirled for the last time, settled and ceased their murmuring) we gossiped on, vaguely and amiably, of affairs in Lancaster, of this Fellow and that award, the renewal of the panelling in the college hall, the resilience and devotion of the ageing Provost. I suppose it was on Penelope's account that Walter was so unwilling to talk of Richard, and I was determined not to raise the subject for my own part. But sooner or later, as we all knew, the talk must turn on him; and finally, steering us with careful nonchalance into what he evidently considered a perilous region, Walter made use of a discussion we were having about the magazine I helped to edit, and asked: "Let's see. You *did* review Richard's second book of poems?"

"We get a bit behindhand," I said, "but we've done them. Miller did a piece."

"Ah, yes. Smart young man, Miller. I can't remember though – was he nice about them?"

"Not very."

"Why not?" said Penelope fiercely.

The topic had already become about as awkward as it could have done.

"I think he felt," I said, "that there was something not entirely genuine about them."

"They weren't intended to go very deep," Walter remarked. "Just as well perhaps."

"Richard is very serious about them," said Penelope. "I've discussed them with him often. He says they reflect an important side of his nature."

"A young man's fancy," said Walter condescendingly. "They have charm and even atmosphere. But as for expressing anything of real importance..." He was now clearly anxious, though he himself had introduced the topic, to get us away from Richard's poetry – but not from Richard. "Tell me, Anthony," he said, circling his glass with his fingers but making no effort to lift it to his mouth, "have you heard much from Richard lately? He was never a good correspondent. I know he's getting on quite well with his research. But he's been very vague about other things – the people he's meeting, his probable movements... I wondered whether... Perhaps you..."

Penelope sat boot-faced. Slowly Walter uncurled his fingers from his glass and then, one by one, wrapped them round it once more.

"I thought you would have known," I said spitefully: "he's coming back this September. If not sooner."

"Ah," said Walter, and forced a smile. "Yes, I rather thought –"

" – No, you didn't," said Penelope sharply; "you knew nothing at all. Neither of us did. He hasn't written for months," she almost shouted in my face.

"Nor to me," I said, regretting my malice, seeking to reassure her. "It's just that someone I know has been in contact with Richard. He told me the other night that it...seemed likely Richard would be back this Autumn."

"Who was this 'someone'?" demanded Penelope. "How should he know?"

"Nobody you've met. Just a friend of mine," I said, "who is normally accurate about this kind of thing."

"And no doubt he's quite right," said Walter. My exchange with Penelope had given him time to pull himself together. Whatever he felt about Richard's impending return, or about the fact that he himself had been in ignorance of it until now, he was going to put a good face on the matter. He lifted his glass, drained it, held it out to me to be refilled. "No doubt your friend is quite right," Walter said. "There's no need for us to upset ourselves. Richard was always independent in some things. He'll let us know in his own good time."

Penelope sniffed.

"Meanwhile," Walter went on, "now's the time to think what's best for him when he gets back. No time better, with Anthony here to help us." He smiled at me, slyly, ingratiatingly, with mistrust and uncertainty lurking behind his little eyes. "What do you think he ought to do next?" Walter asked.

"Write up his research, I suppose. He'll have been away a year. He must have quite a lot to work on."

"Of course," Walter said smoothly, "of course. And then I think we ought to get him settled. He's been wandering about too long. The Army, Greece. It's time he developed some roots."

He glanced at Penelope, who looked haggardly away through the window and over the darkened lawn of King's.

"Some sort of College appointment... Junior Dean, perhaps... A little administrative work can do wonders in calming people down. And later a Lectureship. Old Savage will be retiring next year, and that will mean a vacancy..."

He was well into his stride now. Whether he really believed that Richard would fall in with his plans, whether the easy confidence he displayed in himself and his machinations was the result of habit, vanity or wine, I could not be certain. But Walter was an old soldier and he soldiered steadily on. He brought us to the end of Richard's twenties, to his thirties and his maturity ("a Tutorship and a Readership, and then perhaps a year or two at the British School in Rome"), on to his forties, to a final position of influence and power and esteem. Penelope toyed with her glass, I smoked, the stars blinked between the pinnacles of King's Chapel: and Walter talked.

"I have always had great plans for Richard. Since the day he first came here to take his scholarship examination, I have always thought that he had a splendid future, not only as a scholar, but as a man to guard and guide the affairs of Lancaster

– from without as well as from within. For if we send him into the world at the right time, having first equipped him as only we can do, there is nothing he might not accomplish, and all of it would be to our credit and might – *must* – be used to our advantage. I see him...as my own successor; as a man who imparts knowledge, forms destinies, provides for dynasty. I see him, sometimes, as my son..."

He broke off, and suddenly his face collapsed and he looked desperately tired.

"I have some papers to collect from my rooms," he said to Penelope in a slurred voice, "before we go home. Stay here with Anthony until I get back."

When her father had left us Penelope said quickly, "There's something wrong, isn't there?"

"Yes."

"I knew that. It's not only that Richard was unkind before he left, or that he hadn't written – not at all to me and hardly even to Daddy. It's nothing to do with Daddy or me in any case. But I've had a feeling for months now. Silly of me. I don't believe in feminine intuition, in intuition of any kind. But now, from what you say, I was right, so I suppose... How bad is it, Anthony?"

"I don't know. It should be all right when he gets back to England."

"I'm not going to ask what it is," she said, her face trembling. "You'd tell me if you wanted to. I just want you to know that if I *can* help... You understand?"

"Then don't write to him," I said, "and don't let Walter write or interfere in any way. Let me know of anything you *should* hear. That's all you can do just now."

She nodded, and then, like the sensible girl she was, went quickly (but not very competently) to work with her compact. Walter re-entered the Restaurant, obviously recovered, firm, smiling, radiating all the right attitudes for the end of a pleasant evening with an old friend.

"It's been most agreeable, Anthony. Let us know when you're coming again… And now, Penelope, I think we should go home."

He smiled with determination. Penelope did her best, thanked me with brief formality. Then they both left. I called for some more brandy and sat thinking for a while, watching the constellations wheeling over King's.

Later on, through streets gay with cheap evening frocks, through levies of young men at once arrogant and bashful in their first hired dinner jackets, I walked slowly back to Lancaster again. So Walter and Penelope, I reflected, knew nothing: they were worried and hurt that they had not heard from Richard, and Penelope had sensed, in some strange way dependent, one must suppose, on her loyalty and love, that something was wrong; but they had no inkling of what Tyrrel had hinted to me two weeks before. Nor, for that matter, had I expected them to. For the rest, they would both be pleased to see him back, though Walter at least had seemed rather shaken by the news – partly because he did not like hearing it from someone other than Richard, and partly, I suspected, because there was now a definite prospect of Richard's friendship with Piers Clarence being renewed during Piers' third year in the college. None of this was either surprising or particularly helpful; though I now knew (if indeed I had not always known) that I might call on Penelope for help – in the unlikely event of there being any help she could give.

The next step was to see Marc Honeydew. There was to be no May Ball in Lancaster this year and Marc would not have gone outside the college to a ball in any other: so I could call on him that very evening. Heralded by a fanfare of little shrieks, silver sandals stepped neatly through the revolving door of the Blue Boar Hotel: a froth of muslin bubbled outside Trinity: but Marc Honeydew hated May Week even more than I did, would almost certainly be in his rooms – and alone. At all other times of the year his hospitality was princely; but each summer he let it be known that no one could expect entertainment or even courtesy from him during the first fortnight in June. "If you must show off your frumpish cousins somewhere, then show them, my dears, to Walter. Or to the Provost, for all I care. But I hope you will leave *me* in peace." Indeed, so great was his desire for privacy that on this occasion he had closed his oak, and I had to ring him up from the Head Porter's Lodge to ask for admittance. ("Come straight up, my dear, and I will open the door; but take care that a *hundred* young women don't burst in behind you.")

"Now, Anthony Seymour," he said as soon as I was safely inside, "I will just sport the oak against the legion of females who are *sacking* our beloved university, and I will give you an *enormous* glass of brandy, and you can then tell me exactly what brings you here at this devilish time of the year, hot with desire to have dinner with Penelope and Walter."

"So you know about that already?"

Marc, as usual, was on the scent of news. It would be difficult to get information from him without parting with something substantial in exchange.

"Of course I know. I may lock everyone out, but news, my dear, travels through the thickest walls." He poured a lavish glass of brandy. "Tongue-loosener," he said.

"I simply came," I told him, "to find out if anyone had heard from Richard in Greece. He hasn't written to me for five months and I was getting rather worried. I thought that Walter at least might know what was going on."

"And did he?"

"Not really."

"Of course not. Nobody, my dear, knows a thing. Unless that randy little piece Piers Clarence has heard, and is keeping it from us out of *devilment*."

"Why should he do that?"

"He's a sly one, that Piers. He might want to keep Richard to himself."

"We've been over this before Marc," I said sternly, "we have all agreed that both Richard and Piers are heterosexual by nature and that they are *not* having an affair; and we may therefore presume that the sort of petty possessiveness you are hinting at is out of the question."

"There are times, Anthony Seymour, when you are not at all subtle. Granted they are not having an affair, people can still be very possessive about the most *ordinary* friendships. It's common knowledge that Walter thinks Piers is one of the reasons, however innocent this relationship, for Richard ignoring Penelope. Piers knows Walter thinks this and he may be playing up in consequence. After all, we do know that Richard was using Piers as a Walter-antidote. So what more natural than that Piers should keep anything good to himself?"

"All of which is getting us nowhere," I said. "Whatever Piers may or may not know, he hasn't told it to us. Now *what*, Marc, do you know?"

"Nothing, Anthony Seymour; but what, my dear, about you?"

He raised his stringy body from the sofa, swept up my glass and recharged it. "More tongue-looseners needed," he said. "Quite obviously, my dear, you know something – enough, at any rate, to bring you whizzing down here to see if there's anything more. You can only have one reason for braving the monstrous hordes of students' sisters – sheer curiosity. Now *what*, my dear, set you off?"

You nimble old queen, I thought. Probably you really do know nothing, but you've already seen I'm on to something and you want the best possible value from me you can get. All right, I thought: we'll toss you one crumb and see how keenly you sniff at it.

"I heard in a round-about way," I said, "that Richard's coming back this Autumn."

"So," said Marc. "Well, I certainly thought Walter would try and make him stay another year – to make sure he didn't get in with Piers again. But does Walter know he's coming back?"

"He didn't until this evening."

"One in the pan for him. But what do you mean, Anthony Seymour, by 'heard in a round-about way'? You can't catch an old field-worker like me with that sort of spiel."

"A common friend of Richard's and mine," I lied, "was returning to England from Cyprus, where he had been stationed with the first battalion of our regiment. He took some leave on his way home, ran into Richard in Athens, heard he was coming back, and told me about it in London."

This was much too elaborate to ring true; and in any case Marc spotted an essential flaw that hadn't occurred to me.

"And was this *all* your Army chum had to tell you, Anthony Seymour? But of course," he said, twinkling with the exuberance of his malice, "I forgot. He couldn't have had *time* to ask Richard much, because the Army Council, so my papers tell me, issued an Instruction late last year forbidding Army officers to go to Greece during their leaves in view of the unpopularity there of our military cavortings in Cyprus. So I expect your chum, being *out of bounds*, my dear, got a little nervous and pushed off before Richard told him much."

"My 'chum'," I said stoutly, "was allowed to spend some of his leave in Athens because the General Staff in Cyprus had entrusted him with a top secret report for the military attaché at the Embassy."

"*Intelligence work*," said Marc. "Well, if he was *that* sort of chum, it's a pity he didn't *ferret* a bit more news out of Dickie Fountain."

"I expect he had other things on his mind," I said. "Anyhow, he *did* learn that Richard was coming back this September. So now for a fair exchange, Marc. I've told you my news: what's yours?"

Marc shook his head in a pantomime of sadness.

"Nothing so dramatic," he said. "No secret agents in Athens; no meetings at dawn on the Acropolis. Just stale college gossip, and most of it well known to you. Walter spends much of his time talking of what Richard will do when he comes back – and has certainly *implied*, my dear, that he will be away the full two years. So now he'll have to change his tune about *that*. Penelope hangs her head in sorrow. The Provost, like myself, does not get younger. Piers has been naughty, almost naughty enough to be sent away. But it is whispered, though the results are not yet officially known, that he has done quite creditably in his exams this year. So now they really have no adequate excuse for getting rid of him; and since Dickie is coming back, this will be a great worry to Walter... But nothing at all startling, my dear. And indeed I am very much beginning to wonder what we are *fussing* about with such persistence."

"What indeed?" I said.

"Because," Marc pursued, "all that seems to have happened is that Dickie Fountain has decided to come home this Autumn instead of next, which was always on the cards in any case."

"Exactly so," I said.

"But," Marc said, his eyes glinting with amusement, "here are you rushing about asking us all whether we *know* anything. So bizarre of you, my dear."

"I was just worried." I said.

"You can tell that, Anthony Seymour, to the *Marines*. You're a cool fish, my dear, and you don't run about hysterically giving dinner parties and breaking through sported oaks and telling tales about masked men in Athens simply because you're 'worried'. No, my dear, you're keeping something back. I know that serious old face of yours, and it's *pregnant* with disaster."

"Nonsense," I said.

"Old Mother Honeydew knows her onions, Anthony Seymour. *You're keeping something back.* I'm not going to ask you what, because clearly you don't want to tell me, and I prefer listening to people, my dear, when they're *co-operative*. And in any case, my love, I shall *find out* in time. Just trust Old Mother Honeydew for that.

"And now you'd better go away to bed, so that you're all fresh for tomorrow's *assignations*. Good night, Anthony Seymour; and don't stick your neck out too far, otherwise some *spy*, my dear, may cut your head off with a stiletto."

Feeling a large size of fool, I made my way back to my college guest room. Although the weather had been fine for six weeks, the sheets were palpably damp.

Before going to sleep I came to a decision. I had learned nothing from Walter or Penelope; and as for Marc, I had done even worse: I had learned nothing (because he, like everyone else, knew nothing), but in the process of doing so I had aroused his suspicions. Within twenty-four hours it would be all round Cambridge that "something was up" with Richard Fountain in Greece and that Anthony Seymour was being both secretive and hysterical about it. God alone knew what floods of conjecture would be let loose. This being the case, the best thing I could do was to go – go before people started questioning me and before I did more harm. But one thing I would do first: early in the morning I would see Piers Clarence. I didn't mind him becoming suspicious, indeed I was prepared to tell him all I knew, because I trusted him; he *might* have something of value to say; and in any case I liked him and knew he would think it odd (he wasn't the sort of person who felt "hurt") if I left Cambridge without calling on him. So I would talk to Piers and then leave Cambridge to speculate how it might; and once in London I would replace this particular baby where it properly belonged – firmly back in Inspector Tyrrel's lap.

Piers didn't answer when I knocked on his door the next morning; so I went through his sitting-room and found him, as I had rather expected, in bed.

"Go away, Anthony," he said in a friendly voice.

"That's just it," I said; "I'm going away from Cambridge in two hours, and I want to talk to you first. You can spend the rest of the day sleeping."

"As it happens, I can't. I have a long day of May Week amusements ahead of me." But he got up all the same and splashed some cold water on his face. "However, Anthony, seeing that it's you... So long as you haven't been appointed to lecture me about my course of life..."

He walked into the pantry on the staircase outside, still in his pyjamas, and put a kettle on to boil.

"We'll have a little Nescafé to prepare us for the day's entertainments. Why don't you stay a day or two longer, Anthony?"

The sun was shining through the window on to an expensive fur rug which was in front of the fire place. Piers now lay down on this. His pyjamas were of light-blue silk and several times more expensive than he could possibly afford.

"Why don't you stay and join in the fun?" he said.

"Because unlike you I have responsibilities to attend to. Aren't you feeling cold?"

"No. And I like to show off these beautiful pyjamas. After all, they have not been paid for, and the man may come to take them back. *Carpe diem*, as Walter might say. You've seen him?"

"Yes."

"Did he complain about me?"

"We had better things to discuss," I said. "But I gather from Marc that your behaviour has been *just* tolerable, and that you've done quite well in the Tripos. So accept my congratulations on having survived another year here and pay attention to what I am going to say."

He smiled slightly, and then got up and went out to the pantry. I heard him talking for a moment with the bedmaker; then he reappeared with two cups of Nescafé.

"All right, Anthony," he said: "begin."

He lay down on the rug again, then turned comfortably over on his belly.

"Begin, begin."

"Have you heard from Richard?" I asked.

"Not since February."

"What did he say then?"

"He suggested that I should join him in Greece during the Long Vac."

"And that was all?"

"More or less. As you know, Richard only writes letters in order to make arrangements. He suggested I should join him early in July, and went on to say where I could write to him meanwhile. He would be in or near Athens till late April, he said, then a week or two at Delphi, and after that in Corinth unless he wrote otherwise."

"So he's in Corinth now?"

Piers shrugged and rolled over on his back again.

"He certainly hasn't written to say he's not."

"And are you going to join him?"

"I don't know. It rather depends on whether I can find any money. I wrote to Richard about a month ago saying that if I could fix that I'd be with him by July tenth, and would he still be in Corinth then? Because when he wrote in February he seemed to have some sort of idea that we might meet in Crete and go on a tour of the islands."

"And he hasn't answered?"

"No... You're being very inquisitive, Anthony."

"I'm sorry, Piers. I'll try and explain in a minute. Did he suggest he might come back to England with you at the end of the Long Vac?"

"No. He said nothing about that. I assumed he was going to stay away a second year in any case. Walter keeps saying that to everyone. And this, I thought, was probably why he was keen to see something of me this summer."

"Ah," I said. "You'll forgive me asking, Piers, but just why should it be so imperative for him to see you at all?"

He stretched himself full length on the rug, raising his head and laughing straight into my eyes.

"I thought we'd get on to that sooner or later," he said, relaxing once more, "so I'd better make the position entirely plain. During my first year, Anthony, I went to Richard for supervisions. As you well know, we took a liking to one another, began to go for walks and have meals and so on, and by this time last year we were very firm friends indeed. Now, I know what a lot of people started thinking about this, and I know it looked jolly awkward when he stopped seeing much of Penelope. But whatever anybody may have thought or said, we were, as they say in the papers, just very good friends and nothing more."

"I always knew it," I said.

"Did you now, Anthony? Well, here is something which perhaps you didn't know. It is true that neither Richard nor I am queer. But there's an important difference. I have slept with a lot of people, even while I was still at school, and in no sense whatever can I be called a virgin. Richard, on the other hand, is a virgin all ways round. He's never slept with anyone at all."

"I knew that too," I said.

"Let me finish, Anthony. When I discovered this, I was surprised – and rather shocked. It seemed positively…immoral that someone should have reached the age of twenty-six and still not have slept with anyone. And later on I began to feel downright sorry for him. So I thought to myself that I might not be queer, but if, *if*, Anthony, Richard were to show the slightest sign of wanting me, then such was my affection for him, such was the loyalty I owed him as my friend, I would do anything he asked me and be proud to. And so time went on, and he said nothing, and I began to realise that it wasn't a boy he wanted in any case. But even then, I thought I might be able to help him. And one evening, when we were talking about some girl I'd been seeing and he seemed rather upset about it, I said to him, 'Look, Richard, you've no call to worry about this. Girls come and girls go, and very nice too, but if ever *you* want me,' I said, 'in any way whatever, then tell me so and I'll be happy, *happy*, Richard, to do anything you ask'."

He paused for a moment and reached out for his cup.

"And then...?" I prompted him.

"Well, then he looked a bit dazed for a time. But he soon recovered; he smiled and took hold of my arm and said he appreciated my concern, but that wasn't what he wanted from me. But he still went on being edgy and tiresome, so I wondered whether he might not have been offended by what I'd said. So I asked him straight out, and he said no, that wasn't it, it was something quite different and nothing that need trouble me. However, I kept on at him and wouldn't leave it alone, so finally he told me what it was. He sat up very straight, Anthony, and his face was like stone, and his voice was so cold it might have been coming from the other side of the universe. Have you any idea what he said?"

"None."

"He said...he said he thought he was impotent. I shall never forget it as long as I live. Him sitting so straight and that terrible cold voice. 'I think I'm impotent, Piers,' he said. Well, I pulled myself together as best I could and asked him how he could possibly know if he hadn't *tried*. He said he didn't *know* but he was pretty sure and this was one of the reasons he hadn't tried. I said no one could be sure until they'd tried and that the longer he put it off the worse his doubts would become. He said it was hardly even a question of *doubt*... And so we went on, round and round in a silly and vicious circle, until he got up and said we were never to speak of this again and marched straight out of the room."

82

For a while we were both silent. Piers lay flat on his back looking straight up at the ceiling, his right hand cushioning his head, his left arm stretched out for his fingers to fiddle with his teaspoon. Then I said: "Did he seem to have any idea *why* he should be impotent?"

"There was just one brief hint. He broke away from it almost immediately. But I think he blames Walter Goodrich."

"*Blames Walter Goodrich?*"

"Not so much Walter himself as what he stands for. He gabbled something about a wrong way of life, about schools and institutions which first castrated you and then sucked your blood. It was very quick and difficult to hear, and he stopped almost at once. Then he said, 'Need alien gods' – something like that – and started to laugh rather hysterically. After that he went absolutely silent for about five minutes, until he suddenly said we weren't to discuss this again and went out like I told you."

"If he's prepared to tell you all this," I said slowly, "it's not surprising he wants to see you again. But whether you find the money or not, Piers, there are going to be complications. For one thing, Richard's days in Greece are numbered."

"What can you mean?"

And then, as clearly as I could, I told Piers Clarence the lot. If anyone had a right to know, he did. Tyrrel could like it or lump it, I thought. Because if there was one person, except possibly for Penelope, who could help Richard, it was going to be Piers Clarence.

"So," he said when I'd finished, "he doesn't seem to have found it."

"Found what?"

"What he hoped – *I* hoped – he would. It looks as if he found something though. Not the right something."

"Be plain, Piers."

"He went to Greece," said Piers wearily, "to get away from Penelope and Walter and, most of all perhaps, from Walter's schemes. He liked Walter's schemes and he detested Walter's schemes, and he couldn't make up his mind which he did most, so he went away."

"So I surmised."

"But he *also* went because he thought that Greece might have something to offer him — something Walter and Penelope and this place couldn't give him, but which you gave him for a time, and then the Army gave him, and I gave him most recently of all. Only since none of us had given him enough of it, he wanted more. And he thought he might find it in Greece. The only trouble was that there were *two* things he was after, one of them the *wrong* one, and if he found that first, he'll have stuck with it."

"One of these things being love? Or sex? His manhood?"

"Not exactly," said Piers. "One of these things, the *right* one, is abundance of life. This includes love and sex, his manhood if you like, but it also means truth and liberty, with a strong flavour of adventure and even heroism. You'll have noticed something heroic about him?"

"Certainly."

"But the *other* of these things," Piers went on, "is something that he himself doesn't know about, because it's something that no one could admit to himself and it is, in any case, quite easy to confuse and even equate with heroism and liberty — and still more easy to confuse with love."

"And what might that be?"

"He is looking for *hatred*," said Piers calmly, "because he is, by nature, a great hater. You don't need me to tell you that he can be, for example, very cruel. Now we know that love and hate, and sex and hate, are very much interwoven. As for liberty — well, it implies *hatred* of tyranny; and heroism necessarily permits one to hate one's adversary. In Richard's case there are plenty of targets — this impotence, real or imagined; Walter (whom he sees as the symbol and cause of it), all of what he calls 'the wrong way of life'... So you see, Anthony, it is quite easy for Richard to confuse the good side of his quest with the bad one: to pursue hatred with ferocity while thinking all the time that he is only looking for abundance and love. And from what you say, it is beginning to seem all too likely that he is doing exactly that."

Piers spoke with such confidence, his thesis was so consistent with all I knew of Richard, that I found myself accepting it immediately and without any critical effort, accepting it as something I must always, in a manner, have known for myself. Time and circumstance might give cause for revision, I reflected; but even this, in the face of Piers' cool authority, seemed only the most remote of possibilities.

"Leaving us with the nice little question," I said at last, "of what we ought to do about it."

"Perhaps Inspector Tyrrel will tell you," he said mockingly: "you seem to think highly of him."

"I do. And so will you when you meet him."

"I? Meet Tyrrel?"

"Soon," I said.

"And meanwhile?"

"Stay in Cambridge," I said, "and amuse yourself. And don't leave Cambridge till I tell you. We may want you in a hurry."

"How very *bossing* you are, Anthony. My poor mother expects me home in four days' time. And as I hope to spend most of the summer away – "

" – Never mind your mother, Piers. Do as I say."

I rose to go.

"If *you* say so, Major Seymour," he said, crossing his legs and looking down with pleasure along the silken length of his pyjamas. "But there's just one thing more you ought to know before you leave."

"And that is?"

"Why do you suppose, Anthony, that I've chosen this particular time to tell you about Richard being impotent? When I've known for more than a year?"

"Because I asked you what held you both so close."

"Not a bit of it, my sweet. I told you because it no longer matters — to Richard or to anyone else. Because he's going to die, Anthony. I've seen him three times these last few nights, and each time he was dead."

V

My only real gains in Cambridge had come from listening to
Piers Clarence. For Piers at least had offered a theory, a fantasy
and one concrete fact. His theory, as to the nature of Richard's
real business in Greece – his quest and its possible perversion –
was helpful in that it summed up and gave form to my own
disconnected speculations. His fantasy – that Richard was
doomed to die – was of interest for the light it cast on his own
mental character, though it could scarcely be taken very
seriously, I thought, as an indication of Richard's prospects. (But
for all this his words had left a chill.) As for the fact, it was
established that Richard was keen to see Piers in Greece and
thought of visiting the islands with him. Or rather, that was
how matters had stood in February. Since Richard presumably
knew now that he must leave Greece by the Autumn, he might
have reason to change his plans; but yet again, he had said
nothing of this to Piers.

All of which still left one with the question of what ought
to be done. If Piers was right about the pattern of Richard's
behaviour in Greece, then clearly the sooner he was got out of
Greece the better. People who think they are looking for
abundance of life, and who are not too certain or too
scrupulous as to the best method of finding it, should not be left
alone in distant countries. If Richard was left alone in Greece,
he might do almost anything between now and the Autumn –
and indeed it looked very possible that he had done more than

enough already. But how did one go about retrieving him? Would he let himself be retrieved – by Piers or others? And where, in any case, did one find him?

Well, the last question at least might not be too hard to answer. Piers had said that Richard proposed to leave Athens in late April, to spend a fortnight at Delphi and then go down to Corinth. (An unattractive town, I remembered, except for Acro-Corinth: what could be keeping him there?) In Corinth he would remain, and would hope to be joined by Piers, though possibly the meeting was to be in Crete, in early July. So that when one looked at it, this information was not really so helpful after all; because by intention or otherwise it was quite vague enough to ensure that no one would be able to get hold of Richard unless he wanted to be got hold of. Still, he evidently wanted Piers to find him, in which case, I thought, there will at least be a pilot... But further speculation was futile: the next step, as Piers had so sarcastically indicated, was to ring up Inspector Tyrrel, tell him what little I had found out, and then, as I had determined in Cambridge the previous night, to leave the matter in his hands where indeed it belonged. Loyal to Richard I might wish to be, but this affair was far too serious and too complex for prolonged amateur meddling.

And so I reached my flat, intending to ring up Tyrrel within the hour – only to find that the situation had altered beyond recognition in my absence. The new factor in the case – a factor which was by no means going to exclude Tyrrel but from now on placed a definite and compelling onus upon myself – was a long letter from Richard. It was the first I had had from him for many weeks. I opened it with an apprehension which was to be amply justified by its contents, and I now give it in full here.

Hotel Grande Bretagne,
Athens.
June 7, 1957.

My dear Anthony,

I'm sorry not to have written for so long. But I have been rather occupied with one thing and another, and as you know I'm not one of the world's letter writers – unless there is something to be explained or arranged. At the moment there is probably both, but I am tired tonight, so I shall just attend to arrangements. We shall have the rest of our lives for explanations.

I am leaving Athens by boat tomorrow and going to Crete. Accompanied? Perhaps. But what I want you to do is make ready to come yourself and pass the word on to Piers at Cambridge. You see, I wrote to Piers last Feb., and asked him to join me here during the Long Vac. I gave him a Poste Restante address in Corinth, but if he writes there now it probably won't reach me. So you tell him, Anthony, that the RV is now to be in Crete, and save me writing to him as well. See that he has enough money and everything (I will guarantee anything you have to lend him), gather the pair of yourselves up (and anyone else who might like to come), and meet me in Crete any time after July 1 – I shall be very busy there until then, and anyhow you'll need a few days to get yourselves on the road. And where in Crete do we meet? Well, I'm not quite sure, so I will send you a letter or a wire soon after I get there telling you where I shall be between July 1 and 14. It will be several different places, but I'll be as exact as I can be about which days I shall be at each one.

It would be nice if you could come by car and leave the car either in Venice, Brindisi or Athens – from any of which you can easily get boats to Crete. Then we could drive a lot of the way home. I've always wanted to drive from Athens to Calais, and one can easily get visas for Yugoslavia.

So Richard is coming home? you'll say. Yes, Anthony, Richard is coming home. And the reason he wants you and other friends to come and collect him is that he needs reassurance – one may as well call it that as anything else. Because I've been in rather a muddle, Anthony. So do come, you and Piers and someone else perhaps (not Penelope or Walter), do come, and then you can tell me all the news from England and put me right about everything there, we can have a look at Crete and some of the islands and a bit of the mainland, and then drive home. This will be very pleasant. Anthony, you and Piers at least must come. Please see to this. So much for the arrangements. I'll wire/write to you when I get to Crete, and shall expect to see you some time between July 1 and 14 (the sooner the better) at one of the places I shall mention. It might be Cnossos. I shall be there a lot before you come, as I have things to look at, but whether I shall want to go again... Ah well, we'll see. And of course, I might already have company. But it would be interesting company, and need not deter you in any case...

And now, Anthony, I'm very tired, so forgive me if I don't write any more. Give my love to all in England. My research is a bit disorganised, but I'm on to one or two good things, you can tell them. And don't let me down over this. As if you would. Tell Piers and come as quickly as you can.

Yours with love,

Richard.

This was the letter – rambling, spasmodic, imploring, in no way resembling Richard's usual curt and elegant communications – from which I learnt that I was needed and that I could no longer treat the affair merely as an interested and helpful but largely inactive spectator. Definitely and without question of argument the letter told me I must now take part. It also posed a number of minor problems which only emphasised the impression of mystery that was now beginning to attach to Richard and everything he did. Who or what was this "company" he referred to? Why did he need "setting straight" about matters in England when he had been gone barely nine months? Why was he too "tired" to write to Piers as well as to myself? Why had he left Corinth a full month before he had originally planned? But it was neither essential nor even possible to enquire into such points at the moment. Let them resolve themselves hereafter and as they might. For the import of Richard's message was very plain: the time had come to act.

But first I owed it to Tyrrel to let him know about the new developments and to tell him what I proposed to do. I had no doubt that he would approve my decision, he might make some helpful suggestions, and I was far from averse to renewing our acquaintance. So late on the afternoon of the day on which I had returned from Cambridge and found Richard's letter, I was shown by a courteous and non-committal policeman into a grimy top-floor office in the Charing Cross Road.

Tyrrel rose to his feet with a charming smile of welcome. "I thought," I said, "that all detectives lived in antiseptic offices surrounded by scientific devices."

"Too many of us these days," said Tyrrel. "Too much crime, too many detectives, not enough room. So those of us that don't mind being old-fashioned are…boarded out."

"Better the Charing Cross Road than too much hygiene?"

"Perhaps," he said, and pulled up a chair for me. "It's very nice to see you, Mr Seymour. And looking so healthy after your trip to Cambridge."

"I never – "

"Please." He waved a hand in faint deprecation. "It's not that we're *watching* you, sir. But we were quite keen to know when you'd go to Cambridge, so we took steps to be informed. You've been most prompt...in reporting back, if you'll pardon the expression."

"I'm not sure I shall. But I certainly have something to tell you."

"I shall be grateful."

So I told Tyrrel what I had learned in Cambridge: – that neither Walter nor Penelope had known of Richard's impending return; that Marc Honeydew was full of speculation and empty of knowledge; that Piers had been asked to join Richard for the summer. Having then laid some stress on Richard's confession of impotence, I gave the substance of Piers' theory about his motives for going to Greece and their essentially unstable nature, and I concluded, with some embarrassment, by telling Tyrrel how Piers had spoken of Richard's death. This last item seemed to intrigue him; and since I had nearly omitted it altogether, I found this disconcerting.

"This Piers Clarence," Tyrrel said: "you've described him to me as a young man given to short, sharp and sensible judgements. Why should he come up with dreams and forebodings?"

"I was surprised myself. But he told me this in a most *un*oracular way. Quite coolly, just as if it was another common sense contribution."

"Perhaps he'd been having too much to drink?"

"At nine in the morning?"

"You have a point... It makes me all the more anxious," Tyrrel said, looking up with resignation at his fly-blown ceiling, "to meet Master Clarence."

"I've left him waiting in Cambridge to come when called."

"Aha. I see you're entering into the spirit of the thing, Mr Seymour. And what about Clarence's theory: that Mr Fountain went away to escape being stifled and made impotent by

92

conventional college life, to assert the…heroic side of his nature?"

"It fits."

"I suppose so… And Clarence intends to join Mr Fountain in Greece?"

"He did – if he could get the money. In any case," I said, "he'll certainly be going now. And not alone."

And then I showed Tyrrel the letter I had just received from Richard. He read it through to himself, muttering and grimacing from time to time, slapping with a ruler at the flies who were amusing themselves on his desk.

"Not the sort of letter," he said at last, "that should be written by a scholar and a holder of the Military Cross."

"Not at all."

"Which reminds me that I still have your Cavafis, sir. You're in no hurry to have it back?"

"None."

"Good. I like the historical poems best. The barbarians coming to Constantinople. All that about Alexandria. Do you know Alexandria, Mr Seymour?"

"I'm afraid not."

"It is a city of considerable charm and wickedness. But not heroic, because its…gods, shall we say?…have become urbanised. Whereas in Crete… You *do* propose to go to Crete?"

"But certainly. I came to get your approval and your suggestions."

"And what do you propose to do when you get there?"

"Find Richard. Clear up any mess he may be in. And see that he gets safely home."

"Admirable," said Tyrrel slowly and almost in mockery. "But suppose you can't find him? Suppose he's gone, for example, to… Alexandria?"

"Then we shall have to follow. But why should he do that? His invitation is very clear."

"He might change his mind, sir. People who write that sort of letter change their minds a lot. And whom shall you take with you?"

"Piers Clarence, of course. And I thought one more: Major Longbow."

"Major Longbow?"

"I told you of him the other night. He was Richard's company commander."

"Ah, yes," said Tyrrel, slapping his ruler down with a crack: "but why him?"

"Because Richard likes him and is accustomed to obey him. And because he is a man of great resource, whose occasional and laconic remarks I find amusing."

"So. Good," said Tyrrel, rising to his feet and suddenly becoming brisk and forthright. "Good, good, Mr Seymour. I am not disappointed in you. Take Mr Clarence and Major Longbow. If you need extra currency apply to me. Leave soon, Mr Seymour. Come back soon. Don't fiddle about, sir. And I should like to meet your companions before you go. You will ring up?"

"Indeed."

"Thank you. Go well, Mr Seymour, and go fast. Fast, fast, fast," he sang out like a sergeant-major on a barrack square. And then, in a lower voice, "Theseus triumphed in Crete by making friends with a woman. You might do the same, sir."

"What can you mean?"

"This 'company' of Mr Fountain's, sir, to which he refers in his letter. He's got a woman. Or so they say. Yes, so they say."

He pressed a bell and the whole building seemed to shake. "But I shan't give you any details," he said, "because I don't know them. Anyway, too much detail is bad for an expedition which is just about to leave. Expeditions should go out to the sound of trumpets, sir, not to the nagging whine of detail... Constable Kershaw," he said to the non-committal policeman who had entered, "show Major Seymour out."

The next step was to summon Piers from Cambridge. This I did by letter, asking him to be in London within a week, having done his duty by his mother and totally prepared to spend the rest of the summer abroad. (I added that he need no longer concern himself about money, since I was going to Greece along of him and would see to the matter for him.) A week, I thought, would give me enough time to make the arrangements necessary for us to leave London about June 25 and reach Crete by July 1. There was no point in getting there earlier, despite the exhortations of Tyrrel; for Richard was not prepared to meet us before then, and I must in any case allow time for him to send his list of rendezvous.

Thus far, and as concerned Piers, the arrangements were simple enough: it might not be so simple, however, to persuade Major Roderick Longbow. Yet persuaded he must be; for I had hit on him in a brief moment of real inspiration, and a more suitable man could not have been conceived. He was fond of Richard, Richard was fond of him, they were both used to a relationship in which Longbow gave the orders or at least had the backing of authority. Furthermore, as I had told Tyrrel, Longbow was a tough man and a man of resource. He was accustomed to remain silent, or, when social occasions required it, to talk with an inanity which could only be a deliberate parody of the idiom used by those about him; but from time to time, with a few friends or when an active decision of some sort was required, he would give tongue to a series of downright common-sense statements so supremely apt in substance and pithy in expression that one was reminded of the legends which surround the great Duke of Wellington. He went to the heart of a situation by the most direct route and used a fine sharp knife to cut his way in. He was a realist, he was a tactician, he was a highly practical man who could even use his hands to good effect: in the circumstances which I must anticipate, such assets might be priceless.

But Roddy Longbow was at this time in command of our Regimental Depot at Ludlow. It was not an exacting post, but that was not to say he would be able to come abroad at a week's notice and stay away for an indefinite period. And then, of course, Army Officers were at that time forbidden by the Army Council to set foot in Greece. Not to mention the difficulty Roddy might have in getting a visa if we wished to drive through Yugoslavia — the Yugoslavians being inclined to conceive that all British officers whatever are immoderately given to spying. Still, Roddy had a fine style of clearing obstacles once he was set on a thing; the expedition in prospect was after his heart; and so I packed my bag and went to Ludlow for a night to try how I might win him for our cause.

In the end, and for all my anxieties, this was not difficult. Roddy listened to the story, and pronounced in characteristic fashion that I was too much concerned with theories of Richard's behaviour, too little with ways and means of finding him and fetching him back.

"The thing is to get him out with a whole skin, Anthony. You can see about his neuroses when you've got him home. And what's all this about a woman?"

"Inspector Tyrrel seems to think he has one with him."

"Providing an effective cure for this impotence you talk of?"

"Inspector Tyrrel is not acquainted with the details."

"Well in any case she's going to be a bloody nuisance. The only women people can pick up in Greece are rich American whores or poor Greek ones. The first kind are possessive, the second treacherous."

"Tyrrel thinks we might use her to help us."

"She'd be more use at the bottom of the sea. And who's this Piers Clarence? A chum of Richard's, you say?"

"You'd like him. He has keen wits and a sly tongue."

"I'll take your word for it," said Roddy Longbow: "and if he tries to borrow money from me I shall kick him in the crutch."

"You'll come with us then?"

"I wouldn't miss it for the world."

"And the Depot? And the ACI which says you mustn't go to Greece?"

"I have a second-in-command, Anthony, who spends most of his life and all of his money on racecourses. He can now stay away from them and do some work for a few weeks, no doubt to the benefit of his pocket. And the Brigade Colonel, to whom I must apply for leave, is a second cousin who knows that I know that he is unfaithful to his wife. There will be no trouble from him."

"And the ACI?"

"No one will know where I am."

"You'll have to give a leave address," I said.

"But not necessarily the right one. I never do that in case they actually have the nerve to recall me. I shall say I'm going to Sicily. If they *should* try to get hold of me there, then they won't be able to and I shall simply tell them when I get back that my car broke down and I didn't make it."

"The Greeks may not like it when they see from your Passport that you're a British officer."

"They won't see anything of the kind. My Passport says my occupation is the possession of 'Private Means'. Never put your real profession on your Passport, Anthony. They hate 'journalists' in one place and 'officers' in another, but everybody welcomes a mere man of 'private means'."

"You seem to have everything very neatly arranged."

"All that is necessary," said Major Longbow, "is a little common sense and a lack of superfluous scruple."

When I got back to London from Ludlow, there was a vulgar postcard from Piers which acknowledged my instructions. He would be with me on June 23, wanted a bed in my flat until we left, and had found his own money "thank you very much".

During the next three days I arranged for us to drive to Venice and take a boat from there to Crete. We would leave on June 26, spend single nights at Sens, Aix-en-Provence and Milan, pass two nights and a day in Venice, and catch the boat on July 1st. If Richard liked the idea of driving some of the way home, then there was no harm in it; but for a number of reasons, paramount among them the quality of the food and the roads, I was anxious to avoid Yugoslavia.

On June 23 Piers arrived at my flat in the early afternoon.

"Where did you get your money?" I asked.

"I borrowed it from Penelope Goodrich."

"*You what?*"

"I told Penelope that Richard badly wanted to see me but that I hadn't any money to go. I knew she'd do anything for him, you see. She havered about a bit, but in the end she lent me two hundred pounds."

"You little *shit*. I told you I'd arrange the money for you. Why did you have to go pestering poor Penelope?"

"Because you, my dear Anthony, would have paid all the bills yourself and rationed me to about sixpence a day spending money. But as it is I've got two hundred pounds in my own pocket."

"Well, you can give me a hundred and fifty straight away," I said. "Fifty for travelling expenses already incurred and the rest to make sure you don't spend the lot before we even leave."

He handed it over without a murmur. It was only years later that I learned he had in fact borrowed three hundred from Penelope.

On the evening of June 24, while Piers and I were having a drink, Roddy Longbow appeared.

"All set?" he said.

"We leave Lydd airport by the car ferry at noon on the 26th," I told them. "Tomorrow night we are to have dinner with Inspector Tyrrel, who wishes to meet you both. Then early to bed and leave here at nine sharp. All right?"

"Very officer-like directions," said Piers languidly.

Roddy gave him a short look.

"Little boys who have no money," he said, "do not impress their elders by jangling loose coppers."

In fact, however, Piers and Roddy took to each other very easily. Piers was cheeky and rather tartish, Roddy was amused and affected severity. Piers could play the role of gad-fly: Roddy was happy to answer with an occasional lazy slap. I could only hope that Piers was not going to become whimsical and tiresome, but on the whole I credited him with too much good sense for that. In any event, dinner that night was pleasant, and I found myself looking forward to our journey, and to spending my time in this company, with more enthusiasm than I had felt about anything for years. There was, of course, a shadow over the party; but in London, on a bright June evening, it was not yet a deep shadow. There was more excitement in us than apprehension: for how could we know then, despite all that Tyrrel had told us and we ourselves had surmised, the true nature of the horror we were later to find in Crete?

When the 25th came, the day before we were to leave, there was still no letter or message from Richard. For whatever reason, he had not kept his promise to tell us where to meet him. And yet he had now been in Crete since June 8, and must surely have known long since what his movements were to be...

That evening we dined with Tyrrel as arranged.

"So he hasn't told you where to meet him?" Tyrrel said.

There was a brief silence, during which Piers picked at a fingernail and Roddy scanned the wine list with concentration and disapproval.

"No."

"I warned you," said Tyrrel with a trace of satisfaction. "People who write letters like his change their minds very easily. He may not want you after all. He may hide. He may leave Crete. So how will you go about finding him? You, Mr Clarence," he said sharply to Piers, "how will you find your friend?"

"I shall leave that to my acknowledged seniors," said Piers, glancing at Roddy and myself. He started gaily in on a plate of smoked salmon, while Roddy whispered sternly to the wine waiter.

"You must do better than that, Mr Clarence, I want your ideas on the matter, sir."

"Crete is a small island," said Piers, thoughtlessly eating. "If he's there, then we should be able to trace him. If he's not, then someone will surely know when he left and in what direction."

"Come, come, Mr Clarence. And you a classical man. Crete may not be large but it is mountainous and easy to hide in. You may recall that during the war a handful of men captured and concealed a German general for some considerable time, and then took him off by boat – without *anyone at all* knowing when they left or in what direction."

Roddy gave Tyrrel a look of speculative interest.

"So what do *you* suggest, Inspector?" he said.

"I'm asking Mr Clarence, Major. True, he's much engaged with his salmon. But he must not allow crapulity to dull his wits."

Roddy laughed. Piers, stung, put down his knife and fork with a clatter.

"You forget, Inspector," Piers said. "It seems he is accompanied by a woman. This will make it much harder for him to hide or to leave the island unobserved. Two people take up more than twice the room of one. And women like being seen, not hidden, so that sooner or later, without quite knowing whether they meant to be or not, they *are* seen."

"Better, Mr Clarence, much better… But if he can change his mind about meeting all of you – old friends – then he can certainly change his mind and get rid of a recently acquired woman."

"In which case, if we can get hold of *her*, she'll be very ready to help us if only out of spite."

"Not bad, sir. But suppose, just suppose, that no one knows where Mr Fountain is and no one knows where his woman is. That they haven't, as far as is *known*, left the island, but that is all you have to go on. What are you going to do then, Mr Clarence? Sit on your bottom and eat smoked salmon – which, by the way, you won't be able to get?"

"I should go," said Piers rather crossly, "to Cnossos, where Richard says he has been working. Something might…transpire there."

"It might indeed. And if not?"

Piers shrugged and looked petulantly away.

"And you, Major Longbow?" said Tyrrel, half laughing towards Piers and then turning to Roddy.

"I suppose," said Roddy, "that all we could do would be to cast about a bit and trust to luck."

"Mr Seymour?" persisted Tyrrel.

"As Major Longbow says. If there's nothing better to go on we shall have to trust to luck. But you mustn't forget that I may hear from Richard tomorrow morning before we leave. And I've given an address in Venice to which any message that comes in the next four days will be wired immediately."

"I'll just bet my soul," said Tyrrel, "that you will not hear from Mr Fountain tomorrow or any other morning. I've had one report, gentlemen – if you'll kindly pay attention, Mr Clarence – since I saw Mr Seymour last. And this report says that Mr Fountain has vanished. He and his woman both. They went to Cnossos, as Mr Clarence says, they went here and they went there – and then they vanished. It is *believed* that they are still on the island. People were interested enough, you see, to take note of what Mr Fountain did. And now that he's given them the slip, they are looking for him and his woman, and looking for them hard. Because if they were interested when he first got there, then they're very interested now: since it seems that something else has happened, gentlemen, or rather something has been *found* near Corinth, that suggests, among other things, that women in particular ought to be very careful in the company of Richard Fountain just now. Which gives them two reasons for wanting to find him: to save – yes, save – his companion, and to ask a great many awkward questions of himself."

"They want to arrest him?" Roddy said.

"Not quite, Major. They still don't really *know*, you see – they only suspect. But they suspect enough to be more than anxious about his girl friend and more than hostile to Mr Fountain himself. And what do you deduce from all this – Mr Clarence?"

"That we shall have competitors – who know the island."

"And who, even so, have so far failed to find him. Very good, Mr Clarence. So you do see, sir, that there will be limited time for amusements when you arrive?"

"And do you suggest," I said, "that we compete with our rivals – or get their help?"

"God knows you may need help, sir. But you might do better to get it indirectly, by watching rather than asking. Because, sir, it is very important that when he *is* found it's *you* that takes him away and not them."

"I thought," said Roddy gently, "that you were a policeman, Tyrrel. In which case the Greek Police are, in a sense, your colleagues. It is hardly for you to encourage us to cross them?"

"I wouldn't worry about that, sir," said Tyrrel. "As yet they have no charges to prefer – only questions to ask. If you could get him away before they asked them, then there would be no actual infringement... Anyway, sir, England is what Mr Fountain needs. England and his friends. Once back here, he may be entirely...all right again. So no point leaving him there, getting worse, as you might put it, in a climate that doesn't suit him, and possibly having to face a trial under alien laws. Not much justice in that, Major; or wouldn't you agree?"

"More or less," said Roddy with a smile.

"And besides, sir, I've heard so much about Mr Fountain since all this started that I almost think of him as my friend too. If anything had...happened...in this country, I might have had to take a different view. But as it is, he merely seems to me to be someone very valuable who is in danger. A good soldier, a fine scholar...a poet... They don't grow on every bush..."

For a while he was silent. Then he lifted a large glass of burgundy from the table and drank it down in one.

"And there's good luck to you," he said. "Mr Seymour, Major Longbow, and you, Mr Clarence." He bowed his head to each one of us in turn. "And now, since I've told you all I can, gentlemen, there's no point in spoiling a pleasant evening... Mr Seymour," he said, producing from somewhere about him my copy of Cavafis, "I am now going to return this with many thanks. But first, sir, there are one or two things I wanted to ask, and no time like the present. This poem about the brothels of Beirut..."

Very late that night, long after Roddy had left us to sleep in his club and Piers had gone to bed in my spare room, and as I myself was sitting at my desk doing a last minute check of the tickets and my own correspondence, the telephone rang.

"Mr Seymour?"

It was a woman's voice, faint with distance and in itself uncertain.

"Yes."

"It is Penelope here. Penelope Goodrich. I'm sorry for ringing up so late."

"Penelope... What can I do for you?"

"I'm sorry for ringing up so late, Anthony," she said again. "But Piers – he said he'd tell me what day you were leaving, but he hasn't. And I woke up just now and thought, 'Suppose they're going tomorrow, I shan't be able'..."

Her voice tailed away.

"Able to do what, Penelope?"

"Tell you that I hope...whatever you're going to do...turns out well."

"Thank you, my dear. Because we are going tomorrow and I'm glad of your wishes."

But I said it indifferently. I cared nothing for Penelope's wishes, only for the journey that was to come, the long roads between the poplars, the green plain of Lombardy, the sea...thinking so much of these things that I often forgot even Richard, for whose sake the whole enterprise had been conceived... For a while, as if she sensed my indifference, Penelope was silent. Then the three pips sounded, definitive and fierce, and seemed to rouse her.

"Don't ring off," she said, "don't ring off, Anthony."

"Of course not, Penelope. But what – ?"

" – I know you don't want me there," she said, hurriedly and as if on the verge of tears, "and I know *he* doesn't want me. I won't try to come. You needn't worry. I won't try to interfere. But if you could *tell* me...anything at all?"

But what could one tell Penelope? That the man she loved was in trouble, in danger, with another woman, that no one knew what he might do next, that we had no idea where to find him, let alone how to help him?

"Oh, I don't want to pry," she went on bitterly. "I don't want to know where he is, what's he's doing. I know something's badly wrong and that is enough. But do you think you can help him, Anthony? You and Piers? I've given Piers money, you know. I don't mind that, I'd give him all I've got if it would help. But will it, Anthony? Is there anything that you will be able...?"

Once again her voice trailed away.

"We'll do our best," I said uselessly.

"I suppose so." For one moment she sounded almost sharp. Then, "Give him my love, Anthony. And tell him that... I don't mind what he's done or what he's felt, that if ever he wants me then...he's only got to come."

"I'll tell him," I said, slightly ashamed for a second, but no less aware of the keen pleasure that was filling my bowels as dawn and departure drew nearer.

"Yes, tell him, Anthony," she said softly. "Oh, I know you want to sleep now... That you only care for Richard, you and Piers, not for me... But don't forget to tell him that, in the middle of everything else. Take him my blessing."

"Indeed I will." It was hollowly said.

"And God bless you too, Anthony, you and Piers, for going like this."

And then at last I felt kind towards this woman whom I had for so long respected but never really liked. For one moment I tried to conjure up some word of love or comfort, of gratitude or reassurance or hope; but it was too late. No words came to me, other than such as would have expressed only my pleasure at what was to come, and I remained silent until Penelope said again, "God bless you, Anthony. And bless poor Richard too," and the line went dead.

This was the last word of farewell we had from anybody. For now the blue dawn was showing, and in a few hours it would be time to be away.

PART TWO

The White Mountains

VI

In Heraclion there is a sea front which in some curious fashion seems to turn a blind eye to the sea, although all along it are to be found forts and custom houses erected by the Venetians. Perhaps it is because most of these are now derelict, save for one which has been turned into a tavern, that one has the impression that the sea is being spurned and ignored by a town which is largely dependent on it. However this may be, in the summer the Cretans at least do the sea the occasional courtesy of walking along this front and sitting at outside tables which are served from the tavern; and here, on July 4, having arrived in Heraclion the previous evening, walked Piers and Roddy and myself, holding a rather disjointed discussion as to the next step in our search for Richard Fountain.

For there had been no word from him the morning we left London, nor had any message been relayed to Venice. Furthermore, and consistently with the mood of pleasure in which we had left England, we had spoken little of Richard by the way, had ignored the problems that would shortly confront us. Nor was this entirely due to mere selfish preoccupation with the delights or petty discomforts of the drive and the sea voyage from Venice: it was rather that after what Tyrrel had said the evening before we left there was a general and justifiable feeling among us that much would depend on sheer luck and that there was therefore little point in laying plans for which we had no data to meet contingencies which we could not foretell. So at Sens we ate quenelles, at Aix Piers lost £25 at roulette, in Milan we paid an evening visit to the nightmare cathedral, and in Venice Piers retrieved his £25 at chemin-de-fer; and in all this time you might have thought, to hear and look at us, that we were simply a carefree little bachelor party with cargo of lotus and in summer mood. But now at last we were in Crete; we were at journey's end and must put away the pleasures of the interlude; and on the blank sea front of Heraclion we sat down to drink Turkish coffee and take council.

"The thing is," said Roddy, "that in his letter he talked of going to Cnossos as though it had been an expedition. But Cnossos is barely five miles from where we're sitting, and apart from King Minos' Palace there are, so my guidebook tells me, only three dirty cafés and a collection of hovels. So that even if he wanted to research there, he surely would have slept in Heraclion."

"Wrong," said Piers with satisfaction. "Above the main palace there is another, much smaller, known as the Little Palace. And on the hillside above that is a villa which once belonged to Sir Arthur Evans. He left it in his will for the use of visiting scholars and provided for a caretaker to look after them. Richard might have stayed there!"

"Who told you all this?" I asked.

"The manager of our hotel."

One of Piers' assets was turning out to be a very capable command of modern Greek. Roddy had none, and I myself, for all my lengthy classical education, had little more, for I have a slow ear for spoken languages and I was finding that modern demotic usage bore little resemblance to the pages of Plato. But Piers, agile as ever, had somehow made the transition from the Attic of the lecture room to the demotic of the market place (he had read a lot of modern Greek poetry, he said, and had had a bilingual Greek friend, son of anglophile parents, at school); and from the hour of our arrival he was to prove indispensable as our source of all local information from trifle to tragedy.

"So the manager of our hotel told you there was a villa for archaeologists," said Roddy. "And did he go on to explain just how welcome to the shade of Sir Arthur Evans Richard's woman would have been?"

"I didn't go into that. But I *did* ask if anyone called Fountain had stayed at his hotel."

"And had he?"

Piers picked at a thumbnail.

"The man behaved very oddly. It was clear from his look that the name meant something to him. But he said very curtly that he had heard of no such person, and then just left me without another word. Very rude behaviour – for a Greek."

"It rather looks as if he's heard something of what Tyrrel was telling us," I said: "that the police want Richard for a variety of unpleasant reasons and he's given them the slip. I dare say a lot of people know about it by now."

For a while we sat in silence. The deserted island of Dia hovered in the heat while the tideless sea sucked steadily at the stone beneath us.

"He may go off and tell the police we've been making enquiries," Roddy said.

"In which case we'll just say we're friends of Richard's who had a vague idea he might be in Crete. Which commits us to nothing. In fact," I said, "it might be interesting to make an apparently innocent enquiry along those lines from the Tourist Police and see how they react. What sort of story they fob us off with."

"No point in drawing attention to ourselves," said Roddy. I had a brief vision of the three of us sitting for weeks on the blind, sunny waterfront, talking listlessly on and on and doing nothing.

"Then what do *you* suggest?" I said irritably.

"Calm, Anthony, calm," Roddy said.

"If," said Piers, "we go to Cnossos, then somebody may well be willing to tell us something. But presumably whatever they know there has already been told to the Police, and little good it has done *them*. Richard just went on to other places and then disappeared. Why go to Cnossos just to hear that?"

"Why do anything?" I said. "Why go anywhere?"

My vision of our discussion creaking interminably on in the heat was becoming more insistent.

"Let's just sit here," I said, "drinking Turkish coffee till the sun goes down. We are near enough the East, God knows. Let us all be oriental and fatalistic. If we sit here long enough the world may come to an end and all our problems will be solved."

Roddy Longbow grinned.

"You have a liver," he said, "and you need exercise. So we will go to Cnossos and exercise you by walking you round the Palace of King Minos. Such places are best seen in a romantic light, and dusk is the time when men whisper of matters about which they remain silent in the full light of the sun. So we will go to Cnossos in the early evening. At the very least, it is a sight which no tourist should miss."

"The buses," remarked Piers, "run twice in every hour."

"They say," said Piers, "that the mythical labyrinth was in fact the palace itself. So many passages and stairways and odd little chambers…"

The bus turned and rattled off. The sun was well below the hills now. A small boy stared at us from in front of a flyblown café.

"This is the entrance to the main palace," Piers went on. "The little palace is on either side of the road – about 200 yards back the way we came on the bus. I couldn't see the villa. It must be in the trees."

As we went through the entrance and paid for admission, the man behind the counter muttered something.

"Closes in half an hour," said Piers.

Roddy and I nodded. We all went down a slope through some pine trees, to where we could see a low rampart of stone:

this was surmounted by an obviously recent structure, a prominent feature of which was a row of garish red pillars.

"Sir Arthur's work," said Piers. "Impressive but hardly convincing! His materials strike a wrong note. Yet he selected them with great care…"

We climbed some steps, passed between two of the red pillars, then down some more steps, along a corridor, and into a room with a crude throne against one wall.

"Hardly a throne for a great king," said Roddy.

"It was not the throne of a great king," said a voice from the shadows.

A small, ferrety, bearded man came into the chamber, straight through the wall as it seemed at first, but in fact from a narrow recess, which was concealed behind a stone screen.

"It was not the throne of a great king," repeated the little man, shuffling forward slowly and gesturing towards the stone seat. "It was for one of his noblemen. The steward of the bull ring. This is the room in which he instructed the dancers – the bullfighters I suppose you would call them."

Roddy consulted a plan in his guide book.

"It says quite plainly here, sir," he said, "that this is the Royal – "

"They all say that," interrupted the little man, shuffling up to the throne and seating himself cautiously on the edge of it. "Guide books, scholars, pundits – they all say it. Sir Arthur himself, God rest him, he said it. But it isn't, you know. I know it isn't." He jutted his beard. "Yes, *I* know," he said, "and I've told them all, but they come here from Athens or London or Berlin and they don't listen to me. I can *prove* it, but they wouldn't listen if Minos himself came back from the shades to tell them."

"Oh," said Roddy courteously, "and why not?"

But the little man turned his head to one side and seemed to contemplate, with disinterested passion, the darkened wall over to his right. Then he recollected himself and pulled his head back to face us.

"You'll excuse me," he said. "My name is Arnold. Doctor Arnold, sometime Fellow of Corpus Christi College, Cambridge. I work on the site here."

He nodded his head gently.

"I spend all my time here," he said. "The rest of them come and go, do this, do that. But old Ratty Arnold is always here." He giggled defensively. "That's what they call me, the young men from Athens and London. 'Ratty' Arnold. Ratty Arnold who never leaves Cnossos: who just scrabbles his life away on the site and builds up his crazy theories. Wrote a book which they wouldn't publish. But they let me stay. I'm useful in a way, you see. Ratty Arnold digs about and uncovers things. 'Never mind his theories,' the young men say: 'he does his digging and uncovers things, and it's no sweat off our backs'."

He laughed in a kind of high-pitched whine.

"And then Ratty Arnold takes care of the villa. Keeps the caretaker up to the mark. Reminds him that it's not just his own house, it's for scholars to live in. He waits on Ratty Arnold and remembers his place in life. I'm useful all right."

It was now almost dark inside the chamber. I looked at my watch uneasily. I could scarcely see the ridiculous, wizened head of poor Doctor Arnold as he went on muttering into the gloom.

"But I'm right, you know. The steward of the bull ring had this room, not the King, not the King... But you don't care, do you?" he said, a sort of hysterical resignation in his voice. "You don't give a rap for the King or the bulls."

He paused, and seemed to survey us through the darkness as a cunning child might regard a wild animal through the bars of its cage, pleasurably debating whether or not to cast the beast the morsel it coveted. At last, with great coyness, he said: "You want young Fountain, don't you? He told me some people would come."

"Perhaps," I said, "you could tell us about him somewhere else? In the villa? Because they're going to shut – "

"Please don't interrupt, Anthony," said Roddy quietly but very firmly. And then to the old man: "Please go on, sir."

It was now so dark that the old man and the throne he was perched on could only be seen in the dimmest outline. I was vaguely aware of a nodding head and two crab-like hands clawing at a pair of skimpy knees. And always the high, mad voice, which seemed as though it were striving to contain itself, as though it were desperate to form itself into words, aware that at any moment it might just become a prolonged, meaningless, unmodulated wail.

"He agreed with me, young Fountain, or so he said. But perhaps that was because he wanted something out of me. First, he wanted to have his woman at the villa. So he had to get me to agree. Then he wanted me…to show him things."

At this recollection, the old man burst into an appalling screech of merriment.

"What things?" said Piers.

"Keep *quiet*, will you," hissed Roddy. "Let him get on."

"Things and things," said the old man slyly. "And then he told me what to tell the police. He knew they were coming, you see. Oh yes, he knew. He told me he was going to Phaestos and then to the hills near Mount Ida. I could tell the police that, he said. But after Mount Ida – he didn't want anyone to know. He was going to disappear, see, and he didn't want a mortal man to find him – except for you, the friends he was expecting. There were times when he seemed not to want you to know either, but other times when he did. So all in all I think I might tell you. But what do you think, gentlemen?" Once again he cackled with laughter. "Because if I were you, I should go back to England and forget young Master Fountain. I wouldn't want to catch up with him and his woman, not if it was me."

And then, for all the darkness, I distinctly saw him make, in a wide gesture, a gesture almost of parody, the sign of the cross.

"I'm a scholar," the whining voice went on, "and I know so much that I believe in almost nothing. But if I believed in evil…" He broke off, and there was a sound of scratching: I imagined him clawing at his pathetic old knees. "…Him and that woman," he said, "may God help us all. So what do you think, gentlemen?" – and now his tones were those of the purest Cambridge courtesy – "Do you still want to find your friend?"

"If you will be so good as to tell us where he is," said Roddy.

"He went to Mount Ida," said the old man in tones which seemed to be growing fainter, "and then he disappeared. And nobody can find him at all. But he said to tell you that he liked islands. He liked Crete, he said, and *he liked other islands too*, because, he said, *water is best*. Now you know Greek, gentlemen, classical Greek anyhow. Water is best: ἄριστον μὲν ὕδωρ: *ariston men hydor*. That's what he said. So now you know. But if it was me…"

And then his voice trailed away into nothing and he was silent.

"For Christ's sake," I said, "we must all get out of here and talk sense where we can see ourselves."

"People talk sense when they can see each other," said Roddy very softly in my ear, "but they often cease to tell the truth."

"But *when*," said Piers, ignoring the two of us and walking urgently towards the throne, "when was he going to…disappear from Mount Ida?"

There was no reply.

"Speak up, sir," said Roddy crisply: "When was this to happen? And what is this talk about water?"

At the same time Piers struck a match. The light flickered round the ceiling and the stone walls, wandered over the recess from which the old man had first come, thence on to the stiffly marching figures of a restored wall painting, and finally fell on the crude and now empty little throne.

"Answer me, will you?" shouted Roddy, almost as if he had been on his own barrack square back in Ludlow.

But the only answer he had was his own voice ringing round the throne room, and then the whisper of the wind in the pine trees outside.

"Seek and ye shall find," said Piers at dinner that evening. "Doctor Arnold was certainly most prompt in executing his commission... If I wasn't actually eating this food, I wouldn't have *believed* that food could be so nasty..."

"We're not the only people seeking," said Roddy.

"We know that," I said. "We know the police are after Richard. But they haven't had the full benefit of Ratty Arnold's information."

"Perhaps not. But they're making quite sure that we don't steal a march on them."

"What — ?"

" — You may have noticed," Roddy said, "that two respectable looking gentlemen got on the bus at the first stop on the way back from Cnossos."

"And so?"

"And so they're following us."

"How can you know?"

"I have an instinct about being watched. There were several occasions during the war... Anyway, look there."

He glanced, as though casually, through the window of the Restaurant, across the square with its pretty Venetian fountain and towards a small café. It was now a damp and unpleasant evening, for it had started to rain about an hour before; but two respectable gentlemen were seated outside under the awning, drinking minute cups of coffee and looking calmly back across the square.

"They've rumbled us," Roddy said. "I dare say the manager of the hotel... After Piers mentioned Richard this morning."

"What can we do?"

Roddy shrugged.

"Ignore them. Try to give the impression that we have no idea at all that anyone could conceivably want to bother with us. Then they may deduce that we're not consciously up to anything; or at least they'll take our actions at face value."

"Face value," said Piers meditatively. "Tell me, what would you say was the face value of Doctor Ratty Arnold?"

"He was an old man," Roddy said, "who has gone half cracked after years of obsession with the remote past."

"Agreed. But when I was talking to the hotel manager this morning about Cnossos and the villa, he – well, he seemed to think there was no one there except the caretaker."

"How should he know what goes on up there? He's got his own worries."

"I dare say. Still, when we got back just now, I asked him about Doctor Arnold. After all, if the old boy's been living there for years they must know something about him in Heraclion."

"And did they?"

"Hard to tell," said Piers; "the man just looked at me rather oddly."

"Like when you mentioned Richard to him?"

"Oh no. When I spoke of Richard he was very abrupt and denied knowing of him. But this evening he was more...pitying."

"Hardly surprising," said Roddy. "The poor old man's a clear nut case if ever there was one. I expect the manager's sorry for him."

"He seemed more sorry for me."

"The important point," said Roddy firmly (but with an uneasy look at Piers), "is that the old man has given us all the information we have to go on and he says that we're the only people he's given it to. Now just what did all that nonsense mean? If it meant anything at all?"

"Richard told him to tell us," I said, "that he liked islands, that he liked Crete but other islands as well, because water is

118

best. It very much looks as if he's gone to another island. Though why and how…"

"More to the point," said Roddy, "to ask which."

"Water is best," said Piers: "*ariston men hydor*. I've been thinking about this. There was a legendary town called Hydra; and there has been much controversy among scholars as to whether it took its name from the monster killed by Hercules or from the Greek word for water – *hydor*."

"And the town is still standing?" asked Roddy.

"Not as far as I know – though I fancy there was some talk of excavating it. In any case it is on the mainland. But there is also an island called Hydra – thought to have been inhabited, in the first place, by people from the original city…"

Roddy considered this, and then looked at the index of his guidebook.

"I can't find it here," he said.

"Look under 'I'. In English it is often spelt 'Idra'. To give us a better idea how to pronounce it."

"Idra… Yes, Idra. Island of."

He turned the pages of the guide.

" 'A small island (pop. 3000)'," he read, " 'some four hours by steamship from the Piraeus. The visitor will disembark at the harbour to find himself in the charming town of Idra (or Hydra), which is arranged in the manner of an amphitheatre on the slopes of the surrounding hills. He will be surprised by the opulence of many of the buildings, which were originally erected in the eighteenth century: during which period the privateering families of the island were at the height of their power and wealth, and indeed for some years enjoyed almost entire control of Eastern Mediterranean trade routes…' Sounds pleasant enough," he said, "but I can't think why Richard should want to go there."

"Go on reading."

Roddy shrugged but read on.

" 'Early in the nineteenth century, however, the chief Idriot families gave both their ships and their magnificent fortunes to assist in the struggle against the Turks. The war, as is well known, was ultimately successful, but the Idriots were never adequately compensated for their sacrifice. Since they had no agricultural resources, the islanders were threatened with ruinous poverty; but public outcry compelled the Government of the day to provide assistance, albeit meagre, and the inhabitants were thus enabled to re-equip themselves after a fashion. Meanwhile, however, many of them had left the island, which has shown little sign of regaining its former predominance...' Still want me to go on?" Roddy said.

"Please."

" 'Among other items of interest, it should be noted that certain ancient religious cults of a curious nature, supposedly imported from the legendary parent city of Hydra on the mainland, are rumoured to have been kept alive on the island, sometimes in the guise of local festivals, until within living memory. This has been strongly and repeatedly denied by representatives of the Greek Orthodox Church, it being urged that the festivals in question are of a harmless traditional kind and there is no trace whatever of other or darker observances. Three such protests are recorded as having been made by the Church during the nineteenth century, and one as recently as 1927. The visitor will of course draw his own conclusions, seeing so improbable an allegation only as the product of the romantic and even disordered fancies of earlier Near Eastern travellers, not all of whom were noted for integrity of character. It is said, however, that the poet Lord Byron, on his return from his first journey in Greece, surprised several of his friends by references to some indelicate scenes which he vouchsafed had been described to him in Athens by a trader newly arrived from the Aegean Islands...' I see what you're getting at," said Roddy. "Richard being professionally interested in religious cults?"

"And even emotionally interested," Piers said.

"What sort of cults do you suppose these were?"

"I don't know," said Piers uneasily. "But the inhabitants of the original Hydra did not have too good a reputation. You see, scholars say that the myth whereby Hercules, or Heracles as he should be called, destroyed the hundred-headed monster, the Hydra – that this myth reflects an actual historical occurrence, which was that a *real* king called Heracles sacked the *city* of Hydra as a protest against the cruel and vicious behaviour of the inhabitants."

"This would be *very* ancient history?"

"It would indeed – otherwise it would not have been transposed into the form of a myth. But if one considers," said Piers, "that the mythical equivalent of the city was cast in the shape of a hundred-headed serpent… What does that indicate to you? About the possible nature of the real city and the practices of its citizens?"

"Nothing very wholesome," said Roddy without interest, "but there's no need to go into that kind of detail just now."

"Perhaps not," said Piers, his eyes looking anxious; "but remember that these same practices *may* have survived in some form or other in the *island* of Hydra, having been brought there by the original settlers from the mainland city. And if Richard…"

He broke off and called to the waiter for more wine.

"The trouble with you and Anthony," said Roddy, "is that you're both forever trying to work out Richard's motives and forgetting that we're simply here to get him safely home… But now you've mentioned it, what do *you* think the hundred-headed Hydra stands for? One of those religious whichwhats that Richard finds so fascinating?"

"More or less," said Piers. "But I'd rather not go into it."

"You started it all. Can't back out now."

"Something phallic," I said: "the serpent…"

"Perhaps," Piers said unwillingly. "But the essential point of the hundred heads – and remember that these grew again as swiftly as they were cut off – is that from one main trunk there are growing a great many separate branches, each of which has some sort of identity of its own but renews itself, when destroyed, by virtue of some power it derives from the central body. In other words, you might see the whole thing as some form of contamination or infection, which starts with one person, or a solid central group, but spreads out in various directions and makes whomsoever it touched a part or branch of the original person, infected by him and now forever dependent on him."

"And the renewal of these branches?"

"Some form," said Piers, "of immortality... Does any of this remind you of any particular kind of cult or superstition?"

"It reminds me of *all* superstitions," I said. "Christianity, to take one of the better known. A central group, the apostles, spreading their influence like a particularly malicious growth... Immortality guaranteed by the central authority..."

"Ingenious, Anthony. But in this case – the one I have in mind – the analogy of the Hydra has a far greater exactitude. The similarity is almost *physical*. Have you no idea what I mean?"

Roddy and I shook our heads.

"In which case," said Piers firmly, looking Roddy straight in the the eye, "I do not propose to discuss it further now."

"Anyway," I said, "if Richard is only interested academically..."

"Considering the position he seems to be in, I doubt whether he would be going anywhere just now merely for *academic* interest."

"And that's enough of that," said Roddy in a sharp, practical tone. "Let us just consider what we actually *know* and what, in consequence, we can do. We know we are being followed by the police, who are interested in us because we are interested in Richard. And secondly, if we are to believe old man Arnold – who in any case provides our only evidence – then Piers' interpretation of his gibberish makes sense and may be accepted, for the time being, as knowledge. Richard likes islands; water, or *hydor*, is best. Therefore Richard has gone, with or without his woman, to the island of Idra or Hydra, which is some four hours' sail from the Piraeus and boasts an attractive eighteenth century harbour town. As for these cults, I'll believe in them when I see them. What we want to find is Richard – and without having the police sniffing behind us when we do so. So what action, gentlemen?"

Piers and I looked across at him, inviting him to provide the answer.

"Tomorrow," said Roddy, "we catch a plane to Athens. The police, who still think Richard is in Crete, will then assume we have got nowhere in our search for him, that we are bored or at a dead end and probably never cared very much anyhow whether or not we found him. In any event, they forget all about us and leave us alone. Right?"

"Right…with a little luck."

"We then," said Roddy, "take a boat to the island of Hydra, where, unattended by watch dogs, we set about finding Richard… So we will now go and pack, and Piers, in his fluent Greek, will make enquiries about aeroplanes. After which we shall play a rubber of three-handed bridge, drink two large glasses of brandy each, and then go to bed."

So it was; and the next day, at five in the afternoon, we boarded the aeroplane from Heraclion to Athens.

VII

The island of Hydra is rocky and barren. Nothing grows there, no vines, no olives and no fruit. Everything comes by boat to the small town of Hydra, which, but for a few hamlets by the sea and the scattered monasteries in the hills, is the only inhabited portion of all the island. So the harbour at Hydra is the centre of the island's life. Here, on the waterfront, are the only restaurants and cafés worth speaking of: the cinema itself is only fifty yards away – down a narrow passageway leading direct from the quayside. It is a pleasant harbour, almost archetypal in pattern; the sun beats down on the shining sea beyond the bar, the Hydriots lounge and chatter, little boats go aimlessly in and out, and the white town, with its splendid eighteenth-century houses, rises on to the hills in gleaming tiers above one. There are no cars or motor vehicles of any kind; for the climbing town is intersected only by alleys and winding stairways; and the tracks which lead from it along the coast or away into the mountains are still only fit for mules. So there is peace on the waterfront for all the bargaining and banter of the Hydriots: and here, at half past two on the day after we reached Athens, having booked ourselves in at a little hotel which seemed about to tumble into the water among the fishing boats, we sat down to have a drink.

Before catching the boat that morning, I had had time to call at the Athenian branch of Cook's, to which conveniently central point all my letters were being forwarded from London, to be kept or sent on to Crete or elsewhere, as I might request when our plans were clearer. There were several letters of no interest, but one from Walter Goodrich; and this I now read out to Roddy and Piers.

Lancaster College, Cambridge.
July 1, 1957.

My dear Anthony,

I must confess to being slightly puzzled by your behaviour. The other day, when you were in Cambridge, you told me that Richard was coming back from Greece this autumn – a fact which, I must admit, I found surprising. You did not tell me, however, that you yourself were going out to accompany him home, nor that you were taking Piers Clarence with you, two items of information which Penelope has just thrown off at me, not without implying that she had deliberately withheld them until you *were* safely on your way.

Now of course it is not really any business of mine who goes to see Richard in Greece or what other purpose they may have in going. But since you, more than anyone, know of my interest in Richard's career and well-being, I find it odd that you seem purposely to have concealed your plans from me. I have additional reason for thinking you to have been deceitful, firstly in that you are accompanied by Clarence, Richard's association with whom, as you almost certainly know, I deplore most strongly; and secondly in that Penelope has indicated, without being at all precise, that your journey is far from being a mere affair of pleasure or routine but has some mysterious and disagreeable reason behind it.

Now, Anthony, would it be too much if I were to ask you to let me know just *what* is going on? If only you will do so, in fair round terms, then I am quite willing to assume that you have not been deliberately misleading me

125

hitherto, but have simply been wholly preoccupied with your arrangements to meet whatever problems there may be and have thus lacked for the leisure to consult me. Apart from anything else, it is most important that I should have some idea of what is wrong with Richard (and I infer from Penelope's manner that something is wrong), so that I can see things are made all right here with the Provost and my other colleagues. A year ago I had heavy weather arranging for Richard to change the subject of his research the last minute before he left; and his present determination to return this year instead of next, though I grant you this was always a possibility, is a most unhelpful factor – partly because I surmise that his research will have been inadequately attended to in only the one year, and partly because there are several excellent and practical reasons for keeping him out of Cambridge till the end of 1958.

("Deceitful bugger," interjected Piers: "he means me.")

If, on top of all this, there is to be more trouble sprung on me without warning as to its gravity or its nature, then I really cannot answer for the consequences; and I am sure you do not wish that Richard's career should be laid in ruins any more than I do.

It is annoying to reflect that this letter may not reach you for a considerable time. (I am sending it to London, but I have no notion, nor, apparently, has Penelope, what arrangements you have made for the forwarding of your correspondence.) But if you should get it in good time, then for Heaven's sake, my dear boy, do the following things for me.

Firstly, and if it is at all possible, try to persuade Richard to stay for another year after all: I assure you it will be for the best.

("So evidently he has absolutely no idea," said Roddy Longbow, "of what sort of thing is in the air.")

Secondly, do try to see that Richard does not respond too fully, or at least not too openly, to the detrimental influence of Clarence – who will probably urge him to return with you, quite apart from any other damage he may do.

("He takes you seriously at all events," said Roddy to Piers.)

Lastly, Anthony, and above all, do send to tell me what is the matter. I don't wish to appear self-congratulatory, but I have considerable experience, as you very well know, in arranging even quite difficult affairs to everyone's satisfaction; and if I only know what is going on, however unfortunate it may be, then I am confident that I can deal with any problems which might arise at this end or even at yours. For the point is this: I love Richard and I believe in him and I want to make his life a success, and I do not propose to allow anything at all, let alone some minor scandal on the other side of Europe, to prevent me from so doing. Give me the facts, Anthony; and if these amount to anything short of murder (as they say), then you may safely leave the rest to me.

We have had little rain and the Backs are rather dried up; but the sun suits Cambridge, which somehow seems lovelier than ever.

Penelope sends her best wishes.

Yours ever,

Walter.

"I'll say this for your Doctor Goodrich," said Roddy Longbow: "he's dead loyal."

"He is very jealous of his possessions," said Piers moodily.

"The ironic thing is," I said, "that on his own terms I believe him. He really does want what is best – what he thinks is best – for Richard. And he really could sort out almost any difficulty

127

under the moon. I've seen him at work before now…'Anything short of murder,' as he says."

For a moment a chill fell over the warm, happy quayside and we all looked aside and away.

"We don't really know — " began Piers.

Roddy made a sharp gesture with his hand.

"We don't," he said. "I've told you both before that we must stick to what we do. You intellectuals are too fond of speculation."

"A Greek vice," said Piers, and looked out over the harbour to the deep blue sea. And then — "

"What do you propose to do about Walter's letter, Anthony?"

"He himself is doubtful when I will get it. I could pretend not to have done so."

"But," said Piers rather surprisingly, "that letter deserves a fair answer."

"Any danger of him following us out here?" said Roddy.

"Very little. The long vac term is just coming up. And Walter has so many intrigues running in England at any one time that it's as much as he dare do to go away for a week in September. He's terrified the threads may slip from his loving grasp."

"Then tell him," said Roddy, "that you appreciate his worry, but that Richard is just…unhappy. So that there is nothing Goodrich can do except leave us to provide what comfort we may."

"Yes," said Piers, "I like that. It has a good measure of the truth."

He looked at Roddy with gratitude.

"I'm glad you understand him," Piers said.

"I've known Richard longer than you have," said Roddy coolly, "if never so closely. It is a mistake to assume that soldiers are devoid of sympathy." He made another impatient gesture of the hand. "So what's to do? Anthony will write and reassure Goodrich. And we're here…in Hydra…"

He looked dispassionately at the gently rocking boats in front of him; and then answered his own question.

"There are a limited number of Englishmen here," he said, "even in the summer. One of them will know about Richard. Tonight they will come out of their holes to start drinking. And tonight we will drink with them, and enquire."

And indeed we were lucky enough, though it was not from an Englishman that we had our information.

In Hydra there is a pleasant tavern run by a bulky, smiling Hydriot called Spiro and his pretty twelve year old son. Here one may take an evening meal of sorts; here come sailors to dance and foreigners to watch them – though later in the evening the foreigners will drunkenly ape the sailors' graceful movements on the floor, after which the sailors, now drunk themselves, will ape the foreigners. Here one may drink until the island's electricity is switched off at midnight; and here one may continue drinking, while the oil lamps hiss and the sailors sing sad songs, until the rosy-fingered dawn climbs over the hill behind the harbour. Here we came to dine, and were approached with little ceremony and much friendliness by an American who said his christian name was Milton and who, in the true fashion of the senior expatriate he was, wished to know whence we came and why, and how long we would stay.

"You'll like it here," Milton said. "The people are friendly and there's a lot of English about. Why don't you stay awhile?"

"We haven't much time," Piers said.

"Time doesn't matter here."

"It does to us."

"If you say so..."

He rapped his wine-can hard on the table, then flung it over his shoulder without even troubling to turn his head. It soared over the dancing sailors to where Spiro's pretty son, alerted by the rap, caught it on the other side of the room and scurried away to the barrel.

"If you say so," Milton repeated; "but what's the hurry?"

"We are looking for a friend," said Roddy straight out, "and we must find him without delay. That's the hurry."

"And you think he might be on the island?"

"Perhaps."

"Well then... Describe him."

"He is called Richard Fountain," Piers said. "He is tall and well set, with dark hair, green eyes of great brilliance, and a rather arrogant expression about his mouth. He walks with the bearing of a soldier; and he speaks with the assurance of a prince."

Milton looked curiously at Piers.

"Quite something," he said lightly. "Noticeable, one might have thought. There's no one like that in this town. When do you think he arrived?"

"Mid to late June."

"You'll pardon me. But might he have arrived...in such a way as to avoid notice? People sometimes do, you know."

"He might."

"And perhaps a woman with him?"

"Very possibly."

Milton paused. Then he rapped again with his already emptied wine-can, and again flung it without looking across the room to Spiro's nimble little son.

"There is...something," Milton said. "It's an odd story and worth hearing in any case. It may fit in with what you're after." His can was restored to him by the enchanting Ganymede, who tickled his neck before leaving the table. "Insolent brat," said Milton in a friendly parody of English tones: "he'll charge a drachma extra on the can for that." Then he settled himself forward on his elbows.

"It's a little tricky this," he began, "especially as it may concern a friend of yours. Still, you asked for it. The first thing to know is that some three miles up the coast to the North there's a fine natural harbour, 'most as good as the one here, which the natives use as a kind of crude ship-building yard. There's boat houses and a row of stone buildings, but mostly no one sleeps there. They just work there by day, tearing up the old craft that are sent to be junked there and using the sound timbers to patch the newer boats. Then in the evening they row back here. But sometimes, in the springtime, in the summer, some of the boys take food and stay up there the night as a kind of adventure, I reckon, or to get quit of their scolding old mothers for a while. So one day this June young Michaeli, who's the son of the shipwright Thalassides, took his friend Nico and three bottles of wine and two lobsters, and off they went telling everyone they were going to camp out the night at Thyrias — which is what they call this shipyard."

He took a long draught of wine.

"So no one thought anything of this — until the boys got back the next day and told everyone what they thought they saw. And it was a night, I may tell you gentlemen, with a beautiful round moon, so there's reason enough to suppose they saw it. And what they told everyone was this. They were sitting drinking outside a hut up on the far end of the quay they have there, and because of the moon being so bright they weren't bothered with a lamp, so probably no one would have noticed them. And as they sat there a small sailing boat came round the Northern point of the harbour. Well, at first they thought nothing of this, because it might have been some fisherman who had gone out for a night's fishing, or it might have been some tourist who'd taken a fancy to the moonlight and hired the boat to take him around in it. Anyway, they just watched it without bothering much — until they saw it was putting in towards the quay. So then they got all anxious to see who might be coming to spoil their privacy, and they walked along a strip of beach which lies under the quay for a way; but they kept themselves hidden behind the hulks and all that were lying about, because whoever was coming they weren't keen to be involved with them.

"The next thing that happened was that this sailing boat nosed up on to the strip of beach about twenty yards from where they were hiding behind a rowing boat. Out gets some ragged character whom they don't recognize and ties up the boat to one of the old cannons, which are stuck muzzle down into the sand to act as bollards. Then he looks around him and apparently finds everything in order, so he calls back to the boat. And then... Well, I reckon this is the difficult bit, so I'll try and get it right and you gentlemen must hear me out in peace, so's I don't lose it."

He drank again, a magnificent swig straight from the can that would not have disgraced Jack Falstaff.

"What happened, so Michaeli and Nico said, was this. A tall young woman stepped off the boat, dressed in a sweater and pants, and with a kind of cloak hanging from her shoulders. She too looked around, and apparently she was happy about the beach and all, because she then spoke, very tight and cold, only they couldn't hear the words, back in the direction of the boat. Then there was a deal of fumbling about in the bottom of the boat, and after a bit three other men come up with a kind of stretcher, which they ease forward over the bow, till the tall woman and the man who got out first are able to help them, and they get this stretcher thing lying on the beach. Then the woman kneels down by the stretcher and starts making soft sort of crooning noises, and the boys get to busting themselves to see what's on it, and what they think they see is this.

"They reckon it's a man on the stretcher, wrapped in blankets right up to his chin, and with a face which is bold and proud but...but sort of dead-looking. That is, it's so white, in the moonlight, that it looks like the face of a figure on a tomb – you know the sort of thing, alabaster face looking straight up at the sky, eyes closed, immobile... And they reckon the hair is dark, but it's not a Greek face; while Nico, who's been to Athens once or twice, said it was rather like a picture he saw there of your Lord Byron. Handsome, and proud like I said. But all the time looking so dead. White, they said, with the hair falling over the forehead, and these blankets, held by straps, wrapped tight and coming right up to the chin, so that the body – the man – is rather like some kind of mummy.

"Well, they don't find this any too nice to look at, but they can't move, what with this woman and four men and all, so they just sit tight. Meantime the woman goes on crooning and sort of caresses this figure on the stretcher, strokes him all over, only of course she's only stroking the blankets. She starts at the feet and works up along the body. When she comes to the face, she touches it with the ends of her fingers and tidies the hair back from the forehead for a bit; till suddenly she bends over to kiss the face – or it looks as if she's going to kiss the face, but just as her lips get down there her whole head sort of slips aside and her mouth seems to nuzzle in under the ear, as though she's got some secret to whisper first… But just then one of the men comes up and tugs her to her feet, and starts talking, fiercely but very low, so that once again the boys don't get what's being said.

"Then all the other men come and join in, and they still talk very low, but they seem to be angry over something; until after a time the woman makes a wave of her hand and then seems to be giving them money, and whatever it is it shuts them up for sure. Last of all, two of the men get back into the boat, while the other two pick up the stretcher and start away from the harbour towards the track that leads up into the hills. The woman follows them, with a good strong step and her cloak swinging as she goes, and the whole party vanishes round the shoulder of a hill. Meantime, the two men in the sailing boat untie her and take off out of the harbour, turning back up North when they get to the harbour mouth. As for the boys, they're only a couple of kids, and they just go back to their hut, take a big swig of wine each, and pull their blankets up over their heads. And that's it, gentlemen. That's the story that Michaeli and Nico had to tell when they got back from their all night picnic the next morning."

"They never thought of following...the stretcher?" I asked.

"They thought of it all right. But neither of them would have done it for ten thousand drachmas. They didn't like the woman, see, and they *didn't* like what they saw on the stretcher."

"But presumably," Roddy said, "the police were told about all this?"

"Sure they were told. And they sent men out and made enquiries. But whatever they found out, not a thing did they ever let on. But that's the Greek Police all over. They probably didn't find much, and they couldn't cope with what they did, and in that case they'd just shut up and pretend that nothing had happened. Any case, people here got to reckoning the boys had been drinking too much, or invented the whole thing for laughs, and the police didn't contradict them any. Though that's not to say they don't know more than it suits them to tell..."

"But where in God's name could they have been taking the stretcher from the harbour?"

Milton shrugged.

"There's some monasteries in the hills," he said. "There's a few huts for fishermen round the coast. But nowhere for *that* little party to find much joy... Anyway, who's to think it *was* your friend? Only a face above some blankets."

"The face fits," said Piers, speaking for the first time since Milton had started his story; "and so do several other things."

Roddy and I looked at him, startled by the fierce assurance with which he had spoken. He returned our look very gravely, and said with rather more diffidence – "This is all what I was beginning to think... I hoped... But now..."

He turned away from us and spoke coaxingly to Milton.

"Can you remember the *names* of any of the monasteries?" he said.

Milton swigged at his wine and pulled a drunken parody of a thoughtful face.

"There's the Monastery of the Prophet Elias," he said, "which is high up above the town here. Away to the South West is the Monastery of Hagiou Pneumatos – of the Holy Spirit. And up North you have the Monastery of Haematos Christou, the Monastery of the Blood of Christ – "

" – *The Blood of Christ*," shouted Piers, banging the table so that the cans rattled. He rose from his seat. "We must go *now*," he said. "There isn't a minute – *now*. Richard – OH MY GOD."

White in the face with terror and love, he swept through the prancing sailors.

"*Now*. NOW," he screamed back at us.

The sailors dropped back and the music died. Roddy and I rose to follow Piers. Milton, himself looking scared but understanding no more than the rest of us what Piers meant, simply had recourse to the one action, almost a matter of reflex, by means of which he had for so long sought comfort in the face of difficulty. He rapped his wine can on the table and flung it over his shoulder. But he had forgotten that there was still wine in it; and the pretty pot-boy was too fascinated with the furious face of Piers to answer on his cue. The can hurtled through the air spilling wine like summer rain, till it fell with a clatter at the feet of the pot-boy and rolled aimlessly and with a hideous noise of grinding on the dirty floor of stone.

Fifteen minutes later, Milton having found a guide for us but having prudently elected to remain behind himself, we were walking along a coastal track, which would take us the three miles to the old shipyard whence we must turn up towards the Northern hills of Hydra. The guide, with a powerful flashlamp, walked ahead; just behind him was Piers; while Roddy and I, side by side, brought up the rear. The path was easily wide enough for two but very rough; rocky slopes rose above it and descended from it, almost sheer, into the quiet but expectant sea. There were many loose rocks scattered along the way and a little carelessness could have led to a nasty fall – could have rolled one down over the rock, gasping and clutching with torn arms, into the pitch-black waters below. So Roddy and I walked with care; but Piers, who seemed to have mastered by instinct the technique of this cruel passage, talked on and on into the darkness, often turning his head and walking entirely blind to make sure the two of us could hear.

"We've been misled by what Tyrrel told us," Piers was saying. "Not his fault — for no doubt he was equally misled by what the Greeks told him. Anyway, what they said and what he told us was probably more or less true — once. Once there probably was a time when Richard himself was the danger. You remember what I told you in Cambridge, Anthony? About Richard looking for release, and how this search could quite as easily be for something to hate as for something to love? Well, I stick by that even now. But at some stage the situation has been twisted round. It's Richard that's being hunted now, Richard who's *in* danger...

"Richard being hunted. Not only by the police, but by the very powers he went out to discover. He thought that Greece would give him freedom and manhood — release from Walter and all the things that had been stifling him for so long. All this might have been achieved through love or through hate, but the important thing is he expected to find certain...certain forces...which would propel him onward to release. I don't suppose he knew whether these would operate through love or through hate. Perhaps he didn't care. Perhaps he assumed that they *must* be benevolent — or deceived himself into assuming that. In any case he came here and he found the power he was looking for, and in some way it was working through this woman. He thought he could harness it — harness it to draw his chariot to freedom. But he'd forgotten something very important about himself."

Some stars showed through a gap in the cloud that was drifting across the sky, but the road seemed darker than ever. There was a wind rising and the sea stirred uneasily in its wary rest.

"He'd forgotten something that was embedded in his nature. It is Richard's nature to command *but it is also Richard's nature to obey.* For years he's been obeying – obeying the school rules, obeying Roddy, obeying Walter. He has commanded, yes – but always under higher authority. Sometimes he has seemed temporarily independent of that authority; sometimes he has rebelled against it – snubbed Walter, insulted Penelope: but he's always come back before long. Always knuckled under. So that in the end, when he found the power that was to release him from obedience, he also found that he must still have something to obey. Walter was too far away – the book of rules was back in England, back in the housemaster's study, and there was no help from any of these. Deprived of the familiar, he turned for help wherever he might find it; and so, instead of controlling the power that was going to release him, he has begged for *it* to control *him*, he has chosen, not to use it, but to grovel under it. And since this power has come in the form of a woman...

"What form did he think it would come in? Did he think strength would flow up through his feet out of the soil of Greece? Or that the old gods, the gods of warriors and lovers, of drinkers and travellers, would come down from Olympus to his aid? Or perhaps he longed for even older gods, the gods of Crete, or those that were here before Olympus ever rose from Earth the Mother – herself the most ancient of them all, except the Void. But wherever he thought this power would come from, from Aphrodite or the Earth or the Sky, from the holy soil of Hellas or from the winds of freedom which fly singing off its mountains, he thought it would come in a known guise – known, at any rate, to him, because he knew about the gods, and about Greece which is the giver of life.

"So when he found this woman, he must have thought that here, in human form, was Aphrodite or Demeter, or some power of which he knew and which would bring him where he wished to be – forever out of Walter's clutches. God knows what happened for a time. Those hints of Tyrrel's... But then he started wanting to obey once more, and here was the twist, because having no Walter to obey he now obeyed the woman. Tired of revolt, he turned in obedience to the power through which he had revolted – but thinking all the time that it was a power benevolent towards him, or at least one which he knew of or had read of, a goddess or a guardian or a nymph.

"But it wasn't any of these. This woman was quite different. She wasn't a goddess or a nymph. She wasn't love and she wasn't hate. She was from the ancient world all right, but she was from a part of it he didn't know about. Something he had overlooked in his investigations. Something which has persisted through the ages, firstly in Greece, where it had its birth and where it is still strongest, but later in all of Europe. She was the votary of a cult very different from those, whether good or evil, with which Richard Fountain had concerned himself. She was… She was…"

"Are you trying to say," said Roddy gently, "that she is in some way supernatural?"

"No," said Piers, and now his tone lost its slightly unreal quality and became crisp and sharp again. "No," he said; "she's a woman all right, and she's a mortal woman. But she is the inheritress, if I am not mistaken, of an old and particularly obscene tradition. I've spoken of this before. Do you still not know what I mean?"

"No," said Roddy firmly.

"Well, she…she… It's no good," Piers said. "I can't tell you. Not yet anyway. God send that I am wrong and that you will never need to understand."

We rounded a bend in the track and then started to descend. There were now crude steps at about every tenth pace. When, after a little while longer, we passed to the right of a ramshackle stone hut, I saw we were nearly level with the sea. Although the wind was getting stronger, the sea was calm; because we had come to the old harbour, and there, just discernible in front of us, was a stone quay with a beach beneath it, and on the beach the shapes of forlorn and skeletal caiques lying keeled on their sides. But the guide did not take us on to the quay. He led us past a small white chapel, above the entrance to which the bell seemed to be swinging slightly in the wind; and then on to a far cruder path, along which we had to stumble in single file, and which began to climb in a series of steep twists up towards the mountains and away from the rising sea.

Four hours later, after what seemed a century of torment and curses, a white dawn rose from the East. The wind on the mountains was bitter, the sea far below us huge and angry in its movement. We were walking to the North along a narrow ridge; but after a time the guide led us down a ravine to our right, and then up again on to a parallel but still higher ridge. We continued North, and the ridge started to steepen against us as though we were proceeding to a summit. We passed through a grove of stunted pine trees, then over a minute and incongruous patch of cultivation. Hence up a crude formation of rock, from the top of which we could see the sea to both sides of us, and hence again down into a hollow in the mountain's back. At the far side of the hollow was a wooden palisade, beyond which was a chapel with a small but impressive bell-tower surrounded by several simple and seemly white buildings. As we approached across the hollow, the bell began to ring in the tower; a gate opened in the palisade; and a monk in black stepped slowly forward, then halted to bow in welcome.

We were given bread, wine, water and olives. Then we were taken to the Superior. The conversation which followed was conducted largely through Piers, who put all our questions to the Superior and translated what the grave old man said for the benefit of Roddy and myself; though I suspected him of concealing a good deal from us, in the same wary or fearful spirit as he had refused to reveal, on the night road by the sea, the final answer which he had wrought from his speculations.

The Superior was seated on a stone bench in a large cell, which was lit by high, narrow and unglazed windows, and was decorated by one rather garish depiction of Christ bleeding on the cross. Chairs were brought in for the three of us; and after we had bowed formally to the old man he signed to us to be seated and then made further gestures which might have indicated either welcome or blessing. After which Piers, leaning forward and fixing his eyes full on the Superior's face, started to explain our mission.

After about five minutes the Superior nodded and spoke in reply.

"He says that a woman came here with a sick man," Piers told us. "After a time the police came too, but by then the pair of them had left. He told the police what had happened – but only in the terms they would understand, of physical appearance and symptoms, of arrival and departure. There was another reality, he says, but that would not have concerned the police."

"Does it concern us?" said Roddy.

"Yes," said Piers. "We must be prepared for…what we may find."

He turned and spoke to the Superior.

" 'Your friend,' " translated Piers, who had evidently established Richard's identity beyond doubt, " 'your friend was suffering from …' " – here Piers paused and glanced almost furtively at us – " ' …from an ancient sickness. The woman brought him to be cured. Not because she loves us, but because she knew that we could cure him better and more swiftly than anyone else. Nor does she desire that he should be…properly…finally cured' – cured in the spirit, he seems to mean – 'but she wishes, because after her own way she loves him, that for the time being he should remain alive. When he came here he was sick nearly to death; and we cured him, because we, in the Monastery of the Blood of Christ, have this secret, and because it was our duty, in all charity, to do so. But the cure will not be for long: with the woman he will become sick once more, and sooner or later her love will tire, and when that happens she will not bring him back to us for healing, but will cast him off and let him die. The woman is accursed...' "

The Superior talked gravely on, but Piers, whose expression had slowly become more drawn and despairing, ceased to translate. For two or three minutes we listened to the meaningless voice, then Roddy spoke up sharply – "What does he say, boy? For God's sake tell us."

Piers looked at us, again rather furtively.

"It's all much the same," he said. "The woman is evil, she brought Richard here to be cured, but as long as he is with her he cannot really be well. She only wished him cured so that she might begin to make him sick again. The only real cure is to take him from this woman, and even then..."

The Superior touched Piers' arm and pointed at Roddy and myself with a look of interrogation. Piers seemed to brush off the old man's questions, but he persisted, until Piers shrugged and spoke a few rather halting words.

"What does he want to know?" asked Roddy.

"Whether you have understood what has been said."

"Well I don't," said Roddy flatly. "There are a lot of things I don't understand, and among them what this 'ancient' disease is, which the monks in this monastery can cure but which will apparently recur. I should be obliged, for a start, if you would enlighten me as to that."

"I tried to tell you. The other day and on the road," said Piers, almost in tears. "I tried very hard. Do you remember what I said? That Richard's...trouble...might be connected with the practices of the ancient city of Hydra. That King Heracles destroyed the city, but meanwhile the practices might have come over with colonists to this island."

"Very well. But Richard's trouble must have started in Crete or before. Not here. And what have the monks to do with it all?"

"When they came to the island, centuries after the Hydriots had first brought the curse here with them, the monks tried to fight it. They also found a cure for the...disease which the practices caused."

Roddy considered this.

"The fact remains," he said, "that whatever it was attacked Richard did so somewhere other than on this island. You yourself said last night that this woman represented something which had spread over all Europe. So why this particular knowledge among the monks of this monastery?"

"Because...it...was concentrated here. Here more than anywhere else. The island having a direct connection with the mainland city where it all started. The...thing...only dribbled...into the rest of Europe. But these monks have had it at full flood from the time they first came."

"All right then," said Roddy. "And exactly what form does this disease take?"

"It is...to do with the blood. Hence the name of this place – the Monastery of the Blood of Christ. In gratitude for the discovery of a cure, they renamed their house after the undefiled and undefilable blood of the Redeemer."

"*So what is it they are curing?* Some form of syphilis?"

Piers burst into hysterical laughter. He slapped his thighs again and again, while the scarcely withheld tears now came streaming down his cheeks.

"If only it was," he screamed, "if only it was."

Roddy leant across and smacked him hard across the face. At once Piers became still. He took out a handkerchief and started quietly to wipe his cheeks and eyes. All this time the Superior stared at the three of us, gravely and with no attempt to intervene.

"If you won't tell us, you won't," said Roddy. "It doesn't matter – until we catch up with him. Does the old gentleman know where they've gone?"

Piers, entirely recovered it seemed, began quietly to address the Superior.

"He says they've gone back to Crete," Piers told us after a while.

"Why on earth should they do that?"

"Because the man – Richard – , when he had got his strength back, said that his friends were coming to Crete and he must go there. The woman objected at first, but after a bit she gave in."

"And whereabouts in Crete?"

Piers murmured to the old man.

"He says he doesn't know. But there is a man – a German – who owns a caique. Richard sent one of the monks down to Hydra to charter the caique. Then, a day or two later, they were picked up by night – at the old harbour, where they arrived – and sailed away. The German, he says, will know where they went. If we can find him. He is called Kurt Braunschweig."

"And do the police know?"

More murmuring.

"He told the police only what he knew – and a simplified version of that. That a woman and a sick man had stayed here; and had then chartered a boat and left. They will only know more, he says, if the German has told them."

"And what about the two men who carried the stretcher up from the coast?"

"They left the monastery shortly after they arrived – as soon as they had eaten. No one knows more of them."

"Then the thing is quite plain," said Roddy: "we must find Herr Braunschweig, and wherever he took Richard he must now take us."

We left the monastery with our guide, after a rest and another simple meal, late in the afternoon. The sun was already sinking fast towards the sea, and often, as we descended into a small crevasse or passed under the shoulder of a hill, we were almost in darkness. But at least the wind had fallen now; and there was a kind of treacherous peace over the mountains.

"What I can't understand," said Roddy, "is this. If it's Richard that's in danger, then why did all the reports Tyrrel received get everything the wrong way round? Tyrrel told us in London that the Greek Police were after Richard to ask him some questions and protect this woman. But now…"

"A mixture of national prejudice and genuine misunderstanding," said Piers. "This isn't the sort of thing they handle every day, when all is said. And one may imagine that in the earlier stages of this business Richard was more of an ally and less of a chattel. So that he may even have helped the woman in some of her undertakings. Or appeared to. And then, when the police began to understand the kind of thing their relationship involved, it was a natural Greek assumption that the male partner was the stronger and they concluded that Richard had corrupted the woman rather than the other way about."

"I should like to know," I said, "just how much the police on this island have picked up… Where they got hold of enough to make them get in touch with the Cretans…"

"They got little from the monastery," said Piers.

"But this man… Braunschweig?"

"Wait and see," said Roddy.

"One also wonders whether they'll connect us with what happened. Now we've been up here. Whether they'll see that someone keeps an eye on us after we leave."

"No good worrying about that now," Roddy said. "Much better worry about whether we can find Braunschweig. He may be away in that caique of his. And even if we find him, he may know nothing. He may just have dropped them somewhere – anywhere – on the mainland. So much better not worry at all."

"Difficult," I said.

There was a cry from the guide in front of us.

"Look," said Piers.

Coming towards us, having apparently emerged from a pine grove some hundred yards further down the path, was a woman dressed in black, her hair hidden by a black shawl arranged like a cowl, so that of all her body only the white face was visible. Even her hands were hidden, for they were tucked away into some material which was folded round a large bundle. The face itself was striking, not for any beauty it possessed, although it was not without beauty of a kind, but because of the look of hideous grief – a grief underlain by utter incomprehension – which forced it into a twisted and swollen mask of agony and horror.

Down the path towards us the woman came, while the guide crossed himself and all of us shrank back to allow her wide passage. And as she came she muttered and mumbled and crooned to herself, until, lifting her eyes from the bundle at her breast and catching sight of us for the first time, she gave us a violent stare which conveyed some kind of recognition. She halted some ten paces from us, looked at us intently for a long time, and finally held her bundle out towards us. We saw that it was the body of a young child, perhaps two years of age, the tiny face of which was white and set, its eyes closed, its features immobile. The guide muttered something to her, and she answered him at some length. Piers then walked up to her, gestured kindly, and leaned over to examine the child. When he turned back towards us his face was trembling all over and he retched violently two or three times as he stumbled back up the path. The woman still stood with the child held out before her. Then the guide spoke to her once more; she seemed to recollect herself and passed quietly by us, keening gently over the bundle which was once more clasped to her bosom.

"What did they say?" said Roddy to Piers.

145

"She is taking the child to the monastery," he answered. "It has...the sickness. She says a woman came to her hut some weeks ago, and played with the child, and gave it the sickness."

"The same sickness," said Roddy, "as Richard's?"

"Yes."

"Then the monks will cure it."

"No. She is out of her mind with grief. She has already taken it once, and they could do nothing. That child has been dead for weeks," Piers said. "It was so small, you see. The sickness must have killed it straight away."

Kurt Braunschweig was small and brown and had long, scruffy fair hair. We were lucky to find him, he said, as he was the following day leaving. And what could he for the gentlemen provide?

"A little information," Roddy answered, "about some passengers."

The thin brown face became thinner. Herr Braunschweig preferred his clients' confidence to keep.

"We wish to be your clients also," Roddy said. "We only want you to take us where you took some friends of ours. Some two or three weeks ago a man and a woman..."

Step by step he explained and reasoned. Gradually Braunschweig's face cleared. For Roddy was at once calm, clear and authoritative, and no German lives who does not respond to authority.

Yes, he had taken a man and a woman from the old harbour. He had taken them, via Cape Malea and Cythera, to Crete – a long run for which he had been well paid. They had wished to land in Crete without being conspicuous, so he had landed them on the South coast near Sphakion, asking no questions. He had not liked the woman, but to object to his clients' characters or enquire into their motives was no business of his. So that, when the police had later come asking questions, he simply said he knew no harm of them and had dropped them

146

at Cythera, whence, he understood, they would take another boat, in their own good time, to Naxos.

And would this...misinformation...materially hamper the police?

That he could not say. Sooner or later, no doubt, someone would discover our friends were in Crete. Meanwhile – he had his best attempted.

In which case, Roddy said, would Braunschweig care to take us also to Sphakion? It was a difficult place to get at by normal means, he understood, so the caique would be very convenient. And we too would like to leave Hydra as unobtrusively as possible and arrive in Crete...without fuss.

"I shall cost you one hundred pounds," said Braunschweig bluntly, "and in cash money you shall pay me. And we shall go first to Athens, where I have short business. This thing, understand, may not help the police. Then from Athens to Milos, Milos to Andikithera, and so round Crete the West to Sphakion. Is good?"

"Is good," said Roddy, reaching for his wallet. "Thirty pounds in advance?"

So the next morning, very early, we left the island of Hydra, with its fine houses and its songs and its evil, and started once more for Crete.

VIII

The voyage was swift and, but for its object, pleasant. None of the sudden storms, so common and vicious in the Mediterranean, arose to disturb us. None of the petty delays, so beloved of sailor-folk, was allowed to hamper us. It almost seemed as if the gods, whom Richard might once have been seeking, realised we were going to the rescue of their stricken votary; for they gave us fair mornings, placid evenings, and light, fresh breezes over the wine-dark sea.

During our brief pause at the Piraeus we had gone into Athens to dump the greater part of our luggage; and at Cook's there was a letter from Marc Honeydew.

> Lancaster College,
> Cambridge.
> July 5, 1957.
>
> Dear Anthony Seymour,
> So you're off, you old adventurer, to bring back Dickie Fountain from the Isles of Greece. I knew there was something in the wind that didn't smell quite right. I knew there was something wrong when you told me he was coming back this year. And now he needs an escort, it seems. You and wicked Piers and some soldier chum you've dredged up. Well, bon voyage, my dear, and don't

listen to the Sirens, or *I* may have to come scurrying out to rescue you.

Now Walter, you should know, is furious. A and one, he thinks you've been deceitful. B and two, he is livid that you've let Piers in on this. And C and three, he's in a state, my dear, about what Richard may have been up to. Because Dickie's given quite enough trouble lately and the thought of any more is making Walter simply *blow his top*. Mind you, he's not letting on. He's giving it out that Dickie has been working so hard that he's finished in one year what might well have taken two; and that by way of celebration he's going to have a little jaunt round the islands with you and some other chums (he's doing his best to suppress Piers) before coming righteously home. But underneath, my dear, Walter is boiling; and if your forwarding arrangements allow of any letters reaching you, then besides this one you will be having − if you haven't had already − a *stinkeroo* from Doctor Goodrich.

As for Penelope, she's going around very pale and proud. She affects to be quietly pleased that Richard is coming home and delighted that he's having a little joy ride with his friends first. When malicious ladies suggest that she would have been the proper person to go out to Greece and meet him, she murmurs something dignified about not leaving Walter alone. But underneath, of course, she's in as big a state as Walter. Not angry, but very, very worried. She's got it into her head, I think, that something is very wrong indeed (unlike Walter, who thinks in terms of some mild sexual prank), and she's inwardly biting her nails down to the fist. But England expects, my dear; and Penelope is going to be a credit to the side if she drops dead in the attempt.

So much, Anthony Seymour, for the state of play at this end of Europe. If you have time and inclination, let poor old Honeydew into what's going on at yours. But for once in a way I have something rather important to tell you. Or so I think. Advice, my dear, if you'll take it. You see, the point is this. Whatever Dickie's been up to, Walter is going to fix things up here and then welcome him home with champagne and a brass band. But he's also getting the *clamps* ready. When Dickie Fountain gets back this time, Walter is going to club him unconscious by pointing out how grateful he ought to be, and then tie him down — and tie him down but good — for the next seventy years. (Don't ask me how I know all this: I do know it and you'll admit that the form is true.) Walter is going to get hold of Richard, and marry him to Penelope before the daisies come at Michaelmas, and settle him down with P in the Waltery at Grantchester, and not let him out of his sight, my dear, unless angels blow trumpets from the top of Great St Mary's Church — and not necessarily even then. Dickie is to have a year to write up his Greek research — under strong Walterian supervision; then he will be made Junior Dean or perhaps Third Bursar; and soon afterwards Walter will saddle him with a Junior Lectureship in the Faculty of Classics as well, so that he will be secured under *mountains* of work as firmly as the Titans under Etna. Every day he will bicycle in and out from Grantchester; every night he will either work by Walter's fireside (while Penelope *knits*) or assist in what ever gruesome entertainment Walter has hatched up inside the College. For sheer imprisonment, my dear, the Count of Monte Cristo won't be in it.

So what I'm leading up to is this. You'd just better let Dickie know what Walter's getting ready for him. Hither to, Dickie's had quite a lot of his own way, and even then he's thrown his little rebellions. But from now on it's going to be Walter's way, my dear, and Dickie's going to be nailed so firmly to his cross that not even the tiniest insurrection will be possible. Unless of course Dickie struggles so hard that he kills both himself and Walter in the process – by which I mean *real* trouble. So you tell Dickie what cunning old Walter is cooking up in his kitchen, and if Dickie thinks he can't stomach it, then for God's sake, Anthony Seymour, make him stay in Greece another year (the original arrangements by which he could do this are still valid), during which time he can think whether or not he ought to return to somewhere other than Lancaster College, Cambridge.

Because if he comes back here, my love, he's going to be EATEN UP ALIVE.

Much love from Marc.

"So," I said to Piers, "here we have both Marc and Walter, each for a very different motive, urging us to keep Richard out of England."

"Unfortunately," said Piers, "the motives of both of them are entirely beside the point."

"At the moment, certainly. But if we find Richard all right…"

"It isn't only a question of 'if'," Piers said; "it's a question of 'what'."

It was a good job we had had the sense to leave most of our luggage in Athens, because when Kurt Braunschweig landed us, an hour before dawn, on the South coast of Crete, we were faced with a six mile walk along the shore to Sphakion.

"You must go quickly," Braunschweig said. "There are places where you must cross sand. When the sun comes up the sand will soon be too hot on which to walk."

He accepted the seventy pounds still due to him with dignity, saluted smartly, and turned back to his caique.

"Nice work if you can get it," said Roddy. "Come on." He shouldered the haversack which he had thoughtfully brought with him, while Piers and I picked up our two small grips. Then we started along the beach.

When we reached the village at Sphakion three hours later, exhausted by bare rock and clinging sand, we sat down in front of a small café and called for coffee and bread. A ring of giggling children surrounded us, while behind them a group of adult men, many of them in wide breeches and Cretan top-boots, regarded us gravely. An authoritative face, craggy and moustached, appeared in the background, and both children and adults made way immediately and with respect. A tall man of fine bearing walked through the aisle thus made for him, wearing a black coat of hunting trim together with a pearl-grey tie; his top-boots were immaculately polished and, by local standards at least, of a very superior cut.

"I am the mayor," he said in good English; "you are welcome to Sphakion."

We rose and bowed. Roddy pulled up another chair. The offer was courteously declined.

"You are English," said the mayor. It was not a question. We nodded.

"Then you must finish your breakfast and come with me. I will have the mules made ready."

"I beg your pardon," said Roddy softly.

The mayor gestured impatiently at this mild rebuke.

"There is a countryman of yours in the mountain. He is in grave trouble. We can bring you…near to him. But neither these men nor myself can actually go to him or help him. His own countrymen must do that – if they will. You understand?"

He searched our faces for signs of comprehension. He found what he was looking for in Piers.

"You at least understand me," he said. "Make your friends be swift. There is no time to lose."

"How bad is it?" said Piers.

The mayor shrugged.

"Who can say? We do not go near enough to know. But since they have been together in the mountains for a long time, it will be bad enough. You know that."

"But the police – " began Roddy.

"The police in Sphakion are of the people of Sphakion. We are far from Athens here, far even from Heraclion. The police cannot help your friend... And now please be swift. The journey will be long."

We started fifteen minutes later. The mayor, who had discarded his fine black coat for a rough jersey, and all the three of us, rode on mules. We sat sideways on the harsh wooden saddles, trying to imitate the easy grace with which the mayor let his hands rest on his thighs and swayed to the rhythm of the beast's delicate tread. There was a fifth mule to carry our baggage; and the whole train was escorted by two men on foot, who wore British Army shirts and trousers and ancient, gaping boots.

For a time we went along the coast by a narrow dusty track a few yards above a beach. Then the track turned inland and over a low ridge of rock and scrub, on the other side of which we found ourselves in a beautiful valley with gentle green hills on either side of us. In the valley and on the hills which contained it were olive trees and cypresses, pine and orange and bushes of gay flowers, a grateful sight at any time but never so grateful as in the torrid summer heat. The ground was green and soft; from somewhere nearby came the trickle of water over rock; and for the most part our way lay in the shade.

The mayor noticed our looks of appreciation.

"This is the valley of Hagia Persephone," he said: "the only place of fertility in this part of the island."

"I'm glad," I said, "that it retains its ancient name after a fashion."

"How else? If the name changed, then the goddess would desert it. But then there is also the priests. So to make them happy, the goddess must become a saint."

He spat with elegance and then fell silent.

"What did the mayor mean just now?" Roddy was saying to Piers. "That he and his people could not actually go to Richard?"

"They are afraid."

The mayor was leading, with myself and Roddy and Piers strung out, in that order, behind him. So doubtless Piers had not thought to be overheard. But the mayor pricked up his ears when Piers made his remark, and for a moment I thought he would protest. He simply shrugged, however, and then looked resignedly in front of him. Roddy, seeing what had happened, sought to make amends.

"From what I hear," he said firmly, "Cretans are afraid of nothing."

The mayor squared his shoulders slightly but did not turn his head.

"They are afraid of this," said Piers, "and they do well to be so."

"It's time you made yourself clear."

"You will know all you wish to in time," interrupted the mayor. "And now we must soon be out of this valley. After this the way is hard and steep and hot. It is my advice that you do not waste your strength in arguing."

There were both courtesy and command in his words; so that Roddy said no more.

And now indeed the valley was turning into a re-entrant: the trees were thinner, there was more rock; the hills on either side were closing in and now seemed grudging and even hostile, seemed to shimmer with malice in the heat. The soft path became a crude stone track, which for a time went straight up the re-entrant but soon started to twist and turn, cheating the vicious gradient but causing even the clever mules to falter and jerk, until remaining in one's seat, though never really difficult, became a steady grinding effort of muscles and the will. There was no shade now. The sun, almost at the zenith, beat straight down on mules and men. But the patient animals, for all their occasional faltering, kept steadily on and upwards; while we who were their burden, our heads drooping in weariness and despair, our bodies aching in every inch, went on and upwards with them – and would have been unable, for an Emperor's ransom, to break the silence which had been earlier enjoined upon us.

When we reached the head of the re-entrant, we found we were at one end of a long and narrow ridge. On either side, and stretching for some miles to the North, were groups of foothills, which were dotted here and there with villages and broken by modest patches of cultivation. The ridge itself kept straight on, at approximately the same height as we ourselves had reached though occasionally dipping and rising again, until it was joined by another which swept in towards it from the East. At this point it became broader but it also began to rise; at first fairly gently, so far as we could judge, but then steeply and yet more steeply, until it towered up, many miles distant from us, among a magnificent mass of gleaming peaks and buttresses – The White Mountains of Crete.

An hour or so later we descended for half a mile from the top of the ridge to a group of stone huts which stood on the slope below it. Here we were offered water, olives, some salted fish in oil, and a small quantity of strong and bitter wine. Then, having ascended once again to the crude path on the ridge's back, we rode on through the afternoon towards the looming mass ahead, which reflected, like dull silver, the now somewhat kinder rays of the slowly westering sun.

It was about ten o'clock when the storm broke.

Just before darkness we had paused in our journey to eat and drink once more – white cheese and olives, the same bitter but heartening wine – and had then ridden on to where the ridge from the East joined our own. From here on, as we had foreseen, we were always ascending; the path, straight at first, began to twist and prevaricate as the slope became steeper; and finally we were no longer on a ridge but on a mountain: a bare, cruel mountain, all of it rock, it seemed, rock relieved by only the most occasional patches of scrub.

"Your friend," the mayor had said, "is on the other side of the mountain."

Even so we had seemed to continue upwards, rather than round the mountain flanks. But it was cool without being cold, there was only a hint of wind, and the journey had now been a happy one were it not for the occasion: for the stars had shone with rare brilliance in the thin mountain air, such a sight as may come only once or not at all in a man's life.

"There is the son of Peleus," Piers had said, "and there Orion the Hunter. And there, most beautiful of all, are the Pleiades, of whom Sappho sang in Lesbos."

And in a low voice he had begun to quote the beautiful Greek, until the tears pricked behind my eyelids and I forgot, for a time, that I was riding on a vile wooden saddle toward a friend in deep and nameless distress, and scarcely realised that now at last we had ceased to ascend and were working round a shoulder toward the slopes on the far side of the mountain. For Orion had shone and the Pleiades; and Piers' pleasant voice had murmured to me through the night.

And then the storm broke.

One moment there was calmness and starlight. The next the whole sky was blotted out, there was a great blast of wind, and rain which was half sleet and half hail was lashing across my face. Somewhere just to my left the lightning struck, and at the same moment the thunder crashed on to the rocks about us; while over the mountains came wind to reinforce the gale that was already raging, moaning and shrieking through the pinnacles and bastions, plunging past the summits and wailing over the ravines.

And then I found that I was on a broad shelf of rock and that the mayor in front of me had stopped and dismounted.

"Your friend is not far," he shouted above the wind. He pointed to an ascending path which led from the shelf we were on, up through the rock above us, and disappeared.

"Follow this path," he shouted. "When you are there, you will know. Take light." He handed me a torch. "Take one of your cases." He gestured toward the rearmost mule. "You will need dry clothes."

"And you?" asked Roddy. "And the mules?"

"We will wait here until you have done what is necessary and are ready to leave."

"How long can you wait?"

"We are patient men. We shall be content." He pointed to an overhang which would provide some shelter. "Take food," he said, passing Piers a small canvas sack. "Take food, and do what you must, and return to us. This one," – he nudged Roddy and myself and pointed to Piers – "will know what is to be done. Do not worry about us here. But do not delay more than you must. And now go."

He shook each of us by the hand. The two attendant footmen crossed themselves.

"Go," shouted the mayor through the storm.

Roddy turned, took the torch from me and lifted one of the small valises in his other hand, then started away up the path. Piers and I followed. The storm, from which we had been slightly protected on the ledge, now came at us with fury. But Roddy pressed slowly on and upwards, until we turned a corner and began a gradual descent down and round the slope, a descent which in turn became a level passage and then once more steepened against us…

How long we walked I shall never know. I was conscious only of the vicious lashing sleet, of the agony of the wind, and of the brave figure of Roddy, moving very slowly, but always moving, in front of me. But after a time, minutes or hours, we came to some steps, broad and graceful, which led to a door in a stone wall. Roddy fumbled with a large ring-handle, then flung the door open with a crash; and beyond the door, in the white light of a storm lantern, we saw a woman crouched against a wall and a figure lying on the floor wrapped in blankets. The figure was very still, and its white face stared straight up at the ceiling, sightless and immobile, like a mask of death.

IX

"The place must have been a Venetian stronghold," said Piers. We were outside looking at the low, square tower, with its narrow pointed windows and crenellated walls, which the light of morning revealed. The wind was still strong; but it had stopped raining now, and there was promise that the blanket of white cloud above us might later yield to the sun.

"They must have had a troop of soldiers here," Piers went on, "keeping watch over the mountains."

"I hope," I said, "that they were frequently relieved. One night in the place is enough."

"We shan't be able to move Richard for a day or two," said Roddy, who on account of some slight experience in the field was acknowledged by us as a kind of crude medical expert.

"Just how bad is he?" I asked.

"Very weak," said Roddy with a puzzled look. "As far as I can tell he just needs rest and food. Building up. But it will be some time before he can take much of anything solid."

"So long as we can keep that woman away from him," Piers said, "he will be all right."

Roddy looked at him thoughtfully.

"Will she come back?"

"Oh yes."

"She bolted fast enough when we appeared last night."

159

"She was taken unawares. But soon she will pull herself together, and she will wait for her opportunity, and then she will..." His voice trailed away.

"Will what?" said Roddy.

"...will return, for Richard."

"The three of us should be able to manage her."

"She will have...resources," Piers said.

For a time we were silent. The towering peaks crowded about us, but there was a gap between two of the mountains through which I glimpsed a green plain far below. Familiarity, I thought, security: home.

"We'd best go in and look to Richard."

When we returned into the fort, Richard, for the first time, was awake. He was still as white as marble and he looked desperately weak; but he smiled softly at us and said, without apparent surprise – "So you got here all right. Piers... Anthony...and you, Roddy. It was good of you to come."

"We came as soon as we could."

"Where did you sleep?"

"Here. With you."

"No blankets," said Richard, turning his head with effort and looking round the inside of the fort. "You must have been cold."

"Never mind that," said Roddy; "don't worry about us. Sleep."

"Yes," said Piers, "you must sleep."

But Richard was still gazing, restless and anxious, round the bare stone walls.

"Where is... Chriseis?" he said at length.

"She went away last night when we came."

"We will take care of you now."

"You must watch for her," said Richard. "She will come back. She...is...clever."

Then his eyes closed and he fell asleep.

But later that day, early in the afternoon, he awoke once more. We gave him some yoghurt, which he swallowed with difficulty, and a little wine. And then he seemed disposed to talk.

"You must watch for Chriseis. If she comes back, I shall not be able to fight her. Neither, perhaps, will you. Even when I was well and strong...when I first met her months ago in Corinth... I could not fight her. But then, of course, I thought she was something different...liberation, escape.

"A dreary town, Corinth. Modern and hard. How should such a creature come from those everyday streets, the bright shops, the neat houses? But the was there, and she found me, and I thought she loved me. And indeed I loved her. For herself and the escape I thought she offered. But even then I couldn't... I couldn't..."

He broke off and looked despairingly at Piers, who put out a hand and began to stroke the tumbled hair back from his forehead.

"Never mind, my dear, never mind. We understand. Don't force yourself to tell us."

"But I want to tell you. You must all know."

His voice was becoming urgent and he raised his head from the pillow.

"I couldn't...make love...like a man."

His head sank back and he seemed much relieved.

"But Chriseis, she said it didn't matter, there were other things. And so there were – fearful, ugly things. But I went with her, dazed, not really knowing what I did, but helping her all the same, because, you see, I felt I had betrayed her by my lack of manhood, and now she meant so much I couldn't leave her. And so together we did these things."

He gave a soft moan and looked at Piers once more.

"And then," he went on, "I had to leave Corinth for a time, to go to Athens and then to Delphi, where I had work. Some of the way she came with me, but after a time she had to return to Corinth. For a while I missed her desperately, but then it got

161

better, and I began to realise that what I really needed was to forget her, was to have my own proper friends once more. That was when I wrote to Piers to ask him to come in the summer."

He stretched out a hand to Piers, who took it lightly and rubbed it between his own to warm it.

"But later," said Richard, "when I had done my work and returned to Corinth, she came to me again. I had hoped she wouldn't...that she would have forgotten me and found someone else. But within a week of my return to Corinth – I had more work there, you see, and had to go back – within a week, she came to me. And it was then that something different began between us. We no longer went out and did...the things we used to. She turned herself entirely on to me, and thenceforth all the suffering was mine. You know what I mean, Piers. I can see it in your eye. But you, Anthony? And Roddy?"

A frustrated look appeared on Roddy's face. He opened his mouth as if to ask a question, but thought better of it when he saw Piers shake his head.

"You will find out, Roddy, as time goes on," said Richard, who had apparently noticed this exchange. "You will find out. For the present you must just understand that she made me suffer and began to make me ill. I tried to get away. Although I wanted her to go on making me suffer, at that time I was still strong enough to want to escape from her also, and in the end I decided to leave for Crete several weeks before I had planned. I found the strength to leave without telling her; but she followed me to Athens and found me. Do you know, I was *glad* to be found. But I was also desperate, because I now knew that she was going to kill me. Sooner or later she would have taken everything she could, and then I would be dead. So from Athens I wrote to Anthony, begging him to bring you and follow me to Crete; because I was still strong enough and clear enough to know that I must have help and that you, who were my friends, would help me. And now you have come...

"Now you have come, but there is still danger. For I know she is not far from here, and soon she will come back…"

He broke off, and then returned to the story of his love.

"So when we got to Crete, I became less and less clear, but all the time I knew that you would come. But somehow Chriseis knew too, and persuaded me to come with her to Hydra, thinking to elude you. The police were interested in us, she said, and we must go where we were not known. And then the monks in Hydra would make me strong. They would make me so strong that she would be able to love me, in her vile way, forever, and yet I would never again get weak. So I listened to her lies and believed them; but although she tried to prevent me I left a clue for you, so that you could follow. I managed to speak to the old man, Arnold, though even then her influence was so strong that I found myself speaking in riddles, and whether I was trying to cheat her or trying to cheat you I shall never know. Still, it was a simple riddle, so I suppose you understood…

"By the time we had gone to Mount Ida and then on to Hydra, I was very ill. So ill that I cannot remember how I was brought there. But the monks made me well. In a few days they made me so strong that I could stand up to her; and then I insisted that we went back to Crete. Because I was terrified that you would not find Arnold, or would not understand my riddle, and in any case all this was still in June: so that at this time you had yet to come to Crete, and by going there straight away I might hope to find you. And in the end Chriseis gave way. She let me charter a caique owned by a German, and we came round to the coast near Sphakion. I wanted to go to Heraclion and wait there for you; but she didn't want this, because she hated you and was also afraid, or so she said, that there might be trouble with the police. And since I was already beginning to get weaker again, I gave in to her and let her bring me to Sphakion. From there she took me to several villages, while I was growing weaker all the time; but always the villagers seemed to understand what she was doing, and they would drive us out after a day or two, until at last we ended up here on the mountain. We have been here for days now. And all the time I have been growing weaker and weaker... Why did they have no charity, those villagers? Why did they not try to save me, instead of turning me away with her? I suppose they were afraid of what she might do. For all the time they could see what she was doing to me. How I was growing weaker...

"But now you have come and I shall get well. All I need is rest and food. The monks in Hydra have a special wine, and they did some other things, so that I became well very quickly. But even without their wine and their care, I shall get well in time, if I can only rest. And if that fiend will stay away from me," he said, his voice quivering with anger and disgust, "so that the life within me can grow. Watch for her, Anthony, and you, Piers. Watch for her, Roddy. She is not far away, I know, and she will come again..."

And suddenly, as had happened that morning, his eyes closed and he fell asleep.

By now it was early evening and we must make some sort of plan.

"The mayor must be told," said Roddy.

"He said he would wait."

"He has already waited a night and a day. We must tell him that we shall be here at least another night, and warn him how difficult it will be to carry Richard down... It may be possible to bind him to one of the mules – but then it could be days before he is strong enough to stand it... But in any case we must speak with the mayor. Courtesy requires it."

Piers and I nodded.

"But it is important," Piers said, "that *two* of us stay here with Richard. In case that woman comes."

Roddy looked at him with a question in his eye, but seeing how intent was Piers' face, he just nodded in agreement.

"And whoever goes," said Piers, "must take care. He must go fast and not linger…for anything."

"It is not far," said Roddy, "and there is nothing on this mountain to frighten me. So I had better go."

"That will be good," said Piers. "But remember: *go fast.*"

Roddy gave him another questioning look, but again simply nodded. He rose and made ready to go.

"It is only early evening," he said. "I shall be back before dark."

Richard, disturbed by Roddy's movements, awoke once more.

"Where are you going, Roddy?" he said.

"To speak with friends who have helped us. They are not far."

"You are going alone?"

"Yes."

"Take care, Roddy."

Roddy smiled.

"You needn't worry about me," he said.

A shadow came into Richard's eyes.

"Lift me to the door," he said. "I want to look outside. And to speed Roddy on his way."

Roddy looked startled, then embarrassed, then deprecating. But Piers signed to me, and together we helped Richard from his bed and supported him to the door. It was the first time we had seen him uncovered by blankets; his clothes were tattered and he smelt abominably. Roddy lifted one of the blankets from the litter on the floor and placed it, like a shawl, round Richard's shoulders and over his chest. Then, having made a vague salute, he started down the steps.

"Wait," called Richard.

Roddy turned to face us.

"Some say," said Richard strangely, "that Zeus was reared on this island. Over in the other mountains to the East. Others say that his tomb is in those same mountains. The tomb of Zeus…

But either way, he is strong in this island, and we should pray to him: I for my strength, you for safe passage, and all of us for deliverance."

Roddy shifted uneasily on the steps.

"It is already evening," he said, "I must not wait — "

Richard interrupted him with a movement of his hands. Piers flashed a look at him over Richard's shoulder, a look which said "Pity him and do as he asks."

"I shall not be long," Richard said.

So Roddy stood quiet, waiting politely, impatience still stirring in the muscles under his eyes.

Then Richard, leaning on Piers and myself but lifting his voice in a curiously powerful fashion when one considered the low tones in which he had spoken hitherto, called out his prayer to the mountains opposite. He invoked the deity, he asked for the strength to be put back into his limbs, he solicited a safe passage for Roddy, and he requested a good deliverance for us all. The prayer, as he had promised, was brief; and he concluded by asking for a sign.

"Father," he called out over the mountains, "send us a sign."

For a moment no one moved. Then Roddy, saluting once more, began to descend the steps.

"Wait," called Richard again. And again Roddy turned and stood waiting.

As he turned, a huge black eagle appeared in the sky above us. For a moment it seemed to hover like a hawk, then it swooped down over our heads, so near that the rush of its wings was almost deafening, and soared up again, turning at the same time, till it was once more hovering high above. Again it descended, flying almost into our faces, and again soared up and turned to hover above us. Then it swooped a third time, to ascend, as before, into the sky above our stronghold. And now it hovered, and made as if to swoop yet once more; but before it had come down more than a few yards, it made a wide and beautiful turn and flew away from the declining sun towards the mountains in the East.

"I wouldn't have wanted to miss that," called Roddy cheerfully. "Thank you for making me stay."

He waved gaily. All of us answered his wave, though Richard, who was leaning very hard on the arm I had round him, waved very weakly. Then Roddy turned away; whistling a bar or two of our own regimental march he walked quickly down the graceful steps, turned the corner at the bottom, waved once more as he turned, and was then lost to view. Piers and I made to help Richard inside.

"What did you notice about that eagle?" asked Richard.

"It was a noble bird," Piers said.

"It was," said Richard. "But there are four of us, and the eagle only swooped three times."

As the evening deepened, Richard slept. Piers and I lit the storm-lantern and sat over it on two large rocks we had carried in from outside.

"Why are you so anxious for Roddy?" I said. "What danger could there be for him?"

"The same as there could be for us. If that woman came here."

"And that is...?"

"...best not thought about unless it has to be faced."

I roused myself to press Piers further.

"Piers... It is all very well, this fashion of sparing our feelings. But we are adult men, Roddy and I, and we have a right to know what is going on. When you were still in doubt, then you were probably justified in not committing yourself. But there has clearly been no real doubt in your mind for a long while now. And so now, since Roddy and I are sharing in the dangers, we must be allowed to share in your knowledge."

"I cannot help feeling you have both been slightly obtuse."

167

SIMON RAVEN

"Myself, possibly. But there is excuse for Roddy. His education has been of an uncomplicated nature."

Piers looked over at Richard and stirred moodily above the lantern.

"Very well, Anthony," he said. "But it is not the sort of thing I can bring myself to explain twice. I will tell you both together when Roddy gets back."

He rose to look through one of the windows.

"It is nearly dark now," he said: "I wonder what is keeping him."

"The way may be longer than he remembered."

"Shorter if anything. The storm made it stretch for a hundred miles."

"He may be having a difficult time with the mayor and his men. They can hardly be anxious to stay another night."

"You underrate them. They need never have come in the first place. And I suspect – I know – that it is not only for Richard's sake they have helped us."

"For what other?"

"For their own. That woman is a danger to all men. To all men and all women too."

"Then why did they not deal with her themselves?"

"They are afraid of her in a fashion in which they think we cannot be afraid. They believe in her power."

"But so do you."

"Yes – and that is one reason why I am not anxious to explain it. But I only believe in part. I share their fear all right. But another side of me, the Western, educated, *Lancaster* side forbids me to be afraid. So I can just make shift to face her."

The night was down outside, and still Roddy did not come. "Perhaps the dark overtook him while he was still with the mayor. In which case he might choose to spend the night with him."

"He would know that we worried for him," said Piers: "he would come back."

"And there can be no question of fear…"

"He was brave when you knew him in the Army?"

"Yes. And you can see that he is still brave."

"But perhaps…on the mountain…in the night…"

"He showed no fear last night," I said.

"Last night he was fighting a storm, the kind of enemy to which he is accustomed. But now…"

"It is the only kind of enemy he acknowledges. If there is another, he does not know of it."

"He may begin to…feel that it is there. So long as he does not realise too late…"

But for some time now Piers' eyelids had been drooping. Each time they nearly closed he had forced them back. But plainly the need for sleep was making him desperate.

"I must sleep for a while," he now said. "Can you keep watch, Anthony? Wake me in two hours, and then I will watch for you. It…should be all right like that… I think…unless… But wake me on the instant if you hear any noise at all."

Without another word he settled himself in a corner and fell asleep.

I took a book from the valise we had brought and began to read in the light of the storm lamp. The book was heavy to my hands, however, the words drifted in front of my eyes, there was not a flicker of response in my brain. So putting the book down beside me I began to think. I thought of Tyrrel and the night on which everything had started; of Cambridge and of Walter and of Marc Honeydew; of Piers – "I've seen him three times, Anthony, and each time he was dead"; of how I went to Ludlow to persuade Roddy – "All that is needed is a little common sense, Anthony, and a lack of superfluous scruple." I thought of the dinner with Tyrrel before we left, of Penelope's telephone call that night, and of our light-hearted journey across France and Italy; of Venice; of Heraclion with its blind sea-front; of Cnossos and Ratty Arnold…"He likes islands. He likes Crete, but he likes other islands as well, because water is best…

αριστον μεν υδωρ...*ariston men hydor...ariston men hydor...*
*hydor...hydor...*until I awoke with a start, and this is what I saw.
I saw that the door was half open, and that just inside it was
standing a woman, dressed in black trousers and a kind of black
tunic above them. She also had on a medium length black cape,
which was held together in front by a short gold chain. It was
the same woman as we had surprised the night before; but on
that occasion she had fled so swiftly, and I had been so numbed
by the storm and so dazzled by the white light of the lantern,
that I had taken in no detail about her. But now, though newly
awoken, I saw with great clarity every detail of her dress and her
appearance. That beneath the trousers was a pair of what looked
very like Mess Wellingtons, the upper portions of which were
concealed under the trouser legs; that on her throat, just above
the gold chain which secured her cloak, was a small silver
brooch; that her black hair was long and very glossy in
appearance for a woman who had just spent a night in the open
and many days living in extreme discomfort; that her
complexion was white yet healthy, her nose well proportioned,
her forehead narrow; that her chin was delicate: and that her
eyes were very bright.

It was these bright eyes that were fixed on me now. They
were not looking into my own eyes, but just played generally,
though seemingly without moving, over my face and the upper
part of my body. Sometimes the light caught her brooch and it
would flash; sometimes it caught her eyes, which then became
brighter than ever. So she stood, while her eyes explored me;
and then I realised, not with horror but with a comfortable
feeling of resignation, that I could not move. I could shift my
gaze, turn my head, even raise a hand; but I could not move my
body; and I could not speak. I was not afraid, I was simply
numb. I had realised, dimly and without urgency, that I must
wake Piers, so I had made to get to my feet and go to him; but
my body would not stir. Then I had opened my mouth to call
out to him; but no words, not even the faintest sound, would

come. I was paralysed; I had made my effort and in a distant, theoretical way regretted my failure: but now I knew, with a kind of grim satisfaction, that I could do nothing more, and I settled with interest and almost with pleasure to watch what happened next.

First of all the woman closed the door. She did not turn; she just moved one arm behind her and pushed it gently home. Then, still letting her eyes play over me, she unfastened her cloak and dropped it on the floor. After this, she walked slowly towards me, smiled with considerable charm, and muttered something in Greek which I did not understand. Taking her eyes off me, she passed on to where Piers was slumped in the corner. I was still fixed to my seat, but as before I could still turn my eyes to follow her. I saw her stand over Piers and regard him with attention. For a while she stood there, playing her eyes over him in the same way as she had done to myself, but all the time muttering in a low, soft voice, a neutral voice, neither of hatred nor desire, but perhaps of incantation. After which she stooped down over him, opened one of his eyes with finger and thumb, looked closely into it, and then let the eyelid drop. I was conscious of faint curiosity: why had she paid so much more attention to Piers, who was safely asleep, than to myself who was at least partially conscious? But the thought, vague and untroubling in any case, soon passed from me. Meanwhile the woman was standing up again, and now, after a last low mutter over Piers, she began to move towards Richard.

When she reached the pathetic shape of clammy blankets, she knelt down on the floor beside them and started to moan softly. She passed her hand over the feet and legs, up over the stomach, stroking and fondling, then on to the chest and throat. At this stage, her moaning struck a higher and more intense key; her caresses were slower and more loving; while her face, of which I could see the right profile, became at once fierce with longing and tender with an effort of love. She stroked Richard's forehead and his cheeks. She passed her fingers lightly

171

over his closed eyes. She smoothed his hair and touched him behind the ears. And then she arched her body and brought her face down over his, being about, as I thought, to kiss him on the lips: but just as her face was almost touching his, she seemed to wrench it to one side; she bared her teeth, until her whole face seemed one hideous grin, and then, with a movement as quick as a snake's, she struck into Richard's naked throat.

And still I could not move or speak; still I felt neither fear nor horror, only interest and the very faintest misgiving. Richard was awake now. I was near enough to see his eyes: into them came a look of utter loneliness and despair; a look which, as he saw my eyes on his, turned to one of pleading and of prayer, and thence, as I continued to regard him without moving, to one of sorrowful reproach. "Save me," his eyes had said, "before the life is drained out of me"; and then, "You have yielded to her and betrayed your friend." But still I could do nothing, still I watched with interest and was untouched, in my heart, by the terrible message in those eyes.

Then Richard, seeing that there would be no help from me and knowing that his life was fast leaving him, must have steeled himself to make one final call for help. For the muscles of his face knotted in the desperate summoning of his strength; his eyes bulged and his forehead narrowed and stretched in his agony; and out of his mouth came a great groan of despair and desolation, a call for pity, a call for salvation, a call for love.

The woman, sunk into his throat with lust, did not heed his cry for pity. Myself, lost and paralysed, could interpret but remained indifferent to his plea for salvation. But Piers, whatever the depths to which his sleeping soul had been willed by the woman, awakened to Richard's cry for love. He stirred, sat up, rubbed his eyes and then looked straight at Richard and the woman. His eyes became bright with hatred, brighter than the eyes of the woman had been. He crossed the room in four quick steps; he seized the woman by her shoulders; and with all his strength he wrenched her away from Richard, whose eyes

172

closed, whose head lolled, whose whole body seemed to shrink and sag.

Piers hurled the woman down on the floor. He put one knee on her chest. He placed both hands round her throat and he began to squeeze. He squeezed until the veins and sinews stood out in his neck; until the sweat was running in streams down his face: until his whole body was jerking in spasms, half of rage and half of effort, which struck at him as the multiple lash might strike at a trussed man under the cat. All the time his eyes grew brighter and harder; until at last, after one final and tremendous spasm, which seemed like some supreme and brutish orgasm, he slowly loosened his hands, stood up and back so that I might see what he had done.

"Now are you answered?" he shouted into my face.

On the floor I could see the body of the woman. All of it was limp and easy now. Except for the face: for her mouth was still caught in the hideous grin which she had worn as she struck her face at her victim; and spread over her cheeks and lips, dribbling from the bared white teeth, was the blood, wet and shining red, which she had drunk from Richard Fountain's throat.

For a long time I remained without moving. I have a vague recollection of watching Piers drag the body of the woman into a corner and of seeing him busy himself with Richard; but I related none of this to myself or to any kind of reality, for I was still debarred from reality. Gradually, however, I began to come out of my daze, to think and feel as Anthony Seymour, the friend of Piers Clarence and Richard Fountain, and to comprehend the enormity of what I had seen. I put my head between my knees; then rose slowly from the seat of rock, my limbs cramped and bitterly cold, my stomach heaving and contracting with horror and guilt.

"Richard…will he be all right?"

"I think so," said Piers; "but I only got her in the nick of time."

"What can I...? Oh, Piers. So sorry...I..."

Piers got up from beside Richard and smiled at me.

"It wasn't your fault, Anthony. Why do you think I felt so desperately sleepy so very suddenly? I can usually go for days... No. You couldn't help it, and Richard of all people will understand why."

"How did you awake?"

"I don't know. I heard Richard...with my soul, I think. His call was too strong for her. But even then she nearly...got the better of me. You saw how hard I was...trying?"

"Yes."

"It wasn't anger, Anthony. All that effort, effort of body *and* mind, was really needed. She was a strong woman in more ways than one."

"And Richard will really be all right?"

"I think so," he said. "He's very weak indeed. But when he knows the danger is gone for good..."

He paused for a moment.

"Is it gone for good?" he said.

He looked at me very oddly.

"We have gone through too much," he murmured at last, "to take any more chances now."

He went to one corner where Roddy had left a walking stick which he had been shaping, earlier in the day, from a branch he had found.

"Lucky Roddy forgot this," said Piers softly.

And then, "You realise, Anthony, that if I am *right* in doing...what I am now going to do – and we shall have no way at all of knowing – then there may be...consequences for Richard. Even afterwards. Nobody knows really."

"We must deal with them as and when they arise," I said, not really understanding.

Piers rummaged in the valise and took out a large clasp knife.

"Take her outside, Anthony."

I went to the body of the woman and took it by the shoulders. With some difficulty I dragged it to the door, which Piers opened for me, and then on to the topmost of the wide and graceful steps outside. There was a light cold wind and a trace of dawn.

Piers joined me. He was carrying the storm-lantern and Roddy's stick, which he had sharpened down to a point. He put the lantern down and with great care sawed the stick in two with the knife about nine inches above the sharp end. Then he looked about in the light of the lamp and selected a large, flat-bottomed stone.

"Hold up the lantern, Anthony."

He knelt down on one knee and placed the point of the stake he had made over the heart of the thing which had been Chriseis.

"Now keep this upright with your other hand."

I clasped the stake some six inches above the point; and Piers, drawing a deep breath, raised the stone high above his head with both hands, so that he might be able to strike down again with all the strength of his two arms.

X

When we awoke it was nearly noon.

"We must find Roddy," said Piers, "and let the mayor know what has happened. He will be ready to bring his men and his mules right up here...now."

"I'll go," I said; "you stay with Richard."

I set off down the path the way Roddy had gone the previous evening. It was a warm, soothing day: the sky was unbroken blue over the gleaming mountains, and there was a gentle breeze. So that's what it was, I thought: and now the danger has gone – everything possible has been done to ensure that. But Piers is still afraid: it is in his eyes. What was it he had said the night before? There might be...consequences for Richard. And then I remembered him as he had sat talking, years ago it seemed now, about the taint of the ancient city of Hydra. A number of branches attached to one body: an infection, a contamination, which crept from the main body along all its tributary necks. And I remembered other legends. Yet surely, if you destroyed the source of infection...? But then what were the rules in any case? *Which world were we in?*

For on the one hand you had a superstition: that this thing was infectious, that the victim automatically inherited the taint, that when...one of them...died, then precautions were necessary to ensure his rest. But there was hope of a sort in the superstition: once the parent, the contaminator, was destroyed – as we had destroyed Chriseis – then the taint vanished altogether and all the victims were redeemed. Or so I thought I remembered.

And on the other hand, you presumably had some sort of medical truth – a truth with which, as a civilised and rational man, I must now concern myself. But what was this truth? Did Piers know it? And did he subscribe to it, or did he favour the superstition?

But I was walking in the dark. Whatever the medical theory, the scientific explanation, might be, I did not know it. Perhaps Piers did and perhaps he didn't, but whatever he knew he was far from happy. And that, I thought, is all you've got to go on. In which case, the only thing to do is to look to Richard's present health and safety; time enough to consider the rest when some definite information is available and Richard is strong enough to discuss the matter himself.

At first the path descended; then it levelled out; then, some way later, it ascended again, till it twisted over a rocky mass and down on to the ledge where the mayor was waiting. The walk took me some fifteen minutes, and nowhere on the way was there any sign of Roddy.

I very soon understood why.

When I reached the ledge, the mayor was standing there looking out over the mountains. His two men were under the projecting shelf with their backs to me and were squatting attentively over something; the mayor himself turned to greet me.

"Your news is good?" he said.

"I suppose so. The woman is dead. You will be able to see for yourself."

He nodded.

"That is good. What I must tell you is not so good."

He spoke to the two men under the shelf. They stood up and aside. Roddy was lying on the rock, his face looking straight into the sky.

The mayor took me gently by the arm.

"He came last evening to tell me that you must stay longer because of the weakness of your friend. I agreed to wait also. Then he asks me if I know of a friend of his, who was an officer with your people in Crete during the German occupation. I know this man well, and we talk of him – of him and how he died. We talk of him for a long time, you understand, because we both loved him and he died bravely.

"Then at last, long after it is dark, your friend says he must return. I ask him to stay here with us, because at such a time the mountain is dangerous for a man alone. But he says no, you will be already worrying for him, he must go. So then, for all I do not wish to come near where you have gone, I think of Major Longbow's friend back in those other days and I say I will come with him as far as the fort, and will then come back here to my men, for though they are two I cannot leave them long by themselves. But he says that will mean I must return alone; and he cannot permit this, he says, because it is his fault that he has stayed so long. Anyway, he is not afraid, he says. So I am much in doubt but I let him go."

There was no sign of remorse or guilt in the mayor's face. There had been a situation, his eyes seemed to say, and everyone had acted as he saw fit; for the rest – it could not be helped.

"So he went," the mayor was saying, "and we heard no more. But in the morning I am standing on the rock" – he indicated the mound above us – and I see a body along the path. We go to him and he is dead. His head has been split open with something heavy and hard. A rock. The woman has done this. But even so, perhaps it is better than what she has done to your other friend."

"But he will be well. He is weak now, but soon..."

The mayor shrugged; then he took me by the arm again and led me over to Roddy. His hair was matted with blood, but otherwise he was handsome and calm. Fond, kind Roddy, I thought, who had lingered too long to talk of a dead friend, because he was so happy to find someone else that had known him. Loyal Roddy, who had refused to spend the night in safety lest we should be concerned. Fair-minded Roddy, who had declined help because he held himself to blame for needing it. Brave Roddy, who had known so many battlefields, Dunkirk, Tobruk, Normandy, always where the fighting was thickest. Poor, cold Roddy, who was dead at the hand of a vicious, cunning woman that had sneaked up behind him in the night.

"We shall bury him here?" said the mayor at last.

"Yes. If his people...later... They can send."

"Then this we will do. I and my men will now join you at the fort. We will see the woman who is dead – see that all is attended to. And we shall bring with us your good friend, Major Longbow, and we shall all bury him in a grave of rock by the fort. We shall do this in a manner that is worthy of an honourable gentleman. Then, as soon as may be, we shall take your other friend down the mountain. For we wish him to go swiftly from Crete."

There was hatred and urgency in his last few words.

"But he will do you no harm."

"Not yet. Not for a while. Later. You must see to him among your own people. You will be having wise men, doctors, who know of such things?"

I nodded. There was nothing else to do.

"Then take him to them quickly. But all that must be later, in your own country. Now we have work."

And he called to his men to saddle up the mules.

Some time in the middle of the afternoon the mayor and his men appeared with the mules at our fort. The first thing the mayor did was to inspect the remains of Chriseis, which Piers and I had moved away from the steps and placed among the rocks. Having examined the protruding stake with care, the mayor nodded approval at Piers.

179

"This is good," he said. He spoke briefly to his men, who then placed the body over a mule and disappeared on to the slope above.

"They will see to her," he said curtly. "And your friend? How is he?"

"He has only woken once," Piers said. "He took a little food and wine. He seems stronger."

"Then tomorrow we will take him down," said the mayor.

"But he must have a little longer – ," began Piers.

" – Tomorrow," said the mayor, with unquestionable finality, "we shall take him down."

A little later the two men returned. Then we buried Roddy, making a cairn of mountain stones and paying, so far as we were able, the observances that are becoming at a soldier's funeral.

The mayor and his men disposed themselves early to sleep. We had all, including Richard, eaten well of a broth the Cretans had prepared; and now, while the others slept, Piers and I sat over the dying fire and talked.

"You notice," Piers said, "how anxious they are to be rid of us."

"To be rid of Richard. The mayor spoke of this when I was down at the ledge."

"Did he say why?"

"Not in so many words. It is plain that he regards Richard as being in some way defiled – and even as potentially dangerous."

"He may be right."

"The man is impressive," I said, "but he is still little more than a peasant. From what point of view is he speaking?"

"As a peasant he makes a peasant's interpretation. But I don't need to tell you that such interpretations are often quite accurate reflections, albeit in superstitious terms, of scientific truth. And whatever explanation you chose, the results would be much the same for Richard... Did the mayor suggest any remedy?"

"That Richard should be taken to doctors when we get back to England."

"I wouldn't relish sitting in Harley Street and telling this particular tale... Does it occur to you, Anthony, that technically I am a murderer?"

"I cannot think of you as that," I said.

"Neither can I. The fact remains that I killed this woman by strangulation. Even the plea that I was protecting Richard would not excuse that degree of violence. And I could not readily undertake to convince any jury of the true nature of the circumstances."

"I don't think you need worry. Chriseis is not likely to be found up here. And I doubt if she has many friends elsewhere to miss her."

"True. But if the police catch up with us all, they will want to know what has become of her... We must leave Greek territory, Anthony. The police have been after Richard for weeks. They are probably interested in us as well by now. We do not want to answer any questions."

"With any luck," I said, "the police are still a long way behind... Though the police in this area know for themselves that something is amiss... To judge from what the mayor said they won't interfere, but word may trickle back to someone more resolute... You are quite right, Piers. We must leave Greek waters."

"How?"

"In the same way as we came," I said. "These people know the sea as well as the mountains. The mayor likes us, I think, and is anxious to be rid of Richard. It is reasonable to presume that something can be arranged."

Early next morning we started down the mountain to Sphakion. Richard was still very weak, though he made a tolerable breakfast. In the end they rigged up a high back to one of the mule saddles: so that Richard, riding astride and leaning against this with his spine cushioned, could travel in some sort of comfort. The mayor and his men treated Richard with repugnance. They would not come within ten feet of him, and it was Piers and I who had to hoist him into the saddle, who had to ride by him and watch him throughout the journey.

So down we came. Round the mountain and down the long flank to the ridge; along the ridge, stopping briefly for a midday meal from our own provisions; on through the scorching afternoon; and finally down into the valley of Hagia Persephone, more pleasing than ever in the early evening, with its graceful cypresses and the trickle of running water. Here the mayor halted us; and then went on alone to the village to see what news he should find.

We took Richard from his mule and laid him on his back in the evening sun. He had been unconscious much of the way, and then, having awakened some ten miles from the end, he had been in great pain from his terrible journey; but his present relief gave him heart.

"Where are we going?" he said.

"Home. To England."

"And Chriseis? Where is Chriseis?"

"She will not trouble you now."

He frowned slightly.

"She has left me then?"

"You will not see her again."

"And Roddy?"

"Roddy is dead."

Two large tears welled over on to Richard's cheeks, then ran down his cheek bones to the ground.

"Roddy was always kind. And so was Chriseis. And now Roddy is dead and Chriseis has gone."

It did not seem to occur to him to ask for further details, to attempt any logical assessment of what had happened.

"So kind," he murmured, "the one dead, the other gone."

Piers looked into my eyes and said nothing.

About an hour later the mayor returned.

"There is word from over the mountains," he said. "Any time now the police will come from Heraclion, searching for your friend and the woman. They do not know of you. But when they come, you must all be gone."

"Where? How?"

"Stay here and rest. Tonight I will come for you. There will be a boat to take you to the coast of Italy. You have money?"

"Yes."

"You must pay five thousand drachmas to the captain. He will put you down where he best can. Then you must see to yourselves."

"We can do that... What will you tell the police?"

The mayor shrugged.

"That your friend and his woman went to the mountains. Let them go there if they wish. They will not find the woman."

"Major Longbow?"

"A pile of stones. There are many such in the mountains. They will not notice this one."

"You have our gratitude, Mr Mayor."

He bowed stiffly.

"Rest now," he said. "I will come later."

Late that night we were led to the beach and taken off in a dinghy to a medium-sized motor launch. Once again no one would touch Richard, so that Piers and I had to drag him up from the dinghy to the launch. The stars in the sky were very bright; nearly as bright as they had seemed to me that night on the mountain, in the calm before the storm.

PART THREE

The Michaelmas Feast

XI

"And what happened then?" said Inspector John Tyrrel. The September sun crept slyly into his office in the Charing Cross Road: the flies played on his desk, and periodically Tyrrel thrashed at them with his ruler, causing them to rise in turmoil amid little clouds of whirling dust. I had reached England, with Richard and Piers, late the previous evening; in the morning I had telephoned Tyrrel for an appointment; and now, late in the September afternoon, I had told him all that had happened up to the time of our leaving Crete.

"So what happened then?" he said.

"We got to Italy with little enough trouble," I told him, "and also with little enough luggage. However, we had plenty of money. I had come very well supplied from the start, and Richard turned out to have a letter of credit still on him. So the minute we landed I walked fifteen miles to a discreetly distant village and took a taxi of sorts to come back and pick up the other two – Richard, as you may imagine, being still very weak. We then drove straight to Brindisi to catch the train for Rome. The taxi driver thought we were rather odd, but a journey like that was a real field day for him, so he asked us no questions and thereafter, I dare say, kept his mouth shut in case of trouble with the police. Anyway, nobody bothered us either then or later.

"Once in Rome, we bought ourselves some kit, and I wrote to Athens to tell them to send all our stuff back to London. As for Richard's, God knows what had happened to that, and you'll understand from what I've still got to tell you that Richard himself gave us no help in finding out. Lucky enough, I suppose, that he still had his Passport and that letter of credit… Anyway, from Rome we took him to Orvieto, which is a nice, peaceful place for convalescents, and there we stayed three weeks, by the end of which he was more or less recovered. On to Florence, where it was damnably hot and seething with a hell brew of Germans; on to Venice to collect the car; and then very gently towards home, through the lakes, over the Alps, and so through Switzerland and France. A very nice holiday indeed – if only poor Roddy had been there to share it… But I suppose," I added futilely, "his leave would have been over pretty soon in any case."

"What have you done about Major Longbow?" said Tyrrel. "Have you told anyone yet?"

"I wrote to his Brigadier and said that Roddy had been accidentally killed in the Cretan mountains. Implied it happened while we were climbing. I also did my best with the same story in a letter to his parents. When I got home last night there was a somewhat dignified letter from his father, thanking me for my trouble, and a great packet from the War Office. Why was Roddy in Crete when he said he was going to Italy? Was I aware that Army Officers were forbidden in Greek territory? Where was the Death Certificate or Cretan equivalent? They seem to think that I personally arranged the whole thing expressly to annoy them. They're getting ready to be very awkward."

"Send the whole bag of tricks to me," said Tyrrel, "we can deal with the War House. Provided the parents don't kick up a fuss."

"I don't think they will," I said. "They're old-fashioned people and they know me as Roddy's friend. They trust me. And as his father said in his letter, a man like Roddy could hardly be expected to live for ever."

"You'll be seeing them?"

"Of course. Tomorrow or the day after."

"Hm," grunted Tyrrel. "And what have you told Doctor Goodrich? And your gossipy friend Honeydew?"

"I wrote to them both from Orvieto. I told Walter that we had found Richard suffering from strain and overwork, but that he was now having a nice, restful holiday and was well on the mend. As for Marc, I told him much the same – spicing it up with a few misleading hints to satisfy his sense of drama."

"Will they believe you?"

"Walter should be more or less happy, because my story will be rather a relief. And whatever Marc thinks of it, he will hardly be able to guess the truth."

"You haven't heard from either of them?"

"No. I had enough on my hands... I didn't want Walter nagging at me to make Richard stay in Greece, and I didn't want anyone to start getting at Richard directly... So I told them we'd all be moving around too much to get any letters."

"Hm," grunted Tyrrel again. "So far, so good, I suppose. But now for the real point. What sort of state is he in, this Richard Fountain? How did he behave on the way home? And what about this business of...infection?"

"You can't believe in that?" I said.

"I don't know what to believe, Mr Seymour. Your story is a little unusual, you know."

"So it's me you don't believe?"

Tyrrel smiled with warmth and even with affection.

"I believe you, sir," he said. "It's just that I find it a little difficult to discover...an intellectual framework for all this. I am trying to work out what possible rules there can be. It isn't easy. You know that for yourself."

"I do indeed."

"Anyway, sir, just try to tell me what you've noticed about Mr Fountain's behaviour. That will be the easiest thing. Has he been what you might call 'himself' since you left Crete?"

189

"At first," I said, "he was too weak and delirious to be anything. But as he got stronger – after we'd been about a week in Orvieto – he began to be very much as I'd always remembered him. He started to enjoy things in his rather stiff and reserved way. He made apt and sharp comments about the place and the people. He talked intelligently, though sometimes impatiently, of the things we went to see. He was affectionate, after his slightly proud fashion, to both of us. He seemed grateful for the trouble we were taking. But there was one definitely odd thing. He seemed to have no wish whatever to talk about what had happened to him in Greece and Crete, and no curiosity about what had occurred in the mountains. He did not seem to remember anything or to wish to remember anything. It seemed – how shall I put it? – like a case of deliberate amnesia. As if he had just blotted out of his memory the events of some five or six months, and was going to leave the matter at that – accepting an area of dead time in his past as you or I might accept a patch of dead skin on a finger. If anyone mentioned Delphi, say, or Cnossos, he would just make some very general remark about the place and immediately pass on to another topic."

"And you felt it wise to leave the matter like that?"

"For the time being. Until he was fully recovered. But eventually it seemed to Piers and myself that we *must* make him realise what had happened – how both Roddy and Chriseis had died – and that we must try to find out, in case of future complications, exactly what were the strange things he had helped Chriseis to do in the earlier stages of their association. So one night in Florence – about a month ago now – Piers told him straight out, in my presence, of everything that had happened in the mountains, and then asked him absolutely bluntly for a full account of his relationship with Chriseis from the first day to the last."

"And how did he react?"

"At first, most favourably. Far better than we had hoped. He listened with great attention to Piers' story and interrupted with a number of questions. He was particularly interested to know how the woman had, so to say, hypnotised myself, and how his last minute cry for help had awoken Piers. Then, when the story was finished, he thanked us both, lamented the death of Roddy with a very painful bout of crying, and expressed virulent hatred of Chriseis.

"It was at this stage that Piers went on to say that it was in everyone's interest to know more of what had passed between him and Chriseis when they first met in Corinth, and also how she had later come to persuade him to her own particular type of...intercourse."

"Rushing things a bit?" said Tyrrel.

"Perhaps. But he seemed genuinely moved by the whole topic and fully prepared to discuss it. Piers felt – as I did – that the opportunity, that Richard's favourable mood, must not be wasted. And certainly the enquiries were well enough received. He started to tell us, without any apparent strain, all that happened to him since leaving England last year. At first, while he was talking of his travels and his researches, he went into considerable detail. He spoke clearly and with evident pleasure – pleasure both in the memories and his relation of them – and the further he went the more our hopes were raised. But then, just as he was reaching his first meeting with Chriseis in Corinth, he seemed to get dazed and muzzy: his voice became low, his head drooped: he mumbled and muttered and repeated himself; until he seemed to be talking almost in his sleep..."

"So you *had* overdone it?" Tyrrel said.

"Evidently. We both realised this, and suggested that Richard must be very tired and that we could hear the rest of the story the next day. Piers even made to help him from his chair. But Richard waved him away, seemed to make a great effort to rouse himself to the telling of his story, and then continued, still in very low tones, but quite firmly and consecutively."

"Ah," said Tyrrel.

"I'm afraid you're going to be as disappointed as we were. He went on with his story all right, and in a perfectly sensible fashion: but it came out in exactly the same way as it had done that afternoon on the mountain. All in entirely general terms. How he couldn't make love to Chriseis properly, and how she said it didn't matter because there were 'other things'. How they did these things together, 'fearful, ugly things' – but never a word as to exactly where or what. And then how he returned from Delphi and met her again, and she turned herself entirely on to him; but no explanation of her actual fashion of behaviour, what methods she had used to persuade him, whether he had given in easily or only after a struggle. And so on for the rest of the story: a vague and general account, no real reasons given, only the most broad of motives, and above all no details of any particular thing that *happened*. So that when he had finished we were no wiser at all."

"Did you press him?"

"Oh no. He was clearly too exhausted for that. We just thanked him and saw him to bed… But the next evening Piers brought the subject up again. This time Richard seemed neither anxious nor reluctant to talk of it. Just neutral. So Piers, thinking the prognosis might be worse, forged ahead, and said that while we'd been very interested in Richard's story as he had told it, it was important to us to know it in greater detail. He pointed out absolutely flatly that these 'things' Richard and Chriseis had done might still have embarrassing consequences, and that Richard's health might have been damaged by their later intercourse. He must, said Piers, tell us everything: no detail was too small."

"And then?"

"Well, all the time Piers had been saying this Richard had been looking grimmer and grimmer. No, not exactly grim. A sort of mixture: trapped, sad, petulant, unwilling, uneasy, irritated, even at times uncomprehending – any and all of these he had been looking, and they all seemed to add up to a kind of blank stubbornness, which had been getting blanker and more stubborn with every word Piers said. And when Piers had finished, Richard just got up and left us. He rose from his chair, nodded at both of us, and left. The next morning he was entirely affable; but he made no mention all day of the previous night's conversation – if you can call it that – and no reference whatever to Greece or his own life there. So Piers and I concluded that we had best leave him to talk in his own good time; and that meanwhile we must simply concentrate on making his holiday as pleasant and happy as possible."

"Perhaps it was as you said. Amnesia. Perhaps he really couldn't remember certain things. Or wouldn't."

"I dare say," I said; "and in any case the strain of the whole business must have been very severe. One could quite see he might not often be keen to discuss it. If it had been *only* this – only his refusal to give details of what happened – I should not have worried so much."

"So there was something else?"

"Yes. After we left Florence, Richard was getting stronger and more normal every day, till I dare say he was as fit as he's ever been in his life. As I say, Piers and I set out to give him a good time, and I really think we brought it off. We went to beautiful places, ate good food and drank quantities of wine. Piers was at his gayest and most appealing. The weather was perfection wherever we went. So that Richard really did seem to be happy. After a bit we spoke a good deal of the future. He seemed perfectly content to be going back to Lancaster – Walter, Penelope and all –; and we – Piers and I – judged it best not to mention Marc Honeydew's warning about Walter, not in so many words at any rate, lest it should impair his pleasure. After all, Richard is not wealthy and he must make his living somewhere: if he felt good about the prospect of Lancaster, then so much the better – for the time being at least. So by way of inoculation against future trouble Piers and I made a lot of little jokes about Walter's possessiveness – jokes in which Richard joined –; but in the main the mood was one of peaceable acceptance of Lancaster College and all that it contained.

"But on two of these occasions on which we discussed Cambridge and the future something ·very unpleasant happened. On the first of them we were driving across the Lombard Plain, about three weeks ago now, and Piers was talking about Walter's house in Grantchester, and giving a malicious account of a tea-party he once went to there, and how Penelope presided. And all of a sudden Richard said, just like that and with no particular tone or emphasis – 'I wonder what Penelope will make of Chriseis when she comes to England.'

"Piers and I said nothing at all to this, and Richard went on – 'We thought she might come next spring sometime. I was always telling her how beautiful Cambridge is in the spring.'

"And then he went on to ask what the Backs had been like this year, so the subject was mercifully changed. But you can imagine how sick it had made Piers and me. After all, it was then only four or five days, a week at the most, since Piers had told Richard, with great clarity, everything that had happened in the fort."

I paused for a moment. Tyrrel, swishing his ruler down among the flies, made no other comment.

"And then," I went on, "a few days later, we were having some lunch in Geneva one afternoon when Richard started discussing, without any prompting from us, what he was going to do about his supposed engagement to Penelope. This was a topic everyone had avoided so far, so naturally Piers and I listened with some interest. Richard said he didn't really want to marry anyone for a few years, but when he did – this in an off-hand way – he supposed there might be worse fates than Penelope. And then he said, once again in an entirely normal manner – 'But I'm damned if I know what Chriseis will say if I *do* marry Penelope.'

"Then Piers, who had clearly heard enough of this, leant across the table and said very coldly and fiercely indeed − 'Chriseis is dead, Richard. You know that. And better dead.'

"But Richard just didn't seem to hear him. He didn't look at Piers, he didn't nod, he made no sign of any kind. He sat there looking vaguely thoughtful, and then he started talking again as if he were merely adding to his own remarks, as if there had been no interruption at all other than his own voluntary pause to collect his thoughts.

" 'Of course,' he said, 'I might be able to make Chriseis understand the position if she comes to Cambridge in the spring... Or if I go to Greece again, I can talk to her about it then. It seems a bit hard though... To take advantage of her company in Greece and then, just as I'm getting on the boat, to announce that I'm going home to marry someone else.'

" 'You won't be able to go to Greece again,' Piers said. 'If you do, they'll shove you in gaol. For Christ's sake talk sense.'

"And once again Richard took no notice at all. Just sat there looking thoughtful.

" 'I wonder,' he said, 'how soon Walter would let me go back to Greece. I've gathered up quite a lot this last time, but I could do with a few more months of research.'

"And then, by the mercy of heaven, he started talking about his research, so we heard no more of Chriseis. Either then or later. But what we had heard was more than enough."

"As a matter of interest," said Tyrrel, "what about this research? I imagine that most of his time was...otherwise occupied."

"As far as I can make out," I said, "he's done more than you might have expected. After all, he went to Greece last autumn and he didn't meet Chriseis for some time. Richard is capable of very hard and concentrated work."

"So he'll have done enough to put up a plausible showing? With Doctor Goodrich and the rest?"

"I think so. He seems to have some good stuff on early fertility cults – with a strong sideline on temple prostitutes. That's what kept him so long in Corinth. There was an important temple of Aphrodite in the old city there…"

"Well," said Tyrrel with a broad grin, "that's one practical problem out of the way, Mr Seymour. It would have looked a bit odd if he'd come home empty-handed. But unfortunately it's not the only problem and indeed it's probably the least important. Do you mind if I ask you some more questions? There's one or two things I must get absolutely straight."

"Go ahead."

"Firstly, then, he's given no details at all of these things Chriseis and he did together when they first met?"

"None. He just implies they were very unpleasant."

"That," said Tyrrel, "we don't need to be told… And secondly, he's given you no idea of the way this woman set about…seducing him?"

"Very little. She clearly had a powerful personality."

"And thirdly," Tyrrel went on, "apart from his general evasiveness about a lot of his life in Greece, and apart from these very disagreeable references to Chriseis as a living person, his behaviour has been entirely normal?"

"That is correct."

"In which case I gather you've not taken him to any doctors? In Italy or Switzerland?"

"No."

"And do you intend to?"

"That depends on his future behaviour."

"Umph," said Tyrrel rather crossly. "And where is Mr Fountain now?"

"In the country with Piers. They left this morning. They're going to spend a week watching cricket in Kent."

"A very soothing occupation, Mr Seymour. And will Mr Clarence enjoy it?"

"Not a lot. But Richard will. He nearly got a cricket blue, you remember. They might even offer him a place in one of their Festival Matches."

"Better and better. But the cricket season is nearly over, sir. The days are getting shorter now, and September will draw to a close. 'Farewell, summer, summer farewell'," he murmured across the table with a faint smile. "A sad song, sir. Unlucky too, they say... But what happens then? Doctor Goodrich gets back from his summer holiday, and the stumps are pulled up, and it is time for Mr Fountain to pack away his cricket bat and to put in an appearance at Cambridge; and there, amid the falling leaves of autumn, they are confronted with one another. So what happens then, Mr Seymour?"

"I don't honestly know," I said. "All I can tell you is that Walter is expected back in Lancaster in about a week. I telephoned the Porters' Lodge this morning."

"And how soon must Mr Fountain present himself?"

"He *needn't* go into residence until the beginning of Full Term — October the twelfth or thereabouts. But once it's known he's back in England, after a year away, mind you, it'll be thought very odd if he doesn't pay a courtesy visit to the Provost and at least make his number with Walter."

"And in any case," said Tyrrel, "sooner or later he must meet Doctor Goodrich, not to mention his charming daughter. *And what, Mr Seymour, happens then?*"

We were both silent for a time. The sunlight slunk slowly away across the desk and on to the floor: the flies, tired with their day's sport, were silent. Tyrrel flexed his ruler, aimed a kick at the wastepaper basket, and finally said: "Would you be interested, sir, to hear my view of the situation?"

"Very."

"Well then. In the first place it is clear that rough justice has been done. You have given me an account of something which happened in a territorial area where my powers are not in any case applicable and in the affairs of which it is no duty of mine

197

to interfere. So speaking as a man, Mr Seymour, and as your friend, I say that justice of a kind has been done. In so far as Mr Fountain assisted that woman in her outrages, he was not properly responsible for his actions. In so far as the woman herself has sought to corrupt or destroy others, and to corrupt and destroy Mr Fountain, then she has been quite properly destroyed in her own turn and the world is well rid of her. This is my opinion, and I have little doubt that the Greeks, when they finally come to realise the truth, will share it. I think we shall have no further trouble from them, Mr Seymour; and even if they do want trouble, they are too far away to make it. So far, so good."

He flexed his ruler again and surveyed me almost paternally.

"But now, sir," he said, "Mr Fountain is back in England. So now it is my duty to take thought for the future, not only as a friend, sir, but as a policeman. And the question I must ask myself is this: is Mr Fountain likely to prove a danger, to himself or to the community?

"Now, sir, what do I know to help me make an answer? Very little — except that Mr Fountain is in one respect — one only, as far as we know — behaving very oddly; and that a superior Cretan peasant has hinted, in the light of pure superstition, at the possibility of unpleasant consequences to come. But I also surmise for myself, Mr Seymour, that no one can go through what Mr Fountain has been through without in some way being affected — and perhaps permanently — for the worse. And then I tell myself that if there is one person whom Mr Fountain is liable to hold responsible for all the pain and humiliation he has suffered, if there is one person above all whom he is likely to resent — and even *dangerously* to resent, Mr Seymour — that person is Doctor Walter Goodrich. At which stage, sir, I remember, without any pleasure at all, that if we are to believe your friend Honeydew, then Doctor Goodrich is not going to be very tactful in his future dealings with Mr Fountain.

198

"So what do I conclude? That Mr Fountain must be kept away from Doctor Goodrich? Impossible. Mr Fountain is not a wealthy man, he must pursue his career, he must pursue it at Lancaster College, and he must therefore meet Doctor Goodrich very soon now and suffer daily intercourse with him thereafter. But fortunately, not just yet. We have a week, Mr Seymour, and even a little longer; and during this time, between now and Doctor Goodrich's return, we must make a plan, a plan that will soften the impact between Mr Fountain and Doctor Goodrich and will somehow make them amenable one to another. Do you agree, sir?"

"I do."

"And before making it, Mr Seymour, we must have the best possible information. We must try to ascertain the *rules* about this…thing which has happened to Mr Fountain. There is a mass of superstition, of which we know a certain amount, and there is, we conceive, a scientific truth – of which we know nothing at all. The superstition will be interesting and, since it reflects human experience after a fashion, not entirely irrelevant. As for the scientific truth, it is *vital*. I know a man who will enlighten us fully on both counts. So tomorrow at ten, sir, you will accompany me, if you please, to the British Museum. And there I can promise you a most interesting morning with Doctor Erik Holmstrom, a gentleman of deep learning and most pleasant wit."

XII

Doctor Erik Holmstrom was small and wizened – rather like Ratty Arnold, except that he was palpably sane. Incongruously enough, he had a fine deep voice, which rumbled round his sepulchral office in the basement of the British Museum like the distant thunder which, on a still summer day, heralds the slow approach of rain.

He had already been briefed by Tyrrel, I gathered, but he listened with attention while I told him of our adventures in Crete and Hydra and added what little I could of Richard's experiences in Greece before our arrival there. Then he sat back, pushed his modest stomach comfortably out in front of him, patted it, and lit a cheroot.

"You realise," he growled, "that I am not a consultant for individual cases? I can tell you what I know of this subject, and help you to relate it to these particular circumstances. But I am not to be regarded as a physician. I will take no responsibility. None."

"We know that, Erik," said Tyrrel, who seemed on unaccountably intimate terms with him. "What we want is for you to tell us the rules. This is unfamiliar country: we need a map."

"There are no rules," said Holmstrom. "In this, as in other human afflictions, there are only probabilities. There is no map: there are only occasional signposts – many of which have been turned, by irresponsible people, to point the wrong way."

"Tell us what you know," said Tyrrel abruptly. "Tell us what the superstitious say, and then what the instructed say. We must have something to go on, Erik. Do your best – and then leave the responsibility squarely with us."

"I had no intention of leaving it anywhere else," said Doctor Holmstrom. He tilted his chair back and sent a stream of smoke towards the ceiling. Then he sat forward again, put his chin in his left hand, and began, slowly and with great care, to tell us what he knew.

"Vampirism," he said, "is a phenomenon popularly associated with Central and Eastern Europe. In fact, of course, it is universal – and extremely rare. The reason why we connect it so readily with the Balkan states is that it was in this part of the world that the most substantial and entertaining corpus of legend was first established. Most simple people are good at producing grim superstitions; but the Slav and Magyar inhabitants of Eastern Europe share with certain Scandinavians a genius for spicing their tales with a kind of succinct and plausible nastiness that one seldom finds elsewhere. The vampire myth was just the sort of material they needed. Hence their particular insistence on it, and hence the popular idea that vampires exist only between the Carpathian mountains and the Northern shores of the Eastern Mediterranean. In fact you will find as many, or as few, in Boston as in Budapest. But because of their skilful use of the legend, the East Europeans have a corner in vampirism; and this, roughly, is what their superstition maintains.

"It postulates a taste in a living human being for sucking the blood of other human beings. How, in the first instance such a taste should arise is uncertain; but clearly, from a purely superstitious point of view, there is a connection with the magical notion that by possessing yourself of any living part of another person or animal you increase your own power both over the creature concerned and in nature generally. Nail-parings, hair, testicles…but what could be more significant,

201

what could possibly increase your power so much, as actually drinking human blood? In any case, there it is: a living person has this taste, and he indulges it at the expense of his fellow men. But now we come to one of the most terrifying and also most misleading aspects of the whole affair: for according to the superstition, anybody who is used by a vampire becomes infected with the taste himself. And even worse. He may die from loss of blood, he may, for whatever reason, survive; but *in either case* he himself has now become a vampire and as such will continue to roam the earth in search of human prey even *after he has died his human death* and regardless of how soon or late this may occur.

"Now, as to the exact powers enjoyed by a vampire after death, opinion differs a good deal from region to region. At one end of the scale, the vampire is credited only with the freedom to wander from his grave between sunset and sunrise. At the other extreme, he is supposed to be able to survive in all respects as a normal human being, save that he will always avoid the light of the sun as far as possible and will tend to be languid during the day time. Then there are several ancillary powers, variously affirmed and denied. Most forms of the legend maintain that vampires can induce hypnosis in their intended victims. Some versions say that after dark – whether or not he must spend the day in the tomb – the vampire can transform himself into a bat or a wolf at will – or can even change himself into a kind of thin mist, thus facilitating entrance into places where he is, for excellent reasons, unwelcome. One may remark, incidentally, that some talent of this nature is presupposed by the very condition of his existence, or how would a vampire escape from his tomb in the first place? But it is idle to insist on logic when dealing with matters of this kind. What it boils down to is that any man who has given blood to a vampire, whether to a living vampire or a 'dead' one, becomes a vampire in his turn and is endowed, when he dies, with some form of bodily immortality. Such a creature is nourished by human blood – though he continues to exist when deprived of it –: he dislikes sunlight, garlic, onions, salt water, and the form of the so called holy cross: he may or may not have supernatural powers other than that of surviving death: and he may or may not be able to exist unsuspected with and among other men.

"Finally, the matter of destroying such creatures. There is only one way of doing this. You must discover the vampire when he is inert and powerless, which, according to some, would be between sunrise and sunset, or according to others only when a crucifix is held straight in front of his eyes. You must then take a sharpened stake and drive it through his heart. Once this is done, the creature is finally and properly dead; and all his victims, whether 'dead' or still living, are now released from the spell.

"So much for the superstition. Have you any questions you would like to ask?"

"Yes," said Tyrrel: "I once heard that vampires are able to inspire affection and even sexual passion in their victims. What would you say to this?"

"That it is true," said Holmstrom: "literally and scientifically true. I shall come on to that in a moment."

There was sun outside, the kind sun of mid–September; but no sun came into Holmstrom's basement office, which might almost have been a tomb itself, so damp it was and dreary. Listening to Holmstrom's smooth, deep voice, I had almost begun to wonder if he were not himself akin to the vampires he described so carefully – lurking down in the dark by day, emerging at night, with his bright eyes and soothing voice, to seek his victims along the dull streets of Bloomsbury. But now he rose from his chair and waddled to the door; opening it slightly, he peered out and boomed down the corridor – "Coffee for three, girl" – an earthy statement which I found somewhat reassuring.

He returned to his chair and lit a fresh cheroot.

"So much," he said, "for the superstition. Now for what we may euphemistically call the truth."

He chuckled obscenely – a high-pitched chuckle, in odd contrast to his mellow voice – and spat with care and accuracy into the waste-paper basket at his side.

"Yes," he said, his face twitching with amusement, "the truth... As we understand the matter – and you must realise that only very occasional examples come to our notice – the vampire is in fact a living human being with a peculiar type of sado-sexual perversion. The sexual element is quite obvious; you might consider, in this context, such relatively normal practices as *fellatio* or *cunnilinctus*. Nor is it difficult to see that vampiric intercourse, in a quiet way, has a deeply sadistic tinge to it. It follows, of course, that the victims of vampires tend to be of a masochistic type – and like most masochists, capable of assuming a sadistic role in their turn. You should also be reminded that sadistic practices – and among them this one – are liable to have a strong appeal for impotent males or frigid females.

"But if these are the bare psychological bones, so to say, it still does not do to dismiss out of hand the corpus of superstition. Legends cast in superstitious terms have a way of reflecting scientific reality, and so it is here. Allegations of immortality can be dismissed outright: they are merely the product of the Slav imagination which, confronted with something beastly, delights to make it positively fiendish. Again, tales of transformation into, say, the shape of a bat, clearly originate from the fact that creatures called vampire bats – who amply earn their title – are well known to exist in several parts of the world. But in other ways the superstition is nearer the mark. Take this business of hypnotic powers: it is *not* true that an initiation into vampiric practices confers these powers; but it *is* true that someone who wants to indulge such abnormal and dangerous tastes must possess a very strong and alluring personality to win over his victim in the first place. Thus it is clear that something at any rate comparable to an hypnotic talent is a *precondition* of ever becoming a vampire. This connects very closely with what John was asking about just now – the rumoured skill of the vampire in inducing strong affections and sexual passions. Vampires as such are not endowed with this ability; but plainly it may be necessary to inspire very considerable emotions of an amorous or sexual kind before a victim can be brought to assent to the vampire's proposition. One sums up the matter by saying that sexual magnetism, being one element in the so called hypnotic personality, is a pre-requisite of vampiric practice.

"And then we come to this business of 'infection' or the transmission of taste. Now, quite plainly this taint cannot be passed on in some unspecified magical fashion; and equally plainly it cannot be physically transmitted, like influenza or syphilis, by means of a germ or virus. What there can be, however, is a form of contagion which is partly moral and partly psychological. Look at it this way. We have seen that a victim is likely to have the masochistic tendencies which his passive role requires of him; and we have remarked, as a matter of medical commonplace, that masochists are often apt to reverse the coin, as it were, and wield the whip themselves. Now, suppose you had someone who had been used by a vampire and subsequently felt the need to express himself sadistically. The chances that his sadism will take a vampiric form are clearly increased a thousandfold by the mere fact that he now *knows* about vampiric methods. This is a very simple proposition, and applies, *mutatis mutandis*, to the most elementary forms of sexual behaviour. A small boy at school, for example, feeling without real comprehension the need for sexual relief, will at first resort to some form of masturbation which he has discovered for himself. But once let him be initiated, by a school friend or a girl cousin, into some more elaborate amusement, and henceforth he will scorn self-abuse and seek for a partner with whom to play the new games he has learnt. At first it is a matter of novelty; later it is one of habitual preference and even imperious necessity. It is not so much that a taste has been transmitted as that a technique has been taught – a technique of which time and circumstance may well make an habitual pastime and even an all-governing urge. So with your vampiric initiate: opting, by way of a change, for a little sadistic satisfaction, he tries out the technique which has lately been practised upon himself, and ends up as an addict... Nor is his addiction in any way lessened by the knowledge that what he does not only humiliates his victim but may even kill him; for he is seeking, among other things, to revenge himself on his kind for his own predicament and his own sufferings... You follow the train of argument, Major Seymour? And you, John?"

"Very clearly," said Tyrrel and I together.

"Of course," remarked Holmstrom cheerfully, "I have grossly oversimplified. But it hardly matters, because from what you tell me this friend of yours has been involved in a classically simple situation."

He need not, I felt, have been quite so off-hand about it. I was getting ready to make some mild protest, when I caught Tyrrel's eye. His look carried a clear request to acquiesce in Doctor Holmstrom's academic jocularity (after all, Richard was not Holmstrom's friend), and in any case diversion was now provided by a young slattern, who brought in a tray with three cups of coffee on it and some damp biscuits.

"Made out of some vile essence," said Holmstrom. "Get out this second, you frightful slut."

Whining something about no need to be personal and coffee essence saving trouble, the depressed daughter of humanity slopped through the door.

"And now where were we?" said Doctor Holmstrom.

"Sado-sexual behaviour patterns," said Tyrrel.

"Ah. Well at this stage we start applying what I have been telling you to the actual case in hand. If I am not mistaken, Mr Seymour, your friend was an attractive and vigorous young man, who nevertheless suffered from a condition of impotence and whose past history gives plain evidence of sado-masochistic tendencies?"

"I have never quite thought of them as such," I said.

"I dare say not. But these incidents you have described to John Tyrrel here, which took place at school or Cambridge, and this perpetual willingness, despite occasional revolt, to bide the bidding of his Tutor – these things tell their own tale, Mr Seymour. It is very clear to me, and, I suspect, since your protest is so feeble, to you too, that Richard Fountain, lonely as he must have been in Greece, sexually impaired and psychologically malleable, was the perfect target for the kind of creature I have tried to describe to you… After all, what has Doctor Goodrich been to him these many years other than a kind of…spiritual vampire?"

"All right," I said, "I accept this. It is now a question of what will happen next."

"All questions of what will happen next are also questions of what has happened already. We never really know the answer to either, you see. In this case, what I suggest is as follows. I suggest that when this woman first got hold of your friend she assumed (or pretended to assume in order to flatter him) that because of his bearing and his strength he would not be inclined to play a passive role. This despite his palpable impotence. So she used her charm and attraction to persuade him to join her in acts of a bestially sadistic but very general kind. After a time, however, she realised that this Richard Fountain was in reality a *natural dependant*, a person who both expected and desired that others should dictate their will to him. As you yourself have told Tyrrel, there was now no Doctor Goodrich for him to turn to. So what more probable than that he should turn, in complete obedience, to the woman whom he professed to love – a woman, if I am to believe what I am told, of considerable attraction and power?"

"Very good," I said. "Please go on."

"So what happened? He was subdued by this woman, made ill by her, cured at her instance, and finally nearly killed. He was rescued at the last minute by his friends; but one of them met his death as the direct result of the rescue. And what would you expect to come of all this?"

"It was my hope," I said, "that you would tell me."

Doctor Holmstrom chuckled – once again a nasty, high-pitched chuckle, in most ugly comparison with his smooth, rich speech.

"All right," he said, "I'll tell you. I should expect two things. In the first place, I should expect that sooner or later, when he once again sees fit to assert the aggressive side of his personality – a side, you will recall, that has been often enough asserted in the past – he will do so in a manner consistent with the… instruction that he has received from this woman. Perhaps he will ape the practices which were inflicted on himself, or perhaps those earlier ones which she demonstrated to him at their first acquaintance. In either event, the results will be very displeasing.

"And secondly," he said, "to speak in more general terms, I should expect him at this present time to be suffering from guilt consequent on Major Longbow's death and, more particularly, from resentment and wounded pride. He has once again been proved impotent; he has been used, humiliated and defiled by a woman he thought he loved; he has failed in his revolt against Doctor Goodrich. Two things follow. As one would expect and as you have already seen, he is trying, from pride, to disguise from himself the true nature of the Greek fiasco. He is 'forgetting' the details, pretending the girl who so humiliated him is still alive, trying to convince himself that the whole business is not yet concluded and so may yet turn out well – to his pleasure, that is, and to his honour. And secondly, since inside himself he knows all the time what has in fact happened, he is matching his self-deceit by fostering in himself a condition of vicious and revengeful malice – against Chriseis for so wounding him, against you for preventing her, against everything and everybody that has had part in these events. Does any of this seem plausible in the light of what you have observed of him?"

"Tolerably so," I said grudgingly, "though I have yet to see active malice."

"You'll forgive my professional conscience," interrupted Tyrrel; "but that is just what must concern me. Is he really dangerous and if so to whom?"

"At the moment," said Holmstrom with some self-satisfaction, "he is merely brooding on an intolerable situation. He is too overwhelmed to do anything other than be led – led home from Greece, led off to Canterbury to watch cricket, led back to devouring Doctor Goodrich. But the time will come, as it has before in the pattern of his life, when he will see the need to assert himself. When he does so, he may well be violent: it would not be the first time in his life. And if he makes use of any of the tricks he has learned in Greece, the resulting spectacle will not be seemly."

"And this is inevitable?" asked Tyrrel.

"Not quite, John," said Holmstrom. He pushed his cup away from him and lit yet another cheroot. "Not quite," he said. "If you look into Fountain's past, as described by Seymour here, you will notice that most of his acts of violence have followed on some very definite provocation. The behaviour of a loutish bully at school, for example, or the unwelcome and insulting suggestion that he should come and live in Doctor Goodrich's house. Now, if he is not provoked; if he feels that he is disinterestedly loved, so much so that he need have no occasion for aggressive sexual assertion; if he feels successful, well integrated, that he is welcome back in Lancaster College on his own terms, that he will not be chivied or exploited: if attention is paid to all this, then he may well settle down quite calmly, come to accept what has passed in Greece with a shrug of the shoulders, and address himself to his not unpromising career.

But if, on the other hand, he is to be *got at*; if he is given any sort of shock...then I myself would sooner not be around. Do I make myself plain?"

"Admirably so," I said. "But supposing something should go wrong. What then?"

"As I say," said Holmstrom, "I would just prefer not to be present. I cannot take any responsibility; you know that. I've told you what I can and related it to the case of Richard Fountain as best I can. And that must be that."

"I know," I said. "But we are discussing a valuable man who must, if possible, be helped. I know you cannot be responsible for what may happen. But if the need arises, can you and will you come and be of assistance?"

I did not like Holmstrom. I disliked his manner and his self–assurance, his appearance and his chuckle and his eyes. But John Tyrrel had vouched for him; clearly he was an able man; and help, let alone informed help, was going to be hard to come by. If Holmstrom would agree to help, then he must be suffered, manner and all.

"You know yourself," I went on, "that if we take him to a psychiatrist or even bring him here to you, then he will instantly feel that he is, in your own words, being got at. All we can do is help him after our own light. It is a very dim light. If we could feel that you would help us...if circumstances become extreme..."

Holmstrom looked at me maliciously. He was insufferably pleased that he was in a position to grant or withhold a favour, that his authority was being recognised and courted. His eyes glinted, he ground his cheroot between his teeth, he emitted his ghastly chuckle.

"*Nihil humani alienum*," he said at last in his beautiful, deep voice: "I'll try and come if called."

Tyrrel and I sat down in a pub and despondently drank draught beer.

"Well?" said Tyrrel.

"I don't much care for your chum Holmstrom," I said. "How do you come to know him?"

"He has been helpful to us before in cases of a recondite nature."

"Why is he so pleased with himself?"

"Because he knows a lot of things that we don't."

"I suppose so... And now?"

John Tyrrel took a long pull at his beer mug. He then wiped his mouth very deliberately with the back of his hand and said: "You heard what Erik said about Richard Fountain not being got at...not being got at or shocked. And who, Mr Seymour, is going to get at him?"

"Walter."

"It's what I was saying yesterday. When everything is added up, Richard Fountain is going to blame Doctor Goodrich for what has happened; and if Doctor Goodrich is now to greet him in Cambridge with a sheaf of disagreeable plans, mouthing out unwelcome instructions...then, as Erik might put it, the resulting spectacle could be unsightly. So tell me this, sir: just how reliable is this information of your Marc Honeydew's likely to be? When he says that Walter Goodrich is getting ready to bind Mr Fountain down for good?"

"Marc is as shrewd as he is inventive. There is normally an important element of truth in what he says. And in this case his thesis is only too plausible... Tell me," I said on an impulse, "how would you like to come down to Cambridge and meet him? Cambridge is pleasant in September: empty and melancholy; dreaming, undisturbed by conceited young men, of its own past. And I know Marc is there now. We could go into this question of Walter and I dare say have quite an amusing evening into the bargain. Marc will find us rooms in College for the night."

" 'Come down to Cambridge'," said Tyrrel wistfully: "I thought you always spoke of 'going up'."

211

"Not after one has ceased to be an undergraduate. After all, even Cambridge itself is in the provinces. Undergraduates talk of 'going up' because Cambridge is the centre of their existence. It is dangerous so to think of it as one grows older."

"A perpetual undergraduate being as bad as a perpetual schoolboy?" murmured Tyrrel.

"Not quite."

"And does Richard Fountain still...'go up'?"

"I suppose so. But he is still part of it."

"And therefore still an undergraduate...in some ways at least?"

"Perhaps."

"And Marc Honeydew?"

"Quite possibly."

"In any case," said John Tyrrel, his face suddenly lighting up with pleasure, "I have often wanted to meet this Honeydew. And to go to Cambridge with you, up to it or down to it, will be a pleasure. There is a train, on which we can have lunch, at one twenty-five from Liverpool Street."

"What useful things policemen know."

"We have our compensations," said Tyrrel quietly.

Tyrrel and I walked along the river Cam in the late afternoon. We were to meet Marc for dinner at half past seven. Meanwhile, Tyrrel wanted to renew his scant acquaintance with the colleges; and Cambridge was certainly putting on a good autumnal show for him. Already the leaves were turning gold, were being scattered over the rich, green lawns which would not now be mown again until the spring. In King's the pigeons swirled and cooed, shedding their moulting feathers to flutter down over the empty court. In Trinity the fountain whispered of the departing summer, with none to hear it save ourselves and the ghost of Master Bentley. On Jesus cricket ground, which had been loaned to the County Club, the white figures enacted the season's closing ritual. And then, as we walked slowly back beside the river, Tyrrel said: "I nearly came here, you know. I had a Scholarship – in Mathematics."

"What kept you away?"

"I'm not as young as people sometimes think. This was just before the war. Before the days of county grants and so on. My Scholarship was only worth sixty pounds a year. My parents were very poor... And then the war came anyway. No time for mathematics, I thought, even if we could have found the money."

"They'd have kept the scholarship for you till after the war. And by that time you'd have got a Government grant."

"By that time I was well set elsewhere, sir. I was in the Cavalry, you see, and after a time that meant Tanks. But then I was badly wounded and little by little I made my way into a special branch of the Military Police. Not asking people for their leave passes, but investigations of a more interesting kind. So when the war ended, they fixed me up very well with Scotland Yard... It was too good to refuse. Though I'm often sorry," he said sadly, "that I had to miss all this."

We walked on in silence for a while. Overhead some birds in formation were flying south. The sun was sinking now towards the hidden fields to the West, and a light breeze stirred the leaves at our feet.

"You know," said Tyrrel suddenly, "my duty is really quite plain."

"Oh?"

"Yes. My duty is to insist that Richard Fountain be taken away somewhere for observation. Whatever he did or didn't do in Greece, there is something badly wrong. You know that. So the book says he should be sent away somewhere...until the doctors tell us he's fit to move in the world again. It is all very clear."

"There is such a thing as Habeas Corpus. You can't just take someone away because you feel like it."

"True. But if we have good ground for wanting to investigate people – as we have here – then there are ways and means. Magistrates and judges can be very co-operative. I promise you, we should have no difficulty in detaining Richard Fountain for a while. All those reports from Greece..."

"You've not come to Cambridge with me to tell me that?"

"No. No, I haven't. You see, it's a duty I can't do...*won't* do. I'm willing to cover up and trust to luck we can see this through for ourselves. You know why?"

"Perhaps."

"You do know, Anthony. It's because...for some reason... I regard myself, not only as your friend, but also as Richard Fountain's. Odd, isn't it? I've never met him, never even seen him. But there it is. And so I cannot send him away, as if he were just anybody, to be 'observed'. To be confined and questioned and nagged at and pitied and 'therapised'. I've always dreaded this – the time when all my intelligence and all my instincts would run clean contrary to what was my most clear and official duty. Now it's happened, and I'm *glad*. I'm proud to have a friend who is worth putting before my duty. It's something you nearly learn to do in the Army; but you never quite learn it there, because in the Army there's always so many helpless people, people whom you actually *know*, depending on you to do your duty, and the sight of all those stupid trusting faces – your men – gives you pause, even if it means someone you love must go to the wall. But now I'm the guardian, not of a finite number of men whose faces are familiar to me, but only of the great British public at large. The great British public is too big, Anthony: it's too big and too futile and too anonymous. Let it make shift for itself or let it rot in its sweaty Welfare bed. I don't care. I only care for my friends and the sort of men whom I covet for my friends, men like Richard Fountain, brave, intelligent and rare. And that's what you learnt here in Cambridge, isn't it, Anthony? Your friends before your country? Before the world?"

"Something of the kind," I said: "though one always hopes that interests can be reconciled."

"In this case they can't. The official solution to all this admits of no compromise. Mr Fountain, it says, must be given, if necessary through police action, into responsible medical care. It might just as well say 'Mr Fountain must hang by the neck'. I can't do it and I won't. All those bloody, slimy psychiatrists, preaching away about 'adjustment' and 'normality'... You don't get anything worth having that way. All you get is people sniggering after a man for the rest of his life — 'He had to be put away, you know' — and a poor left over body, making the conventional movements and the conventional noises. A few verses, perhaps, contrived as a 'therapeutic exercise', just about fit to go on a child's birthday card. I'll have no part in it."

"Why are you telling me all this now?"

"Because before we came here I had all but decided to do my duty. I was getting all ready to make the arrangements. I listened to Erik, and I thought, 'There's going to be trouble and I shall be held responsible. Best get this Richard Fountain out of the way and done with it.' But now, now that I'm here, I've remembered something I was in danger of forgetting. I've remembered that it's not *people* that matter but only certain kinds of people — brave, handsome, clever people, or those that you yourself just happen to love — and be damned to all the rest of them with their Government subsidies and their running noses and their dreary, whining voices. So it's not the People you've got to protect — there are far too many of them anyway — but individual persons against the People: special, talented persons, or else those who, if only because they are your friends, mean something special to you. There's no time for the rest, Anthony. Life's too short. I'm glad you brought me here, because I was in danger of forgetting that. But not now. I'm your man now and Fountain's. I'll not forget again."

It was almost dark now. An occasional light betokened the occasional September scholar. It had been a valuable impulse that made me bring Tyrrel to Cambridge. And now for dinner with Marc Honeydew.

"So you're a *policeman*, my dear," said Marc blinking coyly at John Tyrrel. He poured us handsome glasses of dry sherry, and then went to his telephone, through which he instructed the kitchen to send up the dinner he had ordered in a quarter of an hour's time.

"We don't see many policemen in *here*," said Marc, seating himself on the revolving chair by his desk. "Very few." He treated himself to one complete twirl in the chair. "So why have you brought him?" he said to me, as sharp as a slap in the face.

I told him. We wanted Marc's help, and first he must have proper information in exchange. So I told him everything, I swore him to silence, and we were nearly done with his excellent dinner before I had reached the precise object of our visit.

"Quite a story," said Marc thoughtfully. "Who would have thought it? This isn't, my dear, just an elaborate hoax? Silly season joke at poor Honeydew's expense?" He looked at Tyrrel and myself with care. "No." he said. "I'm sorry... It's a little difficult at first, that's all."

He went to the sideboard and fetched a decanter of port.

"Cockburn '27," he said. "Drink hearty, boys. You'll not see much more of it."

He gave Tyrrel a back-hander, filled his own glass, and pushed the decanter on to me.

"So," he said. "That little rotter Holmstrom, who you will all be interested to know, was an undergraduate with me, says that our Dickie's now a dangerous proposition. And he has a way of being so very *right*, that Holmstrom. And you two cunning sleuths have deduced that all we need to trigger Dickie off is a few annoying gestures on the part of organising and possessive Walter. Right?"

"Right," said Tyrrel, lifting his glass with care and appreciation.

"And so you've come to Mother Honeydew to enquire just how difficult Walter is going to be?"

"Right," said Tyrrel again.

"Well, my dear," said Marc to Tyrrel: "you've seen the letter I sent to Anthony Seymour in Greece?"

"I've been told exactly what was in it."

"Dear, accurate, editorial Anthony," murmured Marc. Then, briskly straightening himself in his chair like a governess who has briefly forgotten her "manners" – "The position," he said, "is as follows. When I wrote that letter, Walter was perplexed and angry, no one would tell him what was going on, so he simply resolved to clear up whatever mess there was and to shut Dickie tightly up in a cupboard as soon as he got home so that there should never be any messes again. Then Anthony Seymour's version began to trickle through. Richard, it seemed, was just nervous and overworked, and was, bar the undesirable presence of wicked Piers, in excellent hands. So far – splendid. No trouble: no mopping up for Walter to do: Walter happy for a day or so. But then little question marks begin to appear on that distinguished brow. Why, if Richard was just overworked, all this insistence on bringing him home – against Walter's express wishes, you remember? Or rather, it wasn't so much insistence on bringing Dickie home, but just that the matter wasn't even mentioned: Dickie was being *brought* home, it seemed, and that was that. At this stage, my dears, renewed Walterian annoyance. Next question: why Anthony's deliberate evasion of further correspondence? True, they would all be moving about a bit, but surely they could have given one *poste restante* address which lay on their way home? So Walter deduces – that people are deliberately keeping him out of things, and the pressure rises still higher.

"Then came the final blow. Walter reckons to latch on to Dickie the minute he gets back (which he calculates will be

217

about now) and either turn him round and push him straight back to Greece or, if he won't go, to get off to a flying start with the new Walterian scheme for Dickie-repression by taking him, with Penelope, on a severely regulated tour of the Scandinavian lakes. ('An extra fillip for the dear boy's health.') This, it is thought, will put Dickie finally in his place. Those cold lakes and those *hygienic* Swedes – and Dickie coming home with a date fixed for the wedding and a twenty page schedule, compiled by Walter with Dickie's nominal assistance, for the writing up of his research. But at this stage Penelope, who, I gather, was more or less unbriefed but has an intuitive idea of the probable state of play, tells Walter that she wants to go on holiday now, that it's no good hanging about for Dickie, and that the last thing Dickie will want, after two months of driving across Europe, is to go traipsing off to the fjords. In short, Penelope tells Walter to mind his own business for once. And Walter, who loves the girl and thinks she's looking a bit pasty (she's more delicate than you might think from that Amazonian exterior – something she inherited from her mother, I think) – Walter, my dears, actually does as he's told. Allows himself to be carried off straight away; but *not* without some bitterness and a parting resolve that when he *does* catch up with Richard Fountain, MA, he'll really get his money's worth.

"You see, the point, my dears, is this. Walter is really angrier than ever because, paradoxically enough, he thinks Richard hasn't had trouble in Greece. If he had had trouble, then that would have given him some sort of excuse for coming home despite W's wishes – and would incidentally have put him deeper in W's debt. But since all that's happened, as far as W knows, is that Dickie's been a bit off colour, Dickie's return takes on an aspect of distinct defiance. And when, on top of all this, Penelope does her little bit in helping to ball things up, you can see that poor Walter is feeling rather maltreated. And so, if you want an answer to the question, 'Is Walter still going to be difficult?', the reply, my dears, is 'Yes, he's going to be very difficult indeed'."

The port went its brief round in complete silence. Then Marc got up, carrying his glass, and stood with his scrawny buttocks to the fire.

"Have I answered your question?" he said.

"Very fully," said Tyrrel, looking rather overwhelmed. "So now," said Marc, who was exploiting the privilege of a host in order to dominate the assembly, "I suppose the next question is, 'What is to be done to see that Dickie doesn't hit W on the head with a battle-axe?' "

"Roughly speaking," said Tyrrel.

"Because," continued Marc, "if Dickie doesn't come back here his career and his modest income will be in jeopardy?"

"Exactly so," I said. "But there is one hopeful element in the situation. Up to this present, Richard seemed perfectly content with the idea of coming back here and has – so far – shown no particular animus against Walter or anyone else."

"And according to Doctor Smarty-pants Holmstrom, if I do not mistake you, he will probably stay peaceable as long as he is not kicked about?"

"Correct," said Tyrrel.

"Then surely," said Marc, "the matter is very simple. When Walter and Penelope get back at the end of the week, loyal Penelope must be taken on one side by tactful Anthony Seymour, told the deplorable facts, and made to realise exactly how serious things are. She must then be told that it is up to *her*, since she is one of the few people Walter will listen to, to control her rampaging Daddy. She must be a good, unselfish girl; she must stop Walter nagging Richard into matrimony; and she must explain to Walter daily that Richard, having suffered from overwork and strain, must now be left to work out his own salvation in peace and quiet. Walter, of course, will be told nothing of what has really happened; but if Penelope buckles to, she can make her request seem like good general products of plain common sense – as indeed they are."

"And Doctor Goodrich will listen to her?" said Tyrrel.

"If not to her, then to nobody... Look at the way she's whisked him out of England when he was determined to lie in wait for Dickie."

"You have a point," I said, grudgingly resentful of the fact that Richard's destiny should be so coolly dealt with by, of all people, Marc.

"Of course I have a point, Anthony Seymour, and you needn't look so constipated about admitting it. And there's another thing. I don't suppose you'll trust *me* to look after Richard, but you should remember that wicked Piers Clarence, to whom you seem so very attached, will be here in Lancaster as well. So what with Penelope soothing down Walter and Piers dancing attendance on Richard, and all of us getting ready to bang the warning gong at the least sign of trouble, I don't think you need worry too much. You, Anthony Seymour, can go back to your absurd magazine, and you, John Tyrrel, can go back to your *detection*, and *Alma Mater Cantabrigiensis* can be left to care for her own wayward children in her own wise way."

"If there is trouble," I said, "it's likely to be very sudden."

"So is the Last Trump. There comes a point, my dear, beyond which *prudence* cannot be carried."

"Should Mr Fountain come here at all before the beginning of term?" said Tyrrel – his question, to my annoyance, being aimed at Marc rather than myself.

"He must, I think, come and call upon the Provost. *That* will be no more disturbing than a visit to Salisbury Cathedral. If he comes here before Walter gets back, then he can leave a polite note for W saying he's sorry to find him still away, and that he's now going to the Lake District or wherever for some quiet reading and walking. Then, of course, it will be up to Penelope to see that W does not go charging up to Windermere in hot pursuit, and that he does *not* send Richard four ounces of vituperation through Her Majesty's Mail. I think she can manage that."

"Can she?" said Tyrrel, this time, I was glad to notice, directly to myself.

"I think so," I said. "She is loyal, intelligent and tough."

"On one of her good days," said Marc, "she's a tolerable match for Medusa."

Later that night Tyrrel and I left Marc to go to our own rooms.

"You seemed very much in agreement with Marc," I said.

"I am. What else can we do? If Fountain is to stay free – and we've agreed that he is – then he must come here and he must be dependent on his friends here. You and I cannot spend our lives in Lancaster College. Honeydew's suggestions seem sound enough."

"I wish I could be more certain," I said.

Tyrrel gestured impatiently.

"I've told you," he said. "Either he goes to…some place or other for treatment, in which case you would have the kind of certainty you do not want, or else he stays free and comes here. If the latter, then there will be risk. You can't have it both ways. And if it's your friend in jeopardy, it's also my career."

"I know… I'm sorry…"

"That's all right," said Tyrrel. "I know you're worried. You'll just have to live with it, that's all."

And so it was settled between us. I would tell Penelope, as soon as she returned, all that had happened in Greece, and would urge her to see that Walter was easy and tactful. Piers would always be at hand to be of comfort to Richard; and Marc would be sniffing hard for the least scent of coming trouble. Richard himself would visit the Provost in a few days' time, leave a note for Walter, and then go somewhere quiet with Piers to read and, if he wished, to work: he would return to Lancaster only when October and its mists proclaimed that summer was finally dead and that a new academic year had begun.

And with this, though far from easy, I must rest content. I said good night to Tyrrel and went off to my damp college bed.

XIII

"So all in all," Piers Clarence was saying to Tyrrel and myself, "it might be a great deal worse." A month had now passed since my visit to Lancaster with Tyrrel. Piers and Richard had duly returned from Kent and gone to Cambridge. Richard had been warmly received by the Provost, had left a long and agreeable letter for the yet absent Walter; and had then gone on, still accompanied by Piers, to spend some time in Scotland. Walter and Penelope had then returned from their holiday in Scandinavia; and in the course of a long and painful interview with Penelope – an interview of which Walter knew nothing – I had received her promise that she would do everything in her power to make Walter behave as gently as possible to Richard...

"You surely knew that," Penelope had said. "You surely knew that I would do anything for him."

"Of course," I had answered: "but all of this is not...too easy to understand."

"Why should I need to understand it? If Richard needs my help, that is enough. In any case, I do understand. Richard, for all his strength and his intellect, is a weak man. So this creature was able to get at him."

"You forgive him then?"

"What is there to forgive? I find no cause for blame, Anthony. Only for sorrow...

And then she had left me, but not before she had renewed her promise. Nor had she failed in the keeping of it. Walter had made no trouble; he had merely sent Richard the friendliest of letters, in which he said that he hoped Richard was now feeling stronger and that he much looked forward to seeing him in October.

All this was hopeful. But there was even better news, and it was this which Piers was now telling Tyrrel and myself in my flat. For it was now October 9; Richard had gone to see a friend in Oxford until October 12, when he and Piers would travel together to Cambridge; and so Piers was filling in the days with me, and we had thought it as well to take final conference with Tyrrel before Richard and Piers disappeared to face Cambridge – and Walter Goodrich.

"The great thing," Piers was explaining, "is that he now talks entirely sensibly about Chriseis. Not that he talks of her much – and who shall blame him? – but when he does he talks of her as someone now dead and he is totally frank about his relationship with her.

"He says he can't really explain why he first let her have her way with him. It started as some sort of caress, and then he suddenly realised what she was doing: it was a soothing, dreamy kind of feeling, he said, lying there with her lips against his throat. But later, when she had left him, he realised not only how horrible it was but also how dangerous it might become. He resolved that it should never happen again. When he next saw her, he told her this; but she was so charming, so...loving, that he could not bring himself to be angry. In any case, she apparently accepted what he said, and made no attempt to...seduce him again for several days. Then, after about a week, without a word being said, she started to caress him one night and he found himself waiting, without annoyance and indeed almost, with longing, for her to press her lips to his throat... She did so without being asked; but he says that if she hadn't he might well have guided her kisses there with his own hands... And so it went on. From time to time he would suffer from revulsion or fear, especially when he felt himself growing weaker. But whenever she came to him all disgust and fear vanished: he would just relax contentedly and wait for her to take him…"

"Has he said anything about the things they did together before this started?" Tyrrel asked. "These…activities…which went on when they first met."

"He's mentioned them several times. He says that his memory of them is very clouded; and that on each occasion he had the feeling that he was only dreaming what happened, that none of it was real at all − that even if it was real there was nothing he could do to stop it, so that he was entirely without responsibility. In any case, he says, as far as he knows he was only a spectator: he just sat somewhere near, unable to move or speak, watching what was enacted. 'Enacted' is his word; for it all had the feeling, he says, of some kind of ritual, so that whatever was done, no matter how monstrous, had the sanction of a preordained sequence, like a Liturgy or a dance.

"He says that he can only remember one of these occasions with any clarity − and even then he may be mixing it up with others. But what he remembers is this. Chriseis had asked him to hire a car and drive her into the country to visit a special village. They started after lunch and drove till it was dark − she told him not to worry about getting back as she had arranged somewhere for them to sleep. After it was dark they had a meal of sorts and then drove on still further. Eventually, at about ten o'clock, by which time the road was just a track and he had no idea at all where they were, she said to pull up for a time. Then she got out of the car and told him to sit and wait.

" − Well, after about fifteen minutes she came back and told him to follow her; and they set off down a path and continued until they reached a small olive grove. In the middle of this was a large fire, round which were standing two peasants − men − of an indeterminate age and a pair of children − a boy and a girl − both of them about eleven or twelve. There was a large container of wine, Richard says, and some cups for drinking

SIMON RAVEN

from, and for some time everyone, including the two children, just stood about drinking it. He was sorry for the children, because they looked very dirty and tired, and he thought they should have been in bed; but then he remembered that the Greeks aren't too fussy about that kind of thing, and he was going on to speculate as to where this little gathering had come from, since he hadn't seen a light or a building for miles, when suddenly this feeling of…indifference, of dreaminess, descended upon him, and he found himself sitting down some ten yards from the fire, unable to move or even to think very clearly, just numbly watching what was going on.

"It seems that quite suddenly, at a sign from one of the men, the two children sat down by Chriseis. She then started caressing them, but in a curiously absent and joyless fashion, while for their part they seemed hardly conscious that she was doing anything at all… After a time the two peasants came forward; and one after the other they violated the little girl. No elaboration. They just took her. Nor did she show reaction of any kind. No pain, no pleasure; she just lay there utterly without movement or expression.

"Meanwhile Chriseis was busy about the boy. He too showed no emotion at all; from the look on his face he might just as well have been in church or in school or wondering what he was going to have for breakfast… When the two peasants had finished, they just slunk off through the grove, and that, Richard says, was the last he saw of them. At this stage Chriseis started to encourage the children to make some show of mutual endearments. They didn't seem very interested, but they did as they were shown; while Chriseis knelt over them – becoming, at last, visibly excited. This went on for about five minutes; at the end of which both Chriseis and the boy reached some sort of climax – though the little girl seemed still as indifferent as ever. So then Chriseis lay down on the ground between the children and turned her attention to the girl. Whatever she did seemed to have an effect, because after a little

226

the girl stopped looking so bored and rigid and started to snuggle up against Chriseis with a dreamy, contented look on her face. Meanwhile, the boy had fallen asleep. And it was at this point, Richard says, that Chriseis started kissing the girl's throat. Of course this was before his own initiation, and he couldn't see all that well in the dying light of the fire, so he thought that kissing was all she was doing. Nevertheless, he thinks that in a distant way he was conscious of something being really wrong now — wrong in a far more desperate sense than anything which had happened so far, though God knows most of that was bad enough. So he thinks that he tried to cry out; but whether he did or he didn't, he suddenly felt a wave of exhaustion sweeping over him; and the next thing he remembers is waking up, back in the car, with the sun streaming through the windows."

"None of which," I commented after a long pause, "goes very far towards explaining some of the things the police found."

"Perhaps not," said Tyrrel. "But Mr Fountain seems to have missed a substantial part of the evening's entertainment. And there were other occasions, you remember."

"But did he never...take it up with Chriseis?" I asked Piers. "Try to get an explanation out of her?"

"Not really," said Piers. "He was in love with her, he had failed her sexually, he was simply anxious to be allowed...to be of service. These things, when they happened, happened unexpectedly; and his memories were usually vague and utterly incomplete. He understood that she was a woman of strong sexual needs — and at that time there was nothing he could do about it himself. So he just kept quiet, or so he says. But in any case," Piers went on, "none of that matters now. It's in the past and whatever happened, it was plainly none of Richard's doing. The point is that he is now talking sensibly about all this. And there is none of this obscene pretence that Chriseis is still alive."

"What feelings does he express about her?"

"Hatred and disgust. He realises that she nearly killed him and that she certainly killed Roddy. As a civilised man, he does not condemn her for being perverted: he does condemn her for not keeping her perversion under some sort of control. Though even so, he sometimes remarks that she was very beautiful and that no one could be held to blame for feeling her fascination…"

"All this seems reasonable enough," I said. "Is he looking forward to getting back to Cambridge?"

"Apparently. He's been spending a lot of time going over the notes he made in Greece and seems very keen to start organising them with the help of the authorities."

"Meaning books or people?" Tyrrel said.

"Both… But he doesn't talk much about Walter, though he seemed pleased with his letter; and as for Penelope, he hasn't mentioned her at all…"

Later on we took Piers to tell his story to Holmstrom. The little basement office was damper and more dismal than ever, and this despite the fact that the central heating had now been turned on. The result was not so much warmth as a charnel-house fetidity – an atmosphere which evidently suited Holmstrom, whose voice was riper and whose manner was even more self-congratulatory than they had been a month earlier.

"This tale of the bonfire," he said. "It's a pity your friend didn't stay awake a little longer, but the pattern of the whole affair is quite consistent. The wish to corrupt is a common subcomponent of sadic conditions. The two men had probably produced the children and were allowed to violate the girl as part of their reward; but in any case the near-rape to which she was subjected would be very satisfying to Chriseis. Her next step was to take active pleasure at the spectacle of two 'innocents' defiling one another under her instruction: also very much in keeping. And then she goes on to indulge her most characteristic desire on the girl – and does so with the greater satisfaction as she conceives that a certain amount of male strength and substance has flowed into the child, that she has in some way become richer or riper, a more succulent morsel... You see what I mean?"

"Yes," said Piers nastily. "But all that is in the past – "

" – Is it?" said Holmstrom.

"We can only hope so," said Tyrrel soothingly. "What we are wondering about, Erik, is the significance of Fountain's new attitude; his willingness to talk quite sensibly and openly about this."

Holmstrom lit a cheroot and blew a succession of flawless smoke rings.

"I grant you," he said, "that it seems quite hopeful in some respects. It seems that Fountain is now exercising his memory and his intelligence on what has happened: that he is out to rationalise it, to explain it away, to make the best of a bad job. He is at pains to emphasise his helplessness during the orgy he described: we need not disbelieve him, but we should note that this is an aspect on which he insists. He is also keen to explain that it was impossible for him to resist the later demands on his own person. Nor should I be at all surprised if he does not sooner or later blame his continued impotence on his horrifying experiences with this woman – despite the fact that he was impotent before he met her. For this is the pattern of his thought: to seek excuse, to present everything in the light most favourable to himself."

"Sensible, one would have thought, if not entirely honest."

"Eminently sensible," said Holmstrom, "and in many ways very hopeful. But you remember what I said a month ago? That he must not be shocked or got at?"

"Very clearly."

"Well it's just as important as it always was. If people start getting at him now, it will remind him of the servile side of his disposition – and almost certainly make clear to him that his humiliation in Greece was not only due to Chriseis' unusual

229

strength but also to his own undoubted weakness. If he is reminded too strongly of this, or if he is so shocked that the web of self-justification he is weaving gets torn or destroyed, then he is liable to revert to a condition of pure resentment and to seek satisfaction in a less convenient fashion. It is true that he is now trying to face facts; but he is doing so very much on his own terms. It is clear to me that the position is still very delicate."

"So you think our optimism must be qualified?" I said.

"I do indeed," said Doctor Erik Holmstrom.

In any case, there it was. Two days later, with fair hope but many forebodings, I saw Richard and Piers off at Liverpool Street and made ready to return to the work which I had neglected for so long. But that evening, out of something very near habit, I rang up Tyrrel to tell him they were gone.

"And now perhaps you'll take a suggestion," he said.

"Gladly."

"Forget about this. There's nothing you can do now. We've all got our lives to lead. You and I have both done what we can and stuck out our necks a long way in the process. If we're going to get our heads cut off, the best thing we can do is to think of something else meanwhile... If you feel like coming out for some dinner in the next few days – a meal at which Richard Fountain will *not* be discussed – then you know where to find me. All right, Anthony?"

"All right, John," I said, and put down the receiver.

But a bare forty-eight hours had passed when such peace as I enjoyed was once again disturbed. Not too seriously. The uncertain waters of my contentment were merely ruffled by a light breeze; but there was a chill in the breeze which struck through the skin. The occasion was a letter from Piers.

Lancaster College, Cambridge.
October 13, 1957.

My dear Anthony,

Thank you so much for having me to stay. I'm sorry I drank so much brandy. Next time – you will have me again? – you must lock it up.

Richard and I arrived here safely, but the term has got off to rather a poor start. Walter, despite his nice letter to Richard, has not changed his spots. When we reached Lancaster, the porter on duty took me on one side and said he was terribly sorry but on Walter's instructions I had been moved out of my rooms in College and given digs in the Milton Road. Virtually on Cottenham Race Course. So I told Richard to go ahead with his baggage, and then went hot-foot and red-cheeked to see Doctor Goodrich; because after all I did well enough in my tripos, and I've paid my college bill, and one can't be shifted out of college for no reason at all.

Well, Walter was very busy and looked jolly put out at seeing me, but I insisted on an explanation. So he said that I was being sent to live out because my behaviour was riotous – constituting annoyance to the more serious students and setting a bad example to freshmen. So I said that this was not altogether unreasonable; but why had I not been warned of this decision in the customary manner? For after all, I said, he'd had the whole summer to let me know. At this stage, Walter got rather shifty and said that he understood I'd been abroad and he hadn't known where to find me; whereupon I replied that my home address was filed in the college office along with everybody else's and that he could at least have written there – which I knew for a fact he hadn't, as I'd had Mama start forwarding all my letters as soon as I got back to England. At this very logical complaint, Walter got shiftier than ever, but finally took refuge in ill temper. He said he had other things to bother about during the vacation than the personal convenience of noisy and conceited undergraduates; whereat, having let him put himself well in the wrong, I retired to make further enquiries.

It appeared, then, that Walter – at whatever time he first came to this decision – had only proceeded to act on it some two days before. A mousy freshman, destined for the Milton Road, was installed on arrival in my place and they just had time to paint my name out and his in before I myself appeared. The significance of this will not escape you. Clearly Walter did not want the matter known about until the last possible moment, thus giving me no time for effective protest or appeal and ensuring, in the beginning-of-term hurly-burly, that the affair would excite the minimum of remark in other quarters. Indeed his scheme worked very well; and even Marc Honeydew hadn't heard about my exile – a *very* acid test as you'll agree.

And of course it is not difficult to see what led Walter to this coup. *Tout simple*, he wants Richard and me to see as little as possible of one another – for any number of reasons: Penelope, his own influence, etc, etc. What he *doesn't* know is that this is just the kind of thing which might annoy Richard in the way he mustn't be annoyed at present. So having this in mind, I have loyally represented to Richard that Walter is perfectly justified, that my social behaviour last year was rather exaggerated, and so on – this to persuade Richard that my removal is in no way connected with himself. He has offered to take the matter up for me; but I have told him not to bother (I am sure Walter would prove immovable in this) and have reminded him that the Milton Road is not a thousand miles away.

All the same, Anthony, I am considerably put out. This is my last year at Lancaster and I had naturally looked forward to spending it in College. On top of this, if we are to have many more of these shabby and deceitful tricks of Walter's it will not make things easier with Richard. Incidentally, one wonders what part Penelope played in this. After all, one can understand that she might not be sorry to see me out of Richard's way. But I had a word with her this morning, and to be fair I think she is still very firmly on our side – she is not a girl to break her word – and knew nothing of Walter's little stratagem till I told her. But this in itself reminds us that however willing she may be, even she cannot control Walter as closely as all that.

And this must do for now. I don't think there is any immediate cause for worry, though we shall all do well to keep our eyes open. I cannot tell you how unpleasant it is going to be living in the Milton Road, and I am altogether very displeased with Walter.

Love,

Piers

"Not to worry," said Tyrrel, when I showed him this letter at dinner a few nights later. "Piers has behaved very sensibly. He seems to have matters in hand."

"I dare say. But you see what one's up against with Walter Goodrich."

"I do. It is one of the consolations of this whole affair," said Tyrrel, "that if things should explode they will probably do so right under the broad bottom of Doctor Goodrich."

"I shouldn't bank on that," I said: "Walter is one of those people with an unlimited capacity for survival."

The second warning I received was in a letter from Marc Honeydew, which arrived exactly a week after I had heard from Piers.

Lancaster College, Cambridge.
Oct. 20, 1957.

Dear Anthony Seymour,

I told you I'd bang the gong if things looked like getting troublesome. I'm not actually banging it in this letter, but I am giving it a preliminary pat.

How hard Penelope is trying with Walter, I don't know. Quite hard, I suspect, because she goes about looking very stern and very worried — as if everyone in her hockey team had been nobbled on the day of the match. But the truth is she isn't doing very well. Why, I can't say; perhaps she is only really effective with W over domestic issues. But even here, as I'll tell you later, she seems to have lost her grip. In any case, I invite your attention to the following unsavoury incidents.

Firstly, there is this business of sending Piers out of college. He's told you about that, he says, so we won't go over it again. But I might say that I consider Walter's behaviour to have been underhand and unkind in the extreme. Piers did jolly well in his Tripos last summer and he's never been all that much of a nuisance. If he had been, he should have been told what was to happen. Even the Provost was mildly surprised when he heard about this, and if anyone mentions it openly Walter starts blustering like a failing bookie. His behaviour has been contemptible on any level, and the fact that he doesn't know the real truth about Richard makes no difference at all. Piers is very upset, and if you want to know why, my dear, try living in the Milton Road for yourself.

But worse is to come. As you know, the scheme was — and not too bad a scheme — that Richard should spend his first year back in Cambridge writing up his research. Everyone seems agreed that he's brought back some very good stuff *(clever* Dickie, with everything else that was going on) and Harlow of John's, who's by way of being expert in this line, is impressed. And now what happens? Three days after term begins, Walter announces that he has arranged for Richard to give a series of extension lectures – at the rate of one a week in full term throughout the whole academic year and starting on November 1 – at the University College of Wolverhampton. Have you any *conception* of what this means? Quite apart from a weekly trek across the midlands, Richard has to prepare some twenty-two lectures on a subject – late Greek historians – which is of little interest to him at the moment and which he must now investigate at minimal notice. (One normally has at least six months' warning of this sort of thing.) There is little money in it and virtually no prestige; the whole affair is utterly without point. But Walter calmly maintains that it will be excellent practice for him against the time he starts lecturing here, and if anyone contradicts him, he pouts just like a senior Foreign Official at a rowdy Press Conference. The point is – there is no other possible explanation – that this is just a pure exercise of power on Walter's part. He's simply showing who's master – Dickie-suppression of the exact kind prognosed by your humble servant throughout the summer. But Dickie, I must tell you, has taken it like a lamb – so far. One is left wondering what Penelope was about to permit it. Still, it may be as I say; perhaps she can only get at Walter on domestic issues.

If this is so, then she is seen to have failed most signally on her own ground when we consider the last and most appalling occurrence of which I have to tell you. For this was a domestic affair if ever there was one. Last night Walter gave a party in college – an after dinner entertainment, good wine I grant you, dons and wives and a few carefully chosen undergraduates among whom Piers was not included – and let it be understood that it was by way of being an unofficial welcome home for Richard.

(He'll be officially welcomed back by the Provost at the Feast on the thirty-first; would you like to come as my guest, by the way?) Well this was all very jolly and I was just beginning to think that – for once in a way – Walter was doing something out of pure kindness and niceness, when lo and behold he claps his hands for silence and proceeds to make a longish speech about how glad everyone is to see Richard home again – a speech, my dear, simply *spangled* with references to the 'happy couple' and the 'bells that will soon be ringing', and which concluded with a request that everybody should drink a toast to 'Penelope and Richard – my daughter and my son.' Well, my dear, I can only say that Richard's self-control was a miracle. It was quite clear that he'd had no warning of this, because I was watching him very carefully and Walter's first reference to the 'engagement' was evidently a shock. But he pulled himself together, smiled nicely, and even made quite a pretty little speech in reply, being very careful, you'll be interested to know, to talk only of his return to Lancaster and make no mention whatever of Penelope – which must have been one in the ribs for Walter, though he was at pains not to show it. As for Penelope, my dear, I'm inclined to think that she wasn't warned either, because when Walter started up she looked very embarrassed; but at the same time I don't think she was entirely displeased, and in any case she began to develop a coy, girlish, this-is-my-day sort of look which was indicative of anything but misery. I suppose, like the good girl she is, she was just making the best of things. But if she is not really to blame for any of this, I still think she should have foreseen that Walter might get up to his tricks and given him a firm warning to keep his mouth shut before the party began. Let us not be uncharitable, however; whatever Penelope's shortcoming, she was amply punished for them when she was so pointedly omitted from Dickie's speech; and she was far from floating about in love's young dream when I went to say good night.

And so, you'll ask, have there been any repercussions? Not yet, Anthony Seymour; and when I saw Richard at lunch today he was looking perfectly normal. But remember that twenty-four hours have not yet passed since Walter put that great clod-hopping foot of his through the hot-house window; and remember that this is neither his first nor his only misdemeanour. Indeed, it might be a good thing if you gave Penelope a tinkle and told her to pull her socks up, because one of these peaceful October days Walter will go just too far, my dear, and then the fat will be in the fire for good.

Do think seriously about coming up for the Feast on the 31st, and give my regards to that dear little tame policeman.

Love as ever,

Marc.

"Miss Goodrich, please... Penelope?"

"Yes?"

"Anthony Seymour here. I'm sorry to bother you, my dear, but frankly I've been hearing some rather discouraging reports."

"About that speech of Daddy's, I suppose?"

"That and other things."

"I'm doing my best, Anthony. I cannot be expected to foresee everything that my father is going to do or say."

"I know that. But it really does seem as if the *general lesson* – that Richard is not to be pushed about – hasn't got into Walter's head at all."

"What you must understand is that Daddy doesn't think he is pushing Richard about. He thinks that he's arranging things in Richard's interest. Pushing about, to Daddy, would be if he were trying to punish Richard in some way – get his fellowship taken away, something like that. But fixing up lecture courses or making affectionate speeches... Daddy thinks of these as *kindnesses.*"

"But even he should be able to see that they are...a trifle inopportune."

"Richard and I *are* supposed to be engaged, you know."

"Yes, my dear. But you know as well as I do how he hates being rushed into things. He was bad enough like that even before any of this happened; and now..."

"He seems quite happy today. I saw him in Heffers' this morning."

"Perhaps he does. He probably is. But for Christ's *sake*, Penelope, do try to get Walter to be more careful. To take it *easy.*"

"I sometimes think you're making altogether too much of all this."

"We've taken the best advice we could get."

"Some conceited professor who never sticks his head outside the British Museum."

"And whom else would you suggest?"

"I might suggest that we all use our common sense instead of complicating things."

"There is no question of complication. The basic point is very simple: Richard must be left in peace. If that's not common sense, I don't know what is. And you might be better qualified to make suggestions, Penelope, if you'd been in Crete this summer and seen what happened there."

"I'd gladly have come if you'd let me."

"No point in going into that now. You didn't come and you didn't see. You promised to do as I asked and so far you've made a rotten job of it. Now, are you going to keep your promise or not?"

"You're not being at all fair, Anthony. I've done my best. You don't seem to realise how hard it is..."

"I'm sorry, Penelope. If that is the case, then your best is simply *not good enough.* You know that for yourself."

"Yes, yes. I know. There's no point in talking any more, Anthony. I'll do what I can. But I can't try any harder than I am already, so for God's sake leave me alone and stop being a bloody bully."

And with that Miss Goodrich rang off.

"And serve you right," said Tyrrel, when I told him of the conversation.

"But after that letter of Marc's..."

"For the last time, Anthony. There's three of Richard's good friends down there, all of them in the know and all bending backwards to help him. You and I will only be justified in interfering if things get very bad indeed. So I'm telling you: mind your own business and stop this interminable nagging. All right?"

"I'll do my best," I said.

But then, just over a week later, came a telephone call from Piers.

"Anthony... I'm speaking from Milton Road. A call box. Richard has been out to see me tonight...only just gone. It's very bad, Anthony. You've got to come and help."

"What happened?"

"He thinks Chriseis is alive again. He's been all right until now – even after that party of Walter's. But tonight he came out here, and he sat for a bit saying nothing, and then suddenly he said, 'She's done me wrong, Piers. I'll make her pay for it. Drain the life out of her like she did with me'."

"You're sure he meant Chriseis?"

"Who else? 'Drain away her life,' he said. 'I'm grateful to her in a way,' he said: 'this power of hers has made her free and without meaning it she's taught me the secret – the secret of freedom. *My will be done.* My will of people's bodies and

people's minds. Not yours or Walter's or Penelope's. My will.'
He went on and on, Anthony. He said that at first he thought
he'd failed to find the liberation which he'd been seeking in
Greece. He thought the gods had failed him. But now he knew
he'd been freed in the surest way of all — because of what
Chriseis had taught him. He was grateful, he said—"

Three pips sounded. They were almost visible, like splinters
of ice falling on to glass.

"*I haven't any more change*," said Piers in a note of panic. "For
Christ's sake tell them you'll pay."

"Time's up, caller." A pert, pleased voice.

"Transfer the charges to this number," I said. "Sloane 2766."

"Very well." The voice now stiff with annoyance, still seeking
if it might not after all prevent us. "Slough 2677?"

"No. Sloane 2766."

"And you're willing to pay for the rest of the call?"

"I've already said so."

"No need to be impatient, I'm sure. Carry on, Cambridge."

"Anthony... Anthony... Are you there?"

"I'm here. Go on, Piers."

"So Richard said that in a way he was grateful to Chriseis for
teaching him her secret. But he couldn't forgive her for trying
to kill him. 'Not until I've found her and killed her will I really
be free,' he said: 'the pupil must free himself of his master, of his
master most of all'."

"What did you say? What did you do?"

"What could I say, Anthony? What could I do? I couldn't
even love him while he was talking like that. You can't love an
alien spirit. That's what's in his body, Anthony. An alien spirit.
You must come. You and Tyrrel. Soon. Now. Say you'll come,
Anthony."

"I'll come, Piers. I'm coming to the Feast in any case. I'll ring
Marc and ask him to get an invitation for John Tyrrel.
Meantime you'll do no one any good by being hysterical. So
pull yourself together... Where's Richard now?"

"He went back to College. I wanted to come too, but he wouldn't let me. He seemed a bit calmer when he left, though. More himself. When shall you come?"

"As soon as we can. I'll ring Marc and fix Tyrrel's invitation, then I'll get hold of Tyrrel. Don't worry. Put down the phone and go to bed and expect us as soon as we can make it. There's nothing to be done until then. Go to bed, Piers."

"All right, Anthony. But be quick...be quick..."

"And now?" I said to Tyrrel an hour or so later.

"Now we must go, Anthony. But we must speak with Holmstrom first."

"It won't be only Chriseis that he hates," said Holmstrom with cool satisfaction; "not for long. He'll remember she's dead. Or he'll think to himself that anyway she's in Greece."

"Might he not try to go there?"

"Unlikely. All the time, you see, he really knows that there's nothing he can do to her now − alive or dead. He knows, too, that he is *not* free; that he's really less free than ever before. He will resent this most viciously − and will try to prove that it isn't so. He could choose almost anybody for his purpose...to release his hatred and try to prove his freedom at one and the same time... Almost anyone would do."

"Walter Goodrich?"

"Or Piers Clarence. Or yourself. Anyone who's in any way involved with him. Even someone that isn't."

"How soon?"

"Very soon. When are you going?"

"Tomorrow morning," I said, "the thirty-first. There's a Feast that night. A friend of mine called Honeydew had asked me to it, and now I've got him to ask John as well."

"Marc Honeydew," said Holmstrom. "We were undergraduates together at King's. A buzzing, waspish sort of boy, I remember... So what will happen at your feast?"

"It's the Michaelmas Feast. To mark the safe beginning of the academic year. Among other things, the Provost always makes a speech welcoming back anyone who's been away. This year the only such person is Richard. He will have to make a speech in reply."

"Hm... Will any undergraduates be there? Or only Fellows?"

"All Scholars of the Foundation will be there. Also all undergraduates who are in their last year. And they let Fellows' wives into the Minstrels' gallery to listen to the speeches after dinner."

"So that if anything went wrong," said Holmstrom, "a lot of unsuitable people would know about it. Many guests?"

"A fair number – and some very distinguished ones. The guests of honour this year include an important German scientist, one of the Scandinavian Ambassadors, and a minor Royalty of our own. It's something of an occasion. Marc had great difficulty in getting a place for John Tyrrel at such short notice."

"You must feel very honoured, John," said Holmstrom with a sneer.

"I look forward to it," said Tyrrel quietly.

"But I'll tell you both this," said Holmstrom leaning forward intently: "if you can, you must keep Fountain away from this feast. Pretend he's ill, anything you like. But try to keep him away. An affair like this, with him in the state he is, the excitement and the associations, a speech to welcome him, the necessity to reply... To start with, he may say absolutely anything. Not that His Royal Highness will understand much of what he hears, but even he might realise if something went badly wrong. If only to avoid embarrassment, you must try to keep Fountain from attending – and in any case from speaking. Understood?"

"Certainly. But it may not be easy."

242

"I can see that. You'll just have to use your judgement. If he seems dead set on it, then you may do more harm by keeping him out than letting him in. You must read the signs for yourselves... And another thing. He knows about you, Seymour, and he won't think it odd that you've come as Honeydew's guest. But does he know who John Tyrrel is?"

"They've never met. In all our discussions, we've avoided talk of the police and therefore of John Tyrrel."

"Fair enough. So long as he thinks John is someone you've all got to know since he's been away...so long as he doesn't know he's a policeman."

"We may need your help," I said.

"If you want me, ring me up at home." He tossed a card on to the table. "I don't come here at weekends."

"You wouldn't care to come with us tomorrow?"

"No. With the scope of his researches it's quite possible that he's read some of my stuff and knows who I am. In which case he'd smell what was in the wind the minute I appeared. If anything really bad happens, then let me know and I'll come. But there's little enough anyone can do, you know, unless you're going to hit him on the head and lock him up. The only thing is, see what you can do about keeping him away from that feast. To have him there will be asking for trouble – every kind of trouble in the book..."

And so things were arranged. Holmstrom would come if called. John Tyrrel and I, equipped with tails and miniature decorations, would leave next morning to attend the Michaelmas Feast – and were bound, if we could, to keep Richard Fountain away from it. That evening I gave John his invitation, which had reached my flat by special delivery. He looked at it with interest and a kind of rueful pride.

"What is this expression?" he asked at length. "Down at the bottom...'Doctors Wear Scarlet'?..."

"It means that all those with Doctors' degrees will attend in their scarlet gowns."

"A command or a generalisation?"

"A command, I suppose…"

"And Walter Goodrich will wear scarlet?"

"Most certainly. With dignity and enjoyment."

"I see," said Tyrrel. " 'Doctors Wear Scarlet'… What a very appropriate phrase."

XIV

"Richard…", said Marc Honeydew, "this, my dear, is John Tyrrel."

We were all gathered in Marc's rooms, Piers, Richard, Tyrrel and I, for a drink before the Feast. Any efforts to dissuade Richard from attending or speaking ("You're still a little unsteady in some ways, Richard…the noise and the heat and the nervous strain…") had only seemed likely, as we had thought probable in London, to provoke him to incredulity or indignation. When I had tried remarking that on the following day – November 1 – he would have to leave very early to give his first lecture at Wolverhampton and that he'd be the better for a long night's rest, he had merely laughed in my face. Piers, briefed by Tyrrel and myself and told to do his best, had been equally ineffective.

"There's no good saying any more," Piers told me. "He'll only get angry. He's been at pains to get his speech ready…"

"What's in it?"

"He hasn't said – except that he thinks it very appropriate and we may find it amusing."

"So one hopes," remarked Tyrrel dryly.

And that had been the last of our attempt to keep Richard from the Michaelmas Feast. But now, as I surveyed Marc's room (the decanter of sherry, the cheerful fire, Richard cool and immaculately dressed), I began to think that perhaps our apprehensions had been exaggerated. For after all, what could go wrong in Lancaster College, Cambridge? We should go from Marc's comfortable rooms to the College Hall, with its new panelling, its quietly efficient servants, its careful seating plan; the evening would follow the same course as it had for centuries past – a sung grace, five dishes, three wines and choice of dessert wines, the speeches and the glees – ; and then the Provost would say a final grace in Latin, and we would retire to the rooms of friends to drink the night away in amity and pride. What could go wrong in such circumstances and amid such surroundings? What indeed?

And then again, I noticed with pleasure that Richard and Tyrrel had taken very well to each other. Tyrrel, like Richard, was wearing a miniature MC; and now they were quietly discussing Richard's campaign in the East and speculating about the problems involved in the Kenya dispute.

"People won't realise," Richard was saying; "of course the Kikuyu had a legitimate complaint, but that does not mean to say that the Mau Mau were a lot of knights in shining armour. For the most part they were unoccupied simpletons who were lured into the forest by the promise of money and excitement and kept there by the power of the most atrocious oaths..."

A harmless enough tone, I thought, on which to start the evening.

"And then, my dear," Marc was saying to Piers, "the Professor flew into a huff and said that as far as he was concerned they could all put the Tensor Calculus where the monkey put his nuts. Multi-Dimensional Analytic Geometry was good enough for him he said, and if they thought they could all go swooning off into Matrices and Probability Equations, they had another think coming. So then Freddy got up, and *he* said..."

"I often think that these oaths ought to have been more closely examined," remarked Tyrrel. "Up to now they've only been used, in so far as they have been made public at all, as propaganda – as proof positive of atrocious motivation and intent. But a proper anthropological analysis..."

Tyrrel was warming to the atmosphere: he meant, so far as he could, to enjoy the evening. And that, I thought to myself, is what you'd best do as well.

"So what did the Professor say then?" asked Piers.

" 'Great shades of Eddington,' he said, 'what the devil does it matter if the Universe is starting to contract again? It will last out our time, I dare be sworn, and if you think you can stop it with your ridiculous equations...' "

"I agree," said Richard, who was looking calm and happy. "But these Kikuyu are a difficult, unattractive and very litigious people..."

"...so everyone agreed, my dear, to consult Charles; because though he's given up as a physicist, he's still very strong about Policy..."

"...Litigious, yes. But sophisticated and even mature..."

"...And when Charles said that what they all *really* needed was a long course in Greek Philosophy followed by a good dose of Proust, the roof, my dear, nearly fell off and the Professor swept out with his gown billowing behind him like *Count Dracula's cloak*."

For a second there was a pause in the room. Then, overwhelmed by such absurdity, all five of us burst out laughing. And that settles it, I thought: the evening could hardly have got off to a better start: there was nothing like a bad joke for putting reality in its place.

"Time for din-din," said Marc when the laughter had died down.

"I like your Richard Fountain," Tyrrel whispered to me on the way to dinner. "I hope we shall see more of him later."

"He'll be sitting near the Provost at dinner," I said, "in order to mark his welcome home. But after dinner we shall all drink together in people's rooms."

"Good," said Tyrrel. "I look forward to this evening a lot."

Lancaster College may be puritanically inclined but it is also a Royal Foundation. Certain of its privileges and traditions reflect this fact very adequately; and not the least of these is the Annual Michaelmas Feast.

On the last day of October, so the Royal and pious Founder had ordained, the Provost and Fellows, together with the Scholars of the Foundation and such Noblemen or Gentlemen of esteem as might be resident, must gather together to feast and also to give thanks that once again they were present under the roof of Lancaster College to pass the winter months in the pursuit of godliness and learning. As time went on the tradition altered somewhat. With the introduction of Pensioners, it was decreed by the college authorities that such newcomers might only attend the Feast when they were of reckonable standing in the place — a status which they were conceded to attain only when they were within a twelve month of taking a Bachelor's degree. (Hence the fact that, apart from Scholars, only third year undergraduates were attending the Feast this evening.) The nature of the occasion had also changed in more subtle ways. In early days, when a piety comparable to that of the Founder was still to be remarked in the members of his Foundation, and when the coming of winter ("Farewell, summer, summer, farewell") was still something to be dreaded, the Feast not only signified that its beneficiaries were grateful to God for their winter's refuge but also, one imagines, provided them with occasion for reflecting that the amenities of that refuge might not, after all, be very adequate. The architecture might be dignified, but there were many chinks and flaws through which the insistent snows and cunning draughts might make themselves felt: the Michaelmas Feast might be ample, but who should say whether war or flood might not forbid a similar abundance at Christmas? Thus those early Feasts must have been something of an insurance policy: "let us eat, drink and be merry" while yet we may. Even the songs sung were, by the same token, elegiac in kind, lamenting the death of summer rather than celebrating the approach of long months of academic felicity.

But now all that was changed. Paradoxically enough, the Fellows and Scholars could now observe the Feast in the real and grateful spirit intended by their Founder, for all that it was many years since their Founder's faith had become the subject of bored witticisms and the social order for which he provided had been bitterly questioned and rejected. For now, although the old songs mourning summer's decline were still sung at the Feast, all those who attended were genuinely pleasured by the prospect of the snug winter before them – of the long, warm hours in the libraries and common rooms. Lancaster might still preserve a hint of mediaeval discomfort, but it was only enough to give rise to a joke or a minor complaint. The Fellows and Scholars of Lancaster would be well provided for during this winter and many winters, well provided for with nourishing food, waterproof ceilings, sound learning and contemporary ideas. They acknowledged this truth and they relished it: so that on this occasion at least they drank deep, gave thanks (but not to the God of their Founder) with all their hearts, and basked unashamedly in the golden company and the caressing conversation of their friends.

The form and organisation of the Feast for the most part still followed the Founder's original edict. First of all Scholars and undergraduates, along with the less important Fellows and their guests, entered the Dining Hall and stood at their appointed places at the lower tables. Five minutes later, at the triple sounding of a gong, there entered in rough file the Provost and all who were to sit at high table with him, these being the senior Fellows and their guests, and also the Guests of Honour. (Walter would sit at the high table as of right; Richard, on this occasion, as of privilege; while, as we have seen, there were three guests of honour – a Scientist, an Ambassador, and a Royal Prince.) When the Provost and all the "*majores*" (the title accorded to those sitting at high table) were duly standing at their places on the dais, the gong was sounded five times: after which the Provost called out the traditional blessing "*In nomine beati Henrici, sit felicitas vobiscum*"; whereat all present cried out together, "*Nobiscum et tecum et cum spiritu beati Henrici.*" The gong was then sounded seven times; and as the last stroke died away, the full choir of grown men and treble choristers broke into a wonderful choral Grace, the only one I know of that is sung in Greek, and for ten minutes all stood with heads bowed (a disagreeable obeisance, but nevertheless still performed) until the beautiful and intricate strophes and antistrophes were finally concluded. At this stage there was one mighty stroke on the gong; all sat; and the choir, with an air as of bacchantes set free after an enforced period of abstinence, swung straight into a Latin song of such extreme bawdiness that, if any journalist in the country had but a particle of scholarship, the matter would have been a national scandal these many years.

The seating of the "*majores*", on this occasion as on all, followed the customary protocol. The Provost sat at the centre of the high table and facing down over the Hall. On his right was the senior Guest of Honour (the Scandinavian Ambassador), on his left the Prince. Opposite him was the Vice-Provost, with the third important guest, the German Scientist, at his right hand, and Richard, as "*rediens et acclamandus*" ("the returning one who must be acclaimed"), at his left. Walter, as Senior Tutor, sat at one end of the high table: the Senior Fellow at the other. Dotted around it was a selection of passé Engineers, politicians, Jewish Economists, local worthies and scholarly dotards of uncertain private habits, all being either senior Fellows or their guests; and among them were the official representatives from other colleges and associated establishments – people such as the Bishop of Bangor and the Headmaster of Eton, who, though they came every year, never seemed to get over their bewilderment at the Greek Grace or their consternation at the Latin bawdry which followed it.

Down in the body of the Hall were three long tables, parallel to one another and at right angles to the high table and its dais. At these the rest of us were accommodated – hugger-ugger and without regard to precedence, for it was in essence a democratic occasion, save that Fellows tended to be seated at top and bottom. Piers, as luck would have it, was some way from us; but Marc, with John Tyrrel on his right and myself on his left, was seated at the bottom end of the centre table: thus he had a good if rather distant view of the proceedings on the dais, and for what he could not see he had no scruple in substituting speculation. Both Tyrrel and myself had pleasant undergraduates on our second side; and what with their courtesy, Marc's continuous reportage, and the truly admirable food and wine, what with the purple-hooded candles and the magnificent academic robes all about me, I began to forget I had ever had any purpose in coming to Cambridge other than to relish wit and well found refreshment.

"Walter is having a sticky time," Marc announced with pleasure: "he has Professor Dobbs on one side and Doctor Partridge on the other. Dobbs is telling him about plant life in Scotland, while Partridge has recently developed a strong enthusiasm for Billy Graham. Walter is indifferent to plants and inimical to evangelism… But since Partridge is his own guest, he has brought it on himself."

"Why did he ask him?" said Tyrrel.

"He wants to do a deal with him, my dear, over some faculty matter. It seems that Partridge has got a candidate for the next vacant lectureship – a young man from Leeds who was next to him in the queue for salvation at one of Graham's rallies last summer. Walter, on the other hand, wants the vacancy for Richard; but since Partridge is just that much senior to Walter, his man is the more likely to get it. So Walter has been thinking and thinking, and now he has discovered, by a great stroke of luck, that one of Partridge's other protegés has a reputation for being a tiny bit *naughty* when the students come to him to be supervised. So cunning Walter is setting up a bargain: unless the religious young man from Leeds stands down as a candidate for the lectureship, Walter will create a scandal about the other business."

"What does Partridge say to that?"

"Denies that there is evidence. So Walter has lined up two thesis writers from Girton Coll., and a chorister who was being crammed for a Scholarship to Blundell's, all of whom, he says, will say that Partridge's protégé was very importunate... Partridge hasn't heard about this yet, and that's why he's here tonight. After dinner Walter will get his revenge for all the evangelist chitter-chatter by swingeing him out of court with The Young Chorister's Tale."

"How do you know all this?"

"I'm a mathematician, my dear. Two and two always make four in my world, however many respectable people would prefer, on occasion, that the answer should be five or three... Do you see the enormous man with the totally bald head? The one with the rather pretty Order round his neck?"

"Yes," said John Tyrrel, looking at Marc as a child might look at an adult who was taking him to the pantomime, "yes, I see him. What about him?"

"Well he, my dear, is a sociologist. That Order was given him by the King of Denmark for conducting an enquiry into the drinking habits of the lower class in Copenhagen. Now why do you think he went bald?"

"I've no idea."

"Because one morning, after a night of enquiring into Copenhagen's drinking habits, he woke up in a lavatory of his hotel with the attendant standing over him and asking what he'd like for his breakfast. He was so shaken by the man's *sang froid* that all his hair fell out there and then on to the floor and they had to spend the best part of the morning clearing it up... Richard, I'm glad to say, is making a hearty meal and much enjoying himself. So long as he doesn't drink too much before he makes his speech... We've a long way to go yet."

And indeed we had. We were now at the fish and Chablis stage. This was followed by Goose and Chambertin ("The old man with the red nose spends *all* his time at the University tennis courts") and this in turn by an iced bomb with Krug ("Can you imagine, my dear, screaming out of the boat house like a dervish at Omdurman"). After this came Devils on Horse Back, with whichever of the preceding wines one preferred ("Six foot seven inches, in *riding* boots..."); and then it was time for the cloth to be removed to make way for the port and speeches.

Once again there was a well established procedure to be followed, though by this day and date it was far more elaborate than anything that our Founder could have devised in his own time. As soon as the tables were cleared and the wine had gone round once, the Provost called upon the Vice-Provost to propose the loyal toast. We all stood to drink this; but as soon as we had lowered our glasses the Senior Fellow called out, in accordance with the custom, "*Et rex Henricus, socii*", whereat, with a great shout of "*Rex Henricus, Fundator nobilis*", all drained their glasses and threw them over their shoulders. (When and why this rather Russian ceremony had been initiated, I could never discover: suffice to say that it cost the College a small fortune annually, and that it was considered very lucky to be hit on the head by someone else's glass.) After this we all sat again (Tyrrel looking as if he had wandered through the looking glass), while the choir sang a pretty Elizabethan love song; fresh glass was set, and the detritus was cleared off the floor by squads of bedmakers in black caps, who were traditionally regaled with coins and even bank notes, which they swept into their pans along with the broken glass.

Meanwhile, the wives and other adult female belongings of Fellows had begun to settle themselves in the Minstrels' Gallery above, from which they were graciously permitted to listen to the speeches. This practice had only been introduced, some ten years previously, because of the insistence of an unfortunate Vice-Provost, whose shrewish wife gave him no rest till the College Council had adopted his suggestion. This had finally been passed but had never been generally approved – the less so as some of the wives, albeit they were only admitted on sufferance, complained that the songs and some of the speeches, not to mention the uninhibited drinking, were unsuitable in the presence of ladies. However, they were very properly told that if they did not like it they could stay away; and since they showed no signs of doing this, it seemed that the custom of admitting them was now with us for good and that it was to have, on the whole, no deleterious effect on the evening's entertainment.

Clearly it was having none on this occasion. There would now be half an hour's uninterrupted drinking before the speeches and further toasts began, and all around us the period was being used to good purpose. The decanters wagged merrily down the tables. Glasses were filled and emptied and filled again before the decanter passed. Several young men vomited and were taken away by friends, while discreet servants attended to the mess. The choir sang three songs of death, two of unrequited love, and a challenge to Apollo to inspire better poetry than Bacchus could. The two young men next to us toasted Tyrrel and myself in bumpers and we responded in kind. Marc lit a cigar, informed us that the way people smoked cigars or ate bananas was indicative of their sexual characteristics. ("Anal, my dear, or *oral*"), and began a long story, in this connection, about the Professor of Poetry. Looking up by chance, I saw Penelope Goodrich in the front row of the Gallery; her eyes seemed to be straining towards where Richard was sitting at the far end of the Hall; her face was white and unhappy; she looked, at that moment, very vulnerable. I tried to catch her eye, so that I might wave and communicate my own confidence; but she had no eyes for me. Why are you so dismal,

I thought; can't you see that nothing could go wrong? Not here. Not in Lancaster College on the night of the Michaelmas Feast.

There was a tremendous belt on the gong and sudden silence. Up rose Walter, supposedly knowledgeable about Scandinavian affairs, to welcome the Scandinavian Ambassador and propose his toast.

"Your Excellency: Your Royal Highness: Mr Provost, my Lords and Gentlemen..."

The decanters still passed, but more discreetly now. Walter droned on. Penelope sat aloft with her eyes glued on Richard, who was sitting slightly to one side, was smoking a cigar (anal, my dear, or oral?) and looked entirely composed. Marc fidgeted and my other neighbour giggled. Walter wound up; we rose to drink his Excellency's health; several people, forgetting which stage of the evening they were in, threw their glasses over their shoulders; and we settled down to hear the Ambassador's reply.

Some nonsense about hygiene and democratic monarchies. Mercifully brief. Who next? The Senior Fellow, to welcome the semi-mediatised princeling: "When you look around, Your Royal Highness, at the riches which your distant ancestor saw fit to place at the disposal of learning..." Jesus Christ almighty, and whatever will the little wretch reply? "...When I look awound, Mr Pwovost, at the wiches which my ancestor so wisely placed at the disposal of learning..." God help us all, is the man a travelling advertisement for Wepublicanism? And now what? One of the dimmer college scientists, welcoming Herr Doktor Whatsisname. "Your work, an inspiration to many of us here, appreciated even in Oxford" – Ha! Ha! Ha! – "has revolutionised the world's approach to the Incidental Functions of Independent Cyclonic Factors considered as Asymptotes of the Temporal Co-ordinate."

"Great Balls of fire," said Marc Honeydew *sotto voce*, "they threw that into the dustbin when I was still in knickers."

So now, Herr Doktor: reply, reply: dig your kit out of the dustbin, along with Marc's old knickers, and give us the works. "Excellence: Hochiet" – (?) – "Herr Provost; mein Herren..." By all the gods at once, the insufferable brute is going to talk in German.

And so he did for forty minutes flat. After which the Provost, unrattled, unhurried and radiant, rose to perform a work of love, to welcome back into our midst Richard Fountain, our beloved friend and colleague, *redeuntem et acclamandum*.

"...As the years pass, I sometimes feel very old and lonely, sitting here in this College in which I have lived for so long and which I have loved so much. Of those with whom I was reared, in whose company I came into manhood and learned to explore the secrets of poetry and reason, the few that are not dead are old and scattered. So that it is you, my younger friends, who have come to mean most to me and whose welfare will exercise me until my last day. You will understand, then, that it is always sad for me when any of you leave this College, even though I know that you must necessarily go into the world to get your living. How joyful, therefore, when I am enabled to welcome home someone who has left us indeed, but only for a short time, and who has now returned, his face bronzed by a warmer sun, and his mind filled with deeper knowledge. I tell you all that of all the pleasures this Feast brings me every year, the pleasure of wine and company, of receiving many guests both great and humble, of reflecting, as our Founder would wish, on the good year now before us – of all these there is none which can compare with the pleasure of welcoming home old friends and dearly loved members of this College. And is not a Feast a fitting way for a man to welcome his friends? Is it not meet that those who return should be greeted with well spread tables and flowing wine cups? And so now, dear Richard, I welcome you with all my heart to this our Feast. I give you the greeting of Lancaster College and the blessing of an old man who has served it, in true faith, for as long as he can remember. And I bid the rest of you, all that are here present from the greatest to the least, to rise to your feet and drink, *in nomine beati Henrici*, to the health and happiness of our truly beloved *Magistri Richardi Fountain, redeuntis et acclamandi."*

"*Magister Richardus Fountain.*" A great shout of two hundred voices swelled into the air. "*Rediens et acclamandus.*" And then again, louder this time than before, a welcome home to make a man's heart heave within him, "*Reditus, acclamatus, carissimus sociis*", a mighty roar of affection and inebriety that rang round the ancient rafters while glasses were drained and set down and a storm of clapping burst through the Hall. Then we sat, all save the Provost –

"And so now, Richard, we call on you. Now you must reply to your friends."

And this was it. There was dead silence. Marc sat tensely and wiped his palms with his handkerchief. Penelope gazed along the Hall and her lips, I thought, moved as if in prayer. Tyrrel lowered his eyelids; the Provost reseated himself with unobstrusive dignity; and Walter Goodrich sat back with a beatific smile. And then, calm as a summer morning and cool as a breeze off the sea, Richard Fountain rose to speak.

"Your Excellency: Your Royal Highness: Mr Provost, my Lords and Gentlemen.

"It is an ancient custom that, when a man comes from far away, he should be asked for the news he brings. He is asked for his message. I have brought back a message, a very simple one, and it is this which I shall now pass on to you.

"For it is a message of salvation, which you must all hear. It is a message of hope, of liberation, of escape. I have suffered in acquiring it, but my suffering is now done, and will in any case be well rewarded by the response which I hope to raise in yourselves. In a word, my prize has been my own freedom, and this prize will be many times multiplied in worth if I can share my freedom with all of you; with those of you who are our guests, if you will hear me, and more particularly with those of you, my friends and my colleagues, who have welcomed me home to Lancaster with such abundance of voice and spirit."

Still dead silence, not a single shuffle. What is he going to say? Trite but harmless words about the Greeks and their nobility? Richard is seldom trite. A paean in praise of the old gods? The gods of wine and song? If so, he would have to be partly ironic in his tone; and his tone is not ironic at all.

"The message is this. You must beware, all of you, of those who seek to possess your souls. But we know this already, you will say: here, in Lancaster, the citadel of protest and intellectual freedom, we know all about keeping our souls from other men's possession. But this is not true, my friends. Which of you, from a child, has not been possessed – possessed by parents, or by schoolmasters, by lovers perhaps, or by your elders who are in this very room? Which of you has not been stifled and suffocated, until the breath of life has left you and you remain, a mere shell, to do the bidding of an alien spirit? For a person, or a regiment, a country or a college or a faith – something alien in any case – has drained the life blood from you, until you are no more as the gods would have you be than is a rotten fruit crushed into the gutter.

"And so, you will ask me, how *would* the gods have us be? They would have you in full enjoyment of all their gifts. The smaller gifts, such as wine and laughter. The greater gifts, such as the love of the body and the exercise of strength. Above all, the gift of freedom. For it is freedom which is the oldest and the best of all their gifts. And by this I do not mean freedom simply to come and go as you wish, or even to speak your mind as you see fit on the topic of the day. I mean freedom to live with your whole mind and your whole body – your whole being – in the pursuit of those prizes, prizes of beauty or wisdom or power, which your own soul chiefly covets. You are not to be fobbed off with the petty schemes of academic hirelings, the parochial patterns of prestige and modest earnings which will be coyly but insistently put before you as guides to a suitable life. You are to look into your souls and see what of vision is to be found there; and then, keeping this vision clear, not suffering it to be obscured or tarnished by the quibbling morality or sly vanities of old men, you are to follow your vision through to its end and goal, whether this be a throne or a hermit's cell or the very pit of Hades.

"This is what the gods wish for you. That you follow the visions they have given you in the freedom which they have ordained for you. Like Alexander, you may come a conqueror to the limits of the known world; or like Plato, to the highest mysteries of speculation; like Hector, to a shameful passage behind another's chariot or like Helen to be called strumpet and whore. But Hector's fate and Helen's are as noble as Alexander's, because by following their visions they won the love of the gods, so that their names have come ringing down the centuries in immortal poetry. It is for you to choose: follow your vision, to win the love of the immortals, even if that be joined with present infamy among mankind; or let your vision be clouded by the safe counsel of those who would confine you to the grey world of calculating drudgery. You must choose. But of those who are here to help you make your choice, most of them wish only to wipe out your visions, to corrode or steal away your bright souls. Much of my message is, therefore, a warning, and I sum up my warning thus: *Beware of the thief who comes to take your soul.* He is with you always. There are many of them sitting among us now, making ready, so soon as they rise from table, to slip their nimble fingers into your breast and take from it what is most precious, to seal it away in their cabinets and watch it grow – for grow it still must – on the food which *they* will feed it into some grotesque shape which *they* have preordained. So hide your souls well, my friends; or else there will come the smooth deceiver in the black gown or the scarlet robe – such a man as is sitting there" – he pointed down the Hall to no one in particular – "or there" – once again he

259

gestured vaguely – "or there, worst of all *there*," he screamed out with all his strength; and then pointed with his whole arm, and almost, it seemed, with his whole body, at Doctor Walter Goodrich.

There was a low hum, like that of bees on a summer day, which gradually grew and grew, until it was as though some gigantic piece of machinery, having started very gently, was now gathering all its terrible powers to rend the Hall apart.

Walter sat with his smile frozen on to his cheeks. The Provost looked straight in front of him, his head sagging between his shoulders. Marc, beside me, was twitching like a marionette. From somewhere away in the Hall I heard Piers' voice calling out, "That's enough, Richard. Leave us to drink in peace." But whether Richard heard him or not, he paid him no attention. No longer calm, but swaying and staggering on the dais, he started to speak once more.

"But that is not all," he shouted. "Guard your souls, yes. But there is more you must do before you are truly free. You must make the other – the enemies that threaten – give up their souls to you. For how can you be free if the enemy still watches you? And if you have not tested your freedom by the exercise of your strength? How can you – " He caught at his throat and made a choking sound. He staggered a pace or two forward and nearly fell off the dais. Once again he tried to speak, but he had barely opened his mouth when Penelope's high, stern voice rang across the Hall – "Help him," she called, "for God's sake help him. Can't you see that he's ill?"

And almost before I had had time to understand who was speaking or what she was saying her big bony figure, clad in its black and unbecoming evening dress, was thrusting up one of the aisles toward the dais. Not until Penelope had reached Richard, and was already helping him towards a small side door which led out of the Hall, did anyone else move. Then, as if released from a spell, scores of men scraped back their chairs and made to go to her assistance.

"Too late," she called. "You should have helped him earlier. He's mine now. All of you leave him to me."

And with that she and Richard disappeared through the side door which a tactful servant was holding open; and silence, blank and utter, descended upon the Feast.

"So what now?" I said.

Shortly after Penelope and Richard had left the Hall, the Provost had risen to bring the Feast to an end. Looking bleakly in front of him he reminded gentlemen that certain Fellows, among them Doctor Goodrich and Mr Honeydew, would now be dispensing the customary hospitality in their rooms. He suggested that gentlemen in their first year went first to Doctor Goodrich and only later to Mr Honeydew or the others, that gentlemen in their second year...and so on. He then uttered the curt Latin phrase, half grace and half dismissed, which concluded the Michaelmas Feast for 1957.

"So what now?"

Marc, Tyrrel and myself had been joined, outside the Hall, by Piers. We were all standing by the entrance to the Senior Common Room: Piers drunk and defiant, Tyrrel poised and silent, Marc still twittering and twitching as he had done during Richard's speech.

"And so what now?" I said.

"For Christ's sake stop saying that, Anthony," said Piers, and then belched very loudly.

"Manners, dear," said Marc automatically. And then to me, "You well may ask. But since I must go to my rooms in any case to entertain the students, I suggest you all come too. There will be nourishing whisky."

We started slowly towards Marc's rooms.

"You don't think we should look for them?"

"No," said Tyrrel; "Miss Goodrich is the only person who has shown any ability to cope. She'd best be left to carry on."

"No buts," said Piers thickly. "Whatever he's done, we can't mend it now. So let Penelope have her little evening. Let her be mummy or nanny if she wants to. Perhaps she'll try and drag the poor sod into bed."

He laughed coarsely, staggered and bounced back off a wall.

"No nourishing whisky for *you*," Marc said.

When we reached his room, some ten or twelve undergraduates were already there, talking in low, excited tones but falling silent as soon as we entered. At first things were sticky. But Marc busied himself with beer and whisky, more undergraduates joined us, and gradually we began to pick up the bits of the broken evening. Tyrrel, I noticed, had a knack of getting on with young men, and was soon surrounded by a small and attentive group. I spoke with a young don whom I knew slightly, trying to be polite while he told me with enthusiasm everything that was wrong with my magazine. Piers disappeared and then came back again.

"I've been to Walter's room," he told me. "He's bluffing it out very well. Telling people how Richard has only just recovered from a nervous breakdown due to overwork. He was very good with HRH. If he's not careful Richard will get knighted for the evening's work."

Piers disappeared again; and shortly afterwards Tyrrel and I left Marc and went on to Walter. Here the proceedings were unexpectedly jolly. HRH, palpably drunk, was lolling against the mantel explaining to the Herr Doktor how keen he had been on science at Dartmouth. The Scandinavian Ambassador, rather red round the cheekbones, was talking to the bald sociologist about State Brothels; while a biochemist from King's was explaining, in a very loud voice and to no one in particular, that a creature called the basking shark emitted four and a half gallons of seminal fluid every time it had an orgasm.

"Goot, Highness, goot," said the Herr Doktor with a trapped look.

"State Brothels is just the job," said the Scandinavian Ambassador. "But as yet we do not have. The old ones talk and the young ones burn. 'Let them marry,' say the old ones. 'Let them die and rest their chins in their coffins,' say the young ones. And so there is done nothing." He sat down rather suddenly.

"Four and a half gallons, chums," said the biochemist from King's. "Just imagine. It must take at least ten minutes. *An orgasm lasting ten minutes.*"

"Goot, Highness, goot."

"Nothing, nothing done," said the Ambassador in deep despair.

"Bet *your* orgasms never even last ten seconds."

"...A most interwesting expewiment with a magnet..."

"I wish *I* was a basking shark."

"Goot, Highness."

"...basking and basking, and then – hey presto – another four and a half gallons."

"...hung the magnet from the woof..."

"...basking and basking in the sun."

"*For Christ's sake, Anthony. Come with me.* NOW."

Tyrrel and I followed Piers.

"The oak was sported," Piers mumbled. "I climbed up and looked through the window...a joke, you see...surprise them... Oh God, oh Christ..."

"How will we get in?"

"Marc will meet us there. With the master key. They'll give it to a Fellow."

We went up Richard's staircase. Outside the sported oak we halted to wait for Marc. "What shall we find?"

But Piers was blubbering into the wall. From time to time he retched; a mixture of snot and bile dripped heavily to the floor at his feet. Then we heard Marc. He came straight up the stairs and without a word thrust in the key and swung back the sported oak.

"Through the first room. The bedroom."

The outer room was dimly lit by a reading lamp on a desk. Tyrrel went first. He banged with both fists on the bedroom door and then hurled it open. For a moment he stood quite still, looking in. Then – "Stop it," he screamed.

Coming up behind him, I saw him step over to the bed. The bedside lamp was on and everything was quite clear. Richard and Penelope were lying together, fully dressed, on the bed. Penelope's eyes were open and she was looking straight up at the ceiling. She did not move, she scarcely seemed to breathe; while Richard Fountain, his face wedged into her throat, his cheeks, his shoulders, his whole body heaving with his effort, drank away her blood.

"Stop it," yelled Tyrrel again.

He seized Richard by his heaving shoulders and flung him on to the floor. Penelope lay where she was, unmoved. Richard got to his feet and turned his blood-stained face snarling towards us.

"You see?" he said. "She nearly destroyed me. Now it is my turn. I must use my knowledge to preserve my freedom: drain the life of others before they drain mine. You understand?"

"I think, Richard, you had better come with us," said Piers, from whom all traces of drunkenness had now vanished.

"And leave my adoring Chriseis? Come, Piers."

"And what is all this?" said a bewildered but still fruity voice. Walter loomed in the doorway behind us.

"This is your son," said Richard, "who has been embracing your daughter Chriseis... Your daughter Penelope... It is all one. Ravishing her, you might say, before she could ravish him."

Walter made a loose and hopeless gesture.

"I don't understand you," he said.

"It's very simple. You want to steal my life, and you will use your daughter to help you. But I have moved first. By...embracing Penelope, I have established my power over

264

her. I tried to tell you all tonight, but I couldn't finish. The free man, Walter, must take the souls of his enemies."

"What can you mean? Penelope loves you. She will *give* you her life, her soul. There is no need to take."

"He has already done so," said Piers standing upright. "Penelope is dead."

"*Dead*?" whispered Richard fiercely. "How could she be? This is the first – "

" – She's dead, Richard. You had best come to your daughter, Doctor Goodrich."

"Chriseis...dead..." Richard mumbled to himself..." Penelope... Chriseis...dead."

Walter lurched forward and bent down over Penelope. He ripped away her dress and felt for her heart. He seized her wrist and sought for a pulse. He gave a great moan of despair and swung round on Richard.

"For the love of God," he cried, "what have you done? Raped her? Beaten her? Speak up, boy. What have you done to my Penelope?"

"He has drunk her blood," said Piers, and went into the outer room.

For the first time Walter seemed to begin to understand. He looked at Richard's blood-smeared mouth and he looked back at the ugly gash on Penelope's throat. Then understanding gave place to renewed bewilderment. Walter's eyes stared away into space and his voice became a croak.

"You... *My* Richard.... You did that?"

"Chriseis," muttered Richard, "Chriseis."

Walter seemed to sink towards the floor. Tyrrel caught hold of him and sat him in a chair. Then his head lolled forward, and huge, glistening tears poured over his cheeks and dripped on to his knees.

"Richard... Penelope... My children."

265

Richard was standing, silent and sullen, in a corner of the room. Piers, returning from the outer room, went up to him with a full tumbler.

"Drink this, Richard," he said; "whatever is to happen, you must sleep now."

Richard seemed not to hear him, but he took the glass and put it to his lips.

"Drink it all, Richard," said Piers softly.

"What – ?" I began.

Tyrrel seized my arm and shook his head.

"All of it, Richard," said Piers: "then you will sleep." Once again Tyrrel took hold of my arm, indicating, with a jerk of his head, that I should go into the other room. As I went Marc followed me; a few moments later Tyrrel also came, supporting Walter, and helped the old man on to the sofa. Then he went back, closed the bedroom door, and sat down next to Walter on the sofa.

For ten minutes we waited, hearing nothing and saying nothing. Then Piers came slowly out of the bedroom and halted in front of Tyrrel.

"He is asleep now," Piers said, "and the taint sleeps with him."

XV

On the morning of November 1, 1957, Inspector John Tyrrel presented himself before the Provost of Lancaster College. He was accompanied by a certain Doctor Holmstrom, sometime Fellow of King's College and a man of much curious learning, whom he had summoned from London in the early hours of the morning. Having proved his own office and Doctor Holmstrom's credentials, Inspector Tyrrel then told the Provost of the strange course of events which had led to the deaths of, among others, Miss Penelope Goodrich and Richard Fountain, Fellow of the College. The story was borne out in part by Doctor Walter Goodrich and Mr Marc Honeydew, both of whom were Fellows under the Provost; and borne out in full by Major Anthony Seymour, a respected past member of the College. Doctor Holmstrom confirmed that he had been from time to time consulted and informed in detail of what had passed up to the night of the final tragedy; and he asserted the inherent plausibility of the circumstances described. It was then represented to the Provost that one of his undergraduates, Mr Piers Clarence, was technically guilty of the murder of Richard Fountain; but that this young man had in reality done nothing but his duty to the living ruin of a well loved friend.

The following exchange then took place.

Provost: As I understand you, Inspector, the respective causes of death were loss of blood and an overdose of a sleeping draught compounded mainly of Codeine Phosphate.

267

Tyrrel: That is correct, sir.

Provost: And a qualified physician – we have several in the College – could with good conscience make out certificates to that effect?

Tyrrel: He could.

Provost: Very well. Now, you are aware that Lancaster College, as a Royal Foundation, has privileges which extend well beyond such matters as feasting? That I myself, as Provost, am empowered to act as Coroner in respect of all deaths which occur within the College Gate? I should add that this privilege is not as recondite as it may seem. The Provost of King's has very similar powers, though as far as I know they have not been used since the last century. But if this conception is unfamiliar to you, perhaps you would care to examine the Charter?

Tyrrel: Your word is quite sufficient, Mr Provost.

Provost: Thank you sir. Now again: if I am not mistaken, whatever your official responsibilities may be, you share the opinion held by these gentlemen here as to the *morality* of this whole affair: – That in the first place Richard Fountain was not, and has not been for some months, properly responsible for his actions; and that in the second place Mr Clarence, by taking Fountain's life, was committing an act of mercy and even of piety rather than one of murder.

Tyrrel: I accept this view, sir.

Provost: So that it is the interest of *justice* that the matter should now rest?

Tyrrel: Of justice, but not of the Law. Whatever my personal opinions and affections, Mr Provost, I should not disguise from you that, in Law, we have a murder to consider.

Provost: I am only concerned with justice, Inspector Tyrrel. I am too old to interest myself in the requirements of that unfamiliar science, the Law. On the other hand I have been studying justice, in one sense or another, all my life. Let us therefore reason together, and think what it is meet and fitting that men of liberal understanding should do in these circumstances. Hand Piers Clarence over to the Law? Is this the reward of loyalty, the prize of love? The act of tolerant and humane men? In this College I am chosen to act for the Law; and I say that here it shall follow the reasoned dictates of the mind and the charity of the heart. It is on this assumption that I, with the authority vested in me by our Founder, shall give judgement. But before I do so, I should tell you all that I feel myself morally bound, if any of you wish it, to waive my privilege and give the matter into the hands of outside authority. Do you then undertake to accept my judgement? Because once it is given, it must be final: any further appeal, any reference to those outside, could alter nothing except the esteem in which my office is held. And so, if you think it preferable that we summon outsiders to investigate and pronounce, then you must say so here and now. You must, as my true friends, advise me of your will... Doctor Goodrich?

Goodrich: Penelope is dead and Richard is dead. Any judgment is equally valid, equally irrelevant. Let the Provost judge.

Provost: Mr Honeydew?

Honeydew: We do not need strangers to mix in our affairs. Let the Provost judge.

Provost: Doctor Holmstrom?

Holmstrom: I have given what advice I could. Now I shall forget all this — save possibly as an anonymous and academic example. So for my part, let the Provost judge.

Provost: Major Seymour?

Seymour: The Provost is an honourable man. Let the Provost judge.

Provost: And you, Inspector Tyrrel?

Tyrrel: I protected Richard Fountain in his life and can only wish that he may rest in his death. Let the Provost judge.

Provost: Then hear my judgement, given under the authority vested in me, as Provost of this College, by our Founder, King Henry VI, an authority to this date countenanced by his Royal successors. It is my verdict that Penelope Goodrich and Richard Fountain, being misused by the world and driven to suffer in their minds, did, in equal consent, take their own lives, the one by the letting of blood and the other by drinking a poisonous draught. And may God, and our gentle and beloved Founder, have pity for their souls.

It was a long time since the Head of a Royal Foundation had exercised his right as Coroner; but the right was indisputable, as was that of declining to publish proceedings. Only the verdict need be public; and this, which suggested an occurrence of, after all, a fairly commonplace kind, must be accepted by authority and by the press to make of it what little they could.

In accordance with the terms of the verdict, Penelope Goodrich and Richard Fountain were buried in hallowed ground; to be more precise, in the precincts of the Chapel of Lancaster College, Cambridge. Many people came to their funeral, for both of them had been much loved; but of all those present only four men knew that both bodies were buried only after sharpened stakes of wood had been driven through their hearts.

Athens. March 19, 1960.

SIMON RAVEN

MORNING STAR

This first volume in Simon Raven's *First-Born of Egypt* saga opens with the christening of the Marquess Canteloupe's son and heir, Sarum of Old Sarum. The ceremony, attended by the godparents and the real father, Fielding Gray, is not without drama.

The christening introduces a bizarre cast of eccentric characters and complicated relationships. In *Morning Star* we meet the brilliant but troublesome teenager Marius Stern. Marius' increasingly outrageous behaviour has him constantly on the verge of expulsion from prep school. When his parents are kidnapped, apparently without reason, events take a turn for the worse.

THE FACE OF THE WATERS

This is the second volume of Simon Raven's *First-Born of Egypt* series. Marius Stern, the wayward son of Gregory Stern, has survived earlier escapades and is safely back at prep school — assisted by his father's generous contribution to the school's new shooting-range. Fielding Gray and Jeremy Morrison are returning home via Venice, where they encounter the friar, Piero, an ex-male whore and a figure from a shared but distant past.

Back in England, at the Wiltshire family home, Lord Canteloupe is restless. He finds his calm disturbed by events: the arrival of Piero; Jeremy's father's threat to saddle his son with the responsibility of the family estate; and the dramatic resistance of Gregory Stern to attempted blackmail.

SIMON RAVEN

BEFORE THE COCK CROW

This is the third volume in Simon Raven's *First-Born of Egypt* saga. The story opens with Lord Canteloupe's strange toast to 'absent friends'. His wife Baby has recently died and Canteloupe has been left her retarded son, Lord Sarum of Old Sarum. This child is not his, but has been conceived by Major Fielding Gray. In Italy there is an illegitimate child with a legitimate claim to the estate, whom Canteloupe wants silenced.

NEW SEED FOR OLD

The fourth in the *First-Born of Egypt* series has Lord Canteloupe wanting a satisfactory heir so that his dynasty may continue. Unfortunately, Lord Canteloupe is impotent and his existing heir, little Tully Sarum, is not of sound mind.

His wife Theodosia is prepared to do her duty when a suitable partner is found. Finding the man and the occasion proves somewhat tricky however, and it is not until Lord Canteloupe goes up to Lord's for the first match of the season that progress is made.

SIMON RAVEN

BLOOD OF MY BONE

In this fifth volume of Simon Raven's *First-Born of Egypt* series, the death of the Provost of a large school is a catalyst for a series of disgraceful doings in the continuing saga of the Canteloupes and their circle.

Marius, under-age father of the new Lady Canteloupe's dutifully produced heir to the family estate, is warned against the malign influence of Raisley Conyngham. Classics teacher at his school, Conyngham is well aware of the sway he has over Marius, who has already revealed himself a keen student of 'the refinements of hell'. With fate intervening, the stage is set for another deliciously wicked instalment.

IN THE IMAGE OF GOD

The sixth in the *First-Born of Egypt* series sees Raisley Conyngham, Classics teacher at a large school, exert a powerful influence over Marius Stern. His young pupil, however, is no defenceless victim.

Marius has a ruthless streak and an ability to sidestep tests and traps that are laid for him. Which is just as well because everybody is after something from him…

OTHER TITLES BY SIMON RAVEN AVAILABLE DIRECT FROM HOUSE OF STRATUS

Quantity		£	$(US)	$(CAN)	€
☐	BEFORE THE COCK CROW	7.99	12.99	17.49	13.00
☐	BIRD OF ILL OMEN	7.99	12.99	17.49	13.00
☐	BLOOD OF MY BONE	7.99	12.99	17.49	13.00
☐	BROTHER CAIN	7.99	12.99	17.49	13.00
☐	CLOSE OF PLAY	7.99	12.99	17.49	13.00
☐	THE FACE OF THE WATERS	7.99	12.99	17.49	13.00
☐	THE FORTUNES OF FINGEL	7.99	12.99	17.49	13.00
☐	IN THE IMAGE OF GOD	7.99	12.99	17.49	13.00
☐	AN INCH OF FORTUNE	7.99	12.99	17.49	13.00
☐	MORNING STAR	7.99	12.99	17.49	13.00
☐	NEW SEED FOR OLD	7.99	12.99	17.49	13.00
☐	THE ROSES OF PICARDIE	7.99	12.99	17.49	13.00
☐	SEPTEMBER CASTLE	7.99	12.99	17.49	13.00
☐	SHADOWS ON THE GRASS	7.99	12.99	17.49	13.00
☐	THE TROUBADOUR	7.99	12.99	17.49	13.00

ALL HOUSE OF STRATUS BOOKS ARE AVAILABLE FROM GOOD BOOKSHOPS
OR DIRECT FROM THE PUBLISHER:

Internet: **www.houseofstratus.com** including author interviews, reviews, features.

Email: **sales@houseofstratus.com** please quote author, title and credit card details.

Hotline: UK ONLY: **0800 169 1780**, please quote author, title and credit card details.
INTERNATIONAL: **+44 (0) 20 7494 6400**, please quote author, title and credit card details.

Send to: **House of Stratus Sales Department**
24c Old Burlington Street
London
W1X 1RL
UK

Please allow for postage costs charged per order plus an amount per book as set out in the tables below:

	£(Sterling)	$(US)	$(CAN)	€(Euros)
Cost per order				
UK	2.00	3.00	4.50	3.30
Europe	3.00	4.50	6.75	5.00
North America	3.00	4.50	6.75	5.00
Rest of World	3.00	4.50	6.75	5.00
Additional cost per book				
UK	0.50	0.75	1.15	0.85
Europe	1.00	1.50	2.30	1.70
North America	2.00	3.00	4.60	3.40
Rest of World	2.50	3.75	5.75	4.25

PLEASE SEND CHEQUE, POSTAL ORDER (STERLING ONLY), EUROCHEQUE, OR INTERNATIONAL MONEY ORDER (PLEASE CIRCLE METHOD OF PAYMENT YOU WISH TO USE) MAKE PAYABLE TO: STRATUS HOLDINGS plc ·

Cost of book(s): —————————— Example: 3 x books at £6.99 each: £20.97
Cost of order: —————————— Example: £2.00 (Delivery to UK address)
Additional cost per book: —————— Example: 3 x £0.50: £1.50
Order total including postage: ——— Example: £24.47

Please tick currency you wish to use and add total amount of order:

☐ £ (Sterling)   ☐ $ (US)   ☐ $ (CAN)   ☐ € (EUROS)

VISA, MASTERCARD, SWITCH, AMEX, SOLO, JCB:

☐☐☐☐☐☐☐☐☐☐☐☐☐☐☐☐☐☐☐☐

Issue number (Switch only):

☐☐☐

Start Date: Expiry Date:

☐☐ / ☐☐   ☐☐ / ☐☐

Signature: ————————————

NAME: ——————————————————

ADDRESS: ——————————————————

————————————————————

POSTCODE: ——————

Please allow 28 days for delivery.

Prices subject to change without notice.
Please tick box if you do not wish to receive any additional information. ☐

House of Stratus publishes many other titles in this genre; please check our website (**www.houseofstratus.com**) for more details.